A Winter of Wolves

A Jeff Trask Crime Drama

MARC RAINER

ISBN: 1537610759
ISBN 13: 9781537610757
Library of Congress Control Number: 2016915486
CreateSpace Independent Publishing Platform
North Charleston, South Carolina

To my wife Lea, whose encouragement and belief
in me made this series of books a reality.

*"A nation of sheep will beget
a government of wolves."*
Edward R. Murrow

Chapter One

Jackie Turner began the circle around the Lincoln Memorial, switching her gaze from the road to the huge marble structure from time to time just to make sure nothing was going on. So far, it had been a routine patrol on the graveyard shift. Christmas was only a few days away, and the crowds on the National Mall had dwindled to the usual trickle. The tourists were at home for the season. Whatever they could scrape together in a tight economy was going for gifts to put under their trees.

She looked up again at the Doric columns shining white in the spotlights, guarding the giant figure that sat staring at the Capitol across the Capitol Mall and Reflecting Pool. The park rangers had gone home at 10:00 p.m., about three hours ago. Responsibility for the memorial had shifted to the United States Park Police at that time. Officer Turner's duties included drive-arounds on the circle bordering the Lincoln at random intervals, with an increased emphasis—stressed by the brass at every shift-change roll call—on preventing vandalism.

One crazy woman throws paint from a soda can and everything changes. It's been eighteen months now since the green stains got cleaned off Abe's shoes, and it'll take another year for the captain to think about something else to look for.

She glanced through the branches of the trees bordering the base of the north portico. Most of the steps surrounding the memorial were visible this time of year, with only a few shielded by some evergreens along the base. Something flashed in one of the spotlights, and she squinted at the tiny object, seeing what appeared to be an aluminum can sitting along the edge of the floor at the base of the columns.

Damn. Better check that out—at least toss it in the trash. They'll have my ass if there's more paint in that thing.

I

She steered the white Dodge Charger with the blue stripe to the edge of the circle and pulled out her uniform jacket and gloves before locking the patrol unit. It was just cool enough to be worth the effort. She checked her watch for the shift's log entry she'd have to write: *1:26 a.m.*

She climbed the stairs toward the northeast corner of the memorial and the soda can, silently cursing the thoughtlessness of whoever would litter one of the nation's most iconic monuments. She bent over to pick up the can, not noticing the huge figure rushing out from behind the corner column. A giant hand flashed across the left side of her head as she stood up. The fingers grabbed her upper palate through her open mouth, pulling back so violently that she was denied the breath she needed to scream. She felt herself being dragged back into the shadows behind the column. Her right hand instinctively reached for the gun on her belt, but her assailant had anticipated the move, covering the weapon with another huge hand and trapping hers in a grip so powerful that the bones in her hand cracked like dry twigs. The weapon was tossed to the side, out of her reach.

Jackie felt the top of her head being pulled in one direction, her bottom jaw pulled in the other. The tearing of her flesh and ligaments sent lightning bolts of pain shooting through her head and shoulders. Just as the light and life left her, she had the impression that she was looking down at her own corpse.

―――――

Death is different.

That's what Trask was thinking as he drove toward the District. He had heard the old-timers say it. The ones who had successfully prosecuted death penalty cases—always in other federal districts—all said the same thing. Trask had tried some capital cases before, but until his last trial, he had never gotten the jury to pull the trigger. Ramón Dominguez had been different. A Zeta Mexican drug cartel chief who had the deaths of hundreds on his bloody hands, Dominguez—even more so than the other murderers—had deserved the ultimate punishment. This time, the jury had given it to him.

That had been months ago, but Trask still thought about the trial. Hell, he was still reliving it. He'd persuaded the jury to kill. He had no doubt about the monster's guilt, about the justice of the verdict, and—as he'd told a reporter at the time—he'd have pushed the plungers himself if given the chance. It was the weight of the horrors Dominguez had inflicted that haunted him. The fact that a human being had been—could *even be*—so inhuman. He hadn't been sleeping well as a result, the tales of the hundreds of murders scrolling across the ceiling above him each night, forcing his mind to try to answer questions he could begin to even formulate.

Ross Eastman, the United States Attorney for the District of Columbia and Trask's boss, had ordered him to take a full week off. Eastman had recognized something that even Trask himself hadn't been able to see in the mirror: the exhaustion and the weight on his shoulders of representing all those lost souls as he was trying to get the appropriate verdict for their killer. Some of those souls spoke to him in his dreams. Some simply smiled and nodded at him, grateful for his efforts. Others told him that his job was not done yet, warning him that worse times were ahead. He had trouble wondering what the hell that could mean.

Who could be a bigger son-of-a-bitch than that Zeta bastard?

The downtime was over. It was an early Monday morning, and he was making the drive again into the District from his house in Waldorf, Maryland, a generally quiet bedroom suburb located about five o'clock on the beltway "clock." Despite the week off, Trask felt like he could use another, but that would mean another thousand e-mails to read and another fifty phone calls to return when he got back. He was thankful that it was winter. He never minded the cold, having been raised in the South, where the heat and humidity always fought to see which could climb the highest.

I don't have to mow the yard in the winter, there are no bugs when it freezes, and the cooler temps generally mean cooler tempers. In my line of work that usually means a lighter workload, he thought. *Usually.*

Time to get back on the horse. Maybe the crime critters of DC will take it easy on me for once—let me work my way back into the grind.

A ringing noise—the ringtone for the Bluetooth paired to his cell phone—jolted him.

No such luck.

"Trask." He answered before he looked at the dash display and recognized the number. The caller was Dixon Carter, DC's best homicide detective. "What's up, Dix?"

"You coming in today, Jeff?"

"On the Indian Head now." Trask was on the highway running across southern Maryland into the capital city.

"Good. You had breakfast yet?"

"Nope. I was thinking about pulling off for a fast-food biscuit someplace."

"Don't. You might not be able to keep it down."

"Wonderful." Trask rolled his eyes. "What's up?"

"Don't stop at the office. Meet me at the Lincoln Memorial. North side. You in the Jeep?"

"Yeah."

"I'll have the uniforms look out for you and clear you in."

"Thanks, I guess."

"Don't thank me now." Carter paused. "You won't thank me later, either."

Trask clicked off the Bluetooth from the button on the steering wheel.

I wonder what that was all about?

He turned on an FM station. Music. No news stations for now. Whatever was on the news about whatever he was driving into could only color his judgment. Trask decided he'd get it first-hand, not from some sound bite editor with an agenda. The radio responded, and the mournful lyrics of Ray LaMontagne's "Trouble" floated through the Grand Cherokee.

Trask shook his head. Music had always been a set of audio tarot cards for him, telling his fortune even when he tried to avoid the forecast.

Here we go again . . .

The Indian Head turned into I-295, and he followed the road past what he had known while on active duty with the USAF as Bolling Air Force Base and the Washington Naval Station, now merged into an installation called "Joint Base Anacostia."

He crossed the Anacostia River on the Douglass Bridge, and drove north toward the Capitol before heading west. He passed dozens of government office buildings, the various museums of the Smithsonian, and a couple of pick-up football games in progress on the Capitol Mall.

Not in school or at work, so might as well play, right guys?

There was a collection of flashing lights around the base of the Lincoln Memorial. Trask counted at least a dozen Park Police and Metro units clustered on the north side of the circle. There was an ambulance as well.

I'll bet the ambulance goes home empty, Trask told himself. *No survivor here; they'll need a body van instead to take the victim to the morgue. If Dixon Carter hadn't called me about this, I'd turn around and run. I've never heard Dix sound like he did on the phone, and he's seen the worse this town's had to offer.*

Trask rode the curb around the growing traffic jam as he neared the circle. A uniform saw the Jeep as it approached and waved him in past dozens of other motorists who shot him ugly glances while they waited in their stationary vehicles. Trask parked as close as he could below the north portico and climbed the front steps. He saw a very large, dark-skinned black man in a business suit and wool overcoat sitting about five steps below the main level, smoking a cigarette.

"I thought you'd given that up, Dix," Trask said.

"I did," Carter replied. "Had to mooch this off one of the uniforms."

"What's going on?"

"Go see for yourself. I couldn't describe it if I tried. Wilkes is up there now."

Trask climbed the remaining steps to the floor of the colonnade. A wall of U.S. Park Police officers stood between the last two columns on the right of the Memorial, looking outward, and shielding whatever lay behind them. A small man in coveralls stood beside the corner column, issuing orders to two larger men who were similarly dressed. Frank Wilkes, the chief crime scene investigator for the Metropolitan Police Department, heard Trask's steps and turned to meet him.

"This is ugly, Jeff."

"So I gathered. Dixon Carter called me over. I saw him on the steps. He almost looked pale."

Wilkes snorted and nodded.

Okay, no humor is appropriate today. "What do we have, Frank?"

"She's around the corner," Wilkes said. He turned toward the wall of cops and made a parting motion with his hands. A hole opened and Trask followed Wilkes through the gap. When Wilkes stepped aside, Trask froze in his tracks.

The body of a female was lying on the marble. Trask recognized her uniform as that of a Park Police officer from the light-blue stripe along the side of the dark pants leg. Trask had seen crime scenes before, and the large pool of red around the top of the body was nothing new. It was the woman's head—or what was left of it—that stopped him. The lower jaw was visible inside the blood-soaked collar. There was just nothing above it.

"Jesus!" Trask couldn't move for a moment or two.

"The rest of it's over there." Wilkes waited for Trask to take it all in, and then pointed to his left. The upper half of the woman's head, including the upper jaw, lay on its side at the end of a grotesque, curling trail of dried blood about thirty feet away, toward the interior of the memorial.

"Somebody rolled it over there," Wilkes explained.

Trask tried to focus on the evidence, and not the horror of the event. He noticed a partial footprint to the side of the blood trail, the bloodstained tread markings of a tennis shoe sole—a *very large* tennis shoe sole. "Got all your pics?" he asked.

"Yeah," Wilkes said. "The scene's done except for the body recovery and cleanup. Have a look. You won't hurt anything."

You're right. Trask shook his head again. *I think the hurt's over for this poor girl.*

He walked over to the fragment of the head, Wilkes following. From his counted paces, Trask estimated that the distance from the upper skull to the rest of the victim was about twenty-five feet. He made a mental note to check that later in the crime scene diagrams. He crouched down, noting the auburn hair still neatly tied into a bun at the back. He paused for a moment, looking into the eyes, still wide with shock and fear, frozen in that death stare he'd seen too many times before. Part of the upper spine hung out from under the woman's hair. He almost gagged, but choked it back. Trask gathered himself, and concentrated on what had been the corners of her mouth. The flesh was torn, jagged.

"What kind of weapon does that, Frank?" he asked, looking up at Wilkes.

"I don't think he used one," Wilkes said. "He, it . . . I don't know. My best guess for now is that whoever or whatever did this ripped her head in half with his bare hands. That's why the flesh looks torn instead of cut: it *was.*"

Trask stood up and walked back out past the wall of cops. He looked skyward toward the corner of the top of the memorial. A dark globe mounted on a white stem hung over the edge of the roof, above the top of the columns. The surveillance camera looked like a hawk staring down at the scene.

Trask saw that Dixon Carter was standing nearby. Carter followed Trask's gaze up to the camera.

"Already working on that," Carter said. "Tim's on it. We'll have all the videos in your office ASAP."

Trask nodded. Tim Wisniewski was Carter's junior partner. "Thanks," Trask said. "For warning me about breakfast, that is."

"Yeah. You're welcome." Carter threw the cigarette down and headed down the steps. A uniformed Park Ranger followed him, stopping to pick up the butt.

Trask stood for a moment looking across the Mall toward the Capitol. The world was carrying on, traffic running to and from the seats of government and the museums. The ball games on the mall continued. Everything was normal for most of those in the District. For the dead officer and her family—whatever family she might have—things would never be normal again.

The cold air snapped him back into the present, and he walked toward the Jeep, chewing himself out for leaving his coat on the passenger seat. He pulled away from the curb with the help of a uniform who stepped out and ordered the line of traffic to stop, making a gap. Trask headed for his office.

Minutes later he pulled into the basement parking garage of 555 4th Street, N.W., the Office of the United States Attorney for the District of Columbia, the "Triple Nickel" to the worker bees inside. The elevator took him to the fifth floor, home to the attorneys and staff assigned to prosecute cases in federal district court. The door opened, but Trask wasn't ready to get out yet. He pushed a button and rode back down to the street.

He walked westward half a block to the north end of Judiciary Square. In the center of some older courthouse buildings was a small reflecting pool, surrounded by curved walls with the names of thousands of dead heroes—agents, deputies, and cops killed in the line of duty—etched into the stone: The National Law Enforcement Officers Memorial. Trask walked to an all-too-familiar spot on the wall, and ran his hands along the names of Juan Ramirez and Robert Lassiter. Juan had been Dixon Carter's partner before he had been murdered. Lassiter wasn't a cop; he'd been Trask's mentor and sponsor in the U.S. Attorney's Office before he was gunned down on the courthouse steps. A few feet away he found another slain officer's name. They'd called him Sam when he was alive, before he died in an explosion set off by agents of the Zeta chief Ramón Dominguez.

There's another warrior joining your company today, guys. Welcome her home. Her name will be on this wall soon enough, along with the names of all the cops gunned down after that Ferguson, Missouri, mess. We'll do what we can down here.

Trask walked around the small pool and looked at another wall. A dark, sculpted lioness lay with her paw draped over the edge. Underneath her, an inscription had been carved: *IN VALOR THERE IS HOPE.*

Trask nodded. *I hope that's true.* He walked back toward the office, feeling a familiar fear seeping into his gut. It wasn't a fear of danger; there was no reason for that yet. It was the fear of failure, of not being able to find the killer of a cop, of not finding enough evidence to convict the thug who'd ripped her head in half.

When the elevator door opened this time, Trask didn't bother going to his own office. He turned instead toward the corner suite, the office of Ross Eastman, the United States Attorney for the District of Columbia. Julia Forrest, Eastman's secretary, smiled as she saw him, and waved him into the large room behind her.

"He's been waiting for you, Jeff. I see that you got my voicemail."

"Yep." Trask smiled back as he headed for the door. *I'm lying—I haven't heard it yet—but I know that damned red light is blinking on my desk phone and I know what your message says, which is why I'm here now.*

"Sorry I took a while getting here," Trask said as Eastman looked up from his desk. "Dixon Carter called me from the Lincoln Memorial while I was driving in and I went straight out there."

"No problem. I figured as much." Eastman pushed the glasses back on his nose and sank into a big leather chair. "What do we have?"

"A very dead Park Police officer: a female officer," Trask said. "The Medical Examiner's report will list the cause of death as whatever the official medical term is for having her head pulled apart."

"*My God!*" Eastman shook his head in disgust.

Trask knew his boss's concern was real. Eastman had been a line prosecutor in the office once upon a time. Unlike the states, the District didn't have a senator to make recommendations to the president for the appointment of a U.S. Attorney, and the job here wasn't usually a stepping stone to higher office. Ross Eastman took his job seriously for what it was, and genuinely mourned the loss of any law enforcement officer.

"What are you thinking?" Eastman asked. "Any ideas yet?"

"Not really. The Park Police called in Dix Carter and Frank Wilkes to help. They know they're the best in the metro when it comes to murder investigations and crime scenes, but it will officially be a Park Police investigation since it's one of their own." Trask paused for a few seconds. "I hope to hell our people here aren't under attack like those poor cops who got ambushed in New York and Mississippi. Dix and his partner are pulling the surveillance videos from the memorial. Maybe they'll tell us something."

Eastman nodded. "There are several folks who could have handled that Ferguson mess more productively."

"It's like Bob Lassiter used to say," Trask said. "Politics is always an infection in our business. I've always appreciated your efforts in trying to keep that to a minimum."

"I hope I can keep doing that." Eastman nodded again. "This time I'm not very optimistic."

"That's my biggest worry if this thing *is* a racial revenge attack, Ross." Trask felt his temper rising. "The freakin' attorney general himself goes with the bogus media spin and helps stir this all up. We might have a lot more cops alive if the initial headline from the Missouri incident had been, 'Man robs store, attacks police officer, is shot resisting arrest.' Instead we get, 'White cop shoots and kills unarmed black teenager.'"

"He was a teenager, he was black, he was unarmed, and he was killed."

Trask frowned. "Let's not let the other facts dilute that line of publicity, shall we? The age of majority in Missouri is seventeen, and Michael Brown was eighteen; he was, therefore, an adult by law. A videocam recorded the store robbery, minutes before he attacked the cop, and the forensics, ballistics and bullet holes in the police cruiser backed the cop's story. Those pieces of science aren't something that any grand jury witness fabricated. Despite all that, the AG sends 100 FBI agents to Ferguson and does nothing to douse the flames started by a bunch of race-baiters. Besides, as anyone who has played a single snap of grown-up football can tell you, there's no such thing as an unarmed 300-pound man. That hulk at the Lincoln probably weighed at least that much, and he apparently just pulled our victim apart."

Trask took a breath. "The Garner matter in New York was more troubling for me, since it was a silly-ass arrest for selling loose cigarettes. They could have just written the guy a ticket, but there's nothing indicating it was racial. Even Garner's family is saying that."

"You're right," Eastman conceded. "You just have to understand the background that the AG comes from."

"No, I don't," Trask shot back, "because it's agenda-driven bias and it becomes the very infection we've been talking about. The AG may be one of the guys who appointed both of us, but any racial spin isn't part of the justice we're supposed to be about which, by the way, the police are *also* entitled to receive. At the moment, they're the only ones *not* presumed innocent. We're supposed to be the only federal department where this stuff doesn't matter unless it's a hate crime. We're supposed to be color-blind and let the facts—the evidence—drive our decisions. If Dr. King's 'content of character' test had been put in front of Michael Brown, I'm *not* sure he would have passed it."

Trask paused again. He could feel the heat in his face, and it was not the time or the place to let the anger in him spill over.

"We all know there are bad cops out there, but the vast majority of 'em are straight, and there's no evidence at this point saying the cop in Ferguson was one of the bad ones. He'll get cleared by the FBI sooner or later, but in the meantime good people are dying just for wearing a police uniform."

"I know, and that's why I want you to handle this, Jeff." Eastman got up and stared out his window. "You're my senior litigation counsel—my best investigative *and* trial attorney. Work with Carter and the Park Police on it. I know we owe our best to that murdered officer, and that's you as far as I'm concerned. I just want you to be aware of the pressures we may have to deal with."

"I'd be a fool not to be aware of them," Trask said. "I just need to know that after the usual suspects show up to organize their protests you'll want me to do the right thing, wherever it leads. I promise not to tell the press what I think of their precious politicians and pot-stirrers."

"Thanks," Eastman said sarcastically. He walked back to his desk before looking at Trask again. When he did, he spoke calmly. "Go do your job. Go do the right thing."

Trask walked out past Julia, who gave him just enough of a raised eyebrow to indicate that she had heard the entire exchange. He found Dixon Carter and his partner standing in the hall outside his office. Detective Timothy Wisniewski was as tall as Carter, but about ten years younger, much leaner, and much whiter.

"Video?" Trask asked as he unlocked the door.

Neither detective said a word, but Wisniewski held up an envelope, indicating that the contents were from the Lincoln's surveillance cameras. Trask waived them in, accepting the envelope. He pushed the power button on his office computer and motioned the cops into some seats as he waited for it to warm up.

"Excuse me while I recharge my bat phone," Trask said, pulling an iPhone from his shirt pocket and plugging it into a dock on the credenza behind his desk.

"That's not the number we have for you, is it?" Wisniewski asked.

"No, you've got this one, my personal cell," Trask said, patting a larger phone in a hard plastic holster on the left side of his belt. "To be honest, I don't even know what the number is for that thing." His head tilted toward the iPhone. "Ross makes me carry it, but I never give the number out. One, because I don't know it; and two, because the damn thing is so password-protected that it's virtually useless. We have to use at least two of every type of characters under the sun, change that password every full moon, and try to type that password on that tiny little keyboard in order to try and make any non-emergency call. I just use my own. I can pair it to the Bluetooth in the car, and I can actually communicate with it."

"Why does he make you carry it, then? Doesn't your office have to pay for the account?" Carter asked.

"Yes, we have to pay for it," Trask answered. "Ross wants me to have access to all the office email. Of course, I've never actually checked my e-mail on it. I do that on this dinosaur." He pointed to the computer on his desk.

"Don't you get text messages on it?" Wisniewski was fondling his own cell phone, as if he'd sent Trask a text.

"The phone might get them, but I don't. I still think texting is for sixteen-year-olds who don't want to pay attention in class, or while driving. I prefer oral communications in the manner of humanoids. Those aren't recorded, and don't become something we have to give to the defense after a discovery motion." Trask was looking at the cell phone from his belt. "I've got the number for the bat phone stored in here as a contact if I ever need to call myself."

"What's that number?" Wisniewski stood poised to enter it into his own phone.

"Like I said, I don't know," Trask said, returning his personal phone to the case on his belt. "I could look it up on this one, but I already turned it off."

Wisniewski rolled his eyes toward Carter, who chuckled.

"I'm not really technophobic," Trask said. "I just remember that whole eight-track fiasco. Not every new gimmick or gadget is really an improvement."

A chime on the computer on Trask's desk indicated that it was powered up and ready to use. He put the DVD in the tray and closed it. The computer made a whirring noise, and a menu flashed on the screen. Trask selected the file with the largest data content, and a video from the corner surveillance camera of the Lincoln Memorial appeared. Trask hit the "full screen" icon, and clicked the play arrow after that. He turned the monitor so that Carter and Wisniewski could see the screen.

For several seconds there was nothing to see, just the unchanging view of the outside of the Memorial from the camera perched above it. Trask fast-forwarded the video until he noticed some movement, then he froze the picture. A large hooded figure appeared on the screen, placing a soda can on the outside of the pavement at the bottom of a column.

Trask looked up at Carter and Wisniewski. "Anything?" he asked.

"Big guy. Black sweats, gloves. He hasn't looked up yet," Wisniewski offered. "If he's our subject, it's not much to go on."

Trask looked at Carter again. The senior detective nodded in agreement with his partner.

"What size shoes made those prints at the scene, Dix?" Trask asked.

"Not sure yet," Carter said. "Frank Wilkes said he'd work on both the size and the make. I wear a size thirteen, and I put my foot down next to the best print for comparison. It was at least two sizes bigger than mine."

"Big dude with huge feet who owns a hoodie, sweats, and gloves. No hair color, eye color, or race." Wisniewski was jotting in a pocket notebook. He snorted. "We should have him in custody shortly."

"I don't really want to watch the rest of this, but that's what they pay us for," Trask said, shaking his head. "Maybe there's a lead in this somewhere." He clicked on the play icon again. The big man on the screen headed into the interior of the colonnade, into the shadows and out of camera view. Trask fast-forwarded the video again, pausing it when Officer Jackie Turner appeared on the edge of the pavement, bending over to pick up the can. Trask put the playback into slow motion, and watched as the big figure in black hurled himself from the shadows onto Turner's back, one hand reaching down over Turner's to toss her gun to the side and out of view, the other massive paw gripping tightly around her head, pulling it backward.

Trask paused the video. "Was her gun found at the scene?" he asked Carter.

"No. I asked when I saw it wasn't in her holster. None of the guys there saw it anywhere. We even did a walk through the bushes at the base. Only found that soda can. I told them to bag and mark it. Glad that I did, now."

"Our thug must have taken the gun with him," Trask thought out loud.

"I'll get the make, model, and ballistics, serial number from her unit," Wisniewski said, jotting again in the notebook. "Park Police District One handles the memorials. We'll print the can, even though the killer was gloved up at the scene. Maybe he put the gloves on after having a drink. We might get lucky."

Trask started the video again. The man's right hand joined his left about the victim's head, each hand pulling against the other, until a red spray suddenly spouted from between them.

"*Oh, SHIT!*" shouted Wisniewski, turning his head away from the screen.

"Wilkes was right," Trask said. "The bastard just pulled the top of her head off."

"Look at that," Carter said, pointing at the screen where the video was still running. "He's proud of it."

The killer was holding the top of Turner's head up with both hands, high above the rest of her body. Her arteries were still gushing blood onto the marble at his feet. Then he raised his trophy higher with his right hand, upward toward the corner of the Memorial.

"That asshole knew he was on camera!" Wisniewski growled, just as the figure on the screen tossed the top of Jackie Turner's head into the shadows and jogged out of view.

Trask turned the video off. He activated the computer's Internet browser and typed a phrase into the search engine. When the results of the search appeared, he clicked the mouse pointer on a link to a news article.

"Look," he said as he rolled his chair back to let Carter have a closer look. "The can was bait."

"July, 2013," Carter noted. "Chinese national female arrested for vandalism at the National Cathedral. Investigation revealed she had also vandalized the Lincoln Memorial by slinging green paint all over the place. She had the paint concealed in a soda can. I remember that now. Bet the Park Police were still on high alert for copycats."

"Let's hope nobody copies *this* little stunt," Trask said. "I know you guys have been asked to the party, but it's a Park Police casualty, and they'll want the case. Any idea who's being assigned?"

"Yeah," Carter said. "Nick McCarver. He's out of town on leave, already on his way back. We're supposed to pick him up when he lands at Reagan to take him to the autopsy. You coming?"

"Think I'll skip this one," Trask said. "I hope I'm wrong and that something useful comes out of the body exam, but I doubt it. Our manner and cause of death are on this little horror flick." He removed the DVD from the computer tray and handed it back to Wisniewski. "Keep me posted. You have my number." He patted the cell phone on his belt.

———

Chapter Two

Trask left his office at 4:00 p.m., about an hour earlier than his official quitting time. Having started the day early and worked through lunch, he didn't bother putting a leave slip into the system. He left a voice mail on the phone of Mrs. Jeffrey Trask, telling her that he'd be a little late getting home. He had a stop or two to make first.

The first detour on his way home was to the Cheltenham Federal Law Enforcement Training Center, FLETC or "fletcee" for short, in suburban Maryland. The United States Marshals' firing range was in the back. Ross Eastman had agreed to sponsor his continuing authorization to carry a firearm—or firearms, as was Trask's habit—given the possible danger of the new case assigned to him. Trask had to maintain his skills by qualifying on the Marshals Service's range in order to qualify for this privilege.

He took his gun bag out of the back of the Jeep, checked to verify that he had a couple of boxes of 9mm ammo inside, and went in to fire. On the way to the range he passed a weight room. A poster outside the door showed a huge, burly convict in prison orange doing pull-ups in a prison yard. The words under the photograph warned law enforcement officers: "Every day that you don't work out, he does." Trask paused at the poster making a mental note, when he heard a voice behind him.

"Or, you could just shoot him."

Trask turned to see the smiling face of Deputy Marshal Shane Lightsey, the Marshals Service's range officer for the day.

"I hope I never have to make that call, but just in case, here I am again," Trask said. He pointed toward the poster. "I'm sure not going to win any other kind of fight with that guy."

"Not many of us would. I always wonder why we give 'em any workout equipment at all. Most of 'em come out a lot bigger than they were when they went inside."

Trask nodded, still looking at the poster. "I may have seen him on a video a couple of hours ago."

"I heard you pulled the case from the Lincoln," Lightsey said. "Was it as bad as I've heard?"

Trask nodded. *No secrets among cops. Word travels fast.* "Worse. There's no way anyone could sufficiently describe that horror."

"Come on in." Lightsey motioned toward the doors to one of the firing ranges. "I'll grab you a target."

A half-hour and a hundred rounds later, Trask left the range qualified to carry his weapons for another six months, and slightly overdue to clean the Sig Sauer pistol concealed in a holster around his right ankle. He turned the Jeep eastward when he reached Maryland Route 5, and drove through Waldorf, passing the exit to his house in the St. Charles subdivision. He kept going southeast until he reached what had come to be known among the area's police circles as the FOP (Fraternal Order of Police) East, a bar and grill with a neon sign on the front identifying the establishment as "The Beverly."

The place had been a chain restaurant before its conversion. It had a bar on one side, which had remained in place. Most of the restaurant tables on the other side had been removed to make room for a decent-sized dance floor, with a small stage centered against one wall. When a band wasn't hired for the evening, a large jukebox could be heard playing compact discs of songs that had been recorded long before CDs had replaced cassettes and eight-tracks. The Stones' "Time Is on My Side" was entertaining only the owner of the joint as Trask stepped inside.

"Well, if it isn't my favorite federal prosecutor," the voice chirped from behind the bar.

Trask smiled, and reached over the counter to shake the man's hand. The bartender was pushing sixty now, his thinning hair almost completely white, topping an angular face that sported a goatee of the same color. Prior to his retirement from the District of Columbia's Metropolitan Police Department, Commander William "Willie" Sivella had been in charge of the Violent Crimes

Division of the force, and the commanding officer and long-time mentor of one Detective Dixon Carter.

"Thought I might see you here today," Sivella said. "You picked up the case from the Lincoln Memorial, didn't you?" Sivella slid a cold mug of draft Michelob across the bar.

"Yeah. Dix tell you?"

"Yep. I knew before that, though. I just figured that if Ross Eastman still had a brain in his head, you'd get this one. You're his best guy."

"Thanks, Willie. After seeing that gal's poor head this morning, I don't think *her* brain was all that intact."

"That's what I heard. Kathy called me after the autopsy. I just got off the phone with her before you walked in."

Trask nodded. Kathy Davis, the District's Deputy Medical Examiner, had been Sivella's significant other for a significant number of years.

"I'm surprised you weren't at the exam for this one," Sivella said.

"I watched the film from the memorial's surveillance cam," Trask said. "It didn't leave many questions unanswered. Dix and Tim were there for the autopsy. They said they were picking up McCarver from the airport, too. Park Police guy. You know him?"

"Yeah. You don't?"

"Only when I see him. A couple of conferences or ceremonies here or there. We've never had a case together. I thought you might be able to give me a scouting report, since you seem to know every cop who's come through these parts since they *buried* Lincoln."

"Remind me to give you a warm beer next time, smartass." Sivella shot Trask a mock warning glare. "Anyway, Nick McCarver's a good man. No nonsense, no games. Loves his people and they love him. The only issue I could see Nick having on this would be if anybody tried to take the case away from him. It's one of his own who's gone, and he won't let the world forget that. He also won't stop 'til the bad guy's down for the count, whichever way that has to go. He'll be happy to have the help from Dix, Tim, and from you, as long as everybody knows who's running the investigative side of things."

Trask nodded, and sipped the beer from the frosted mug. "I'll try not to step on his toes."

"Then you'll be making a mistake."

Trask frowned. "I don't follow . . .?"

"You're as good an investigator as you are a prosecutor, Jeff, which makes you pretty damned scary." Sivella pointed a finger at him. "You owe it to the victim—and to Nick and everybody else—to speak your mind and let the chips fall where they may, the same way you always operated with me. I'm sure Dix and Tim are giving Nick the run down on you while you're here getting one on him, so he shouldn't resent your input. They should be here in a few minutes, anyway."

"I kind of figured that. That's why I'm here."

"And I thought it was my company and the beer—the *cold* beer."

Trask looked up and smiled. "The beer *is* pretty good." He took another sip from the mug. "Something else is pulling on me pretty hard, Will. The murder this morning has all the markings of a targeted assassination. I'm worried that the race-baiters are stirring these things up nationally."

Sivella grunted. "You mean the media coverage and politicians have stirred things up. That and the anti-police mentality that's already been boiling in some of our neighborhoods for years. Looks like it's now in the White House and at Main Justice."

"Exactly."

"You can't worry about that. It'll mess with your mind. I've gone through every form of 'alternative' policing you can think of, every kind of community interaction training that some shiny-faced sociology major who's never been on a street at night could think of writing up for his dissertation. There are some out there who hate and kill. Simple as that. Always have been. It'll never change. They kill more of their own than cops. Find 'em and put 'em inside. All you can do is be fair and do the right thing. Get the right guy and convict him."

"I got those orders from Eastman already."

"Then he's got your back."

"Maybe, but I'm not sure who has *his*. The whole goal of the department these days seems to be letting people *out* of jail and claiming that we all need to be more sensitive." Trask pulled a folded paper from his jacket. "I got this today in official email. It's from the National Institute of Justice, claiming that some study they ran proves that 'sending an offender to prison' and 'increasing the severity of punishment does little to deter crime.'"

"Somebody never got spanked as a kid," Sivella snorted. "Sounds like the same guys who wrote those 'alternative policing' papers. They must have just sent the surveys to convicts, who—what a surprise—said they didn't like jail and that we should try something else. I'm pretty sure that whoever's serving a prison term is deterred from crime while he's there, and if he's there longer, he's deterred longer."

"It's not doing much for the morale on our side of things." Trask shook his head. "The sentences we work for get cut back or commuted. Bad guys get put back on the streets, more victims are dead or suffering, and cops are dying just for being cops."

"And that's something we're not going to allow to continue, isn't it?" a voice from behind Trask asked.

Trask turned to see a tall, lanky figure in a Park Police uniform holding out his hand. The collar brass identified the man as a captain. Dixon Carter and Tim Wisniewski were flanking him.

"Jeff Trask, Nick McCarver," Sivella said.

Trask shook the offered hand. "We're going to sure as hell *try* to stop it. We were just trying to figure out who was on which side of the fight."

McCarver nodded. "You saw the surveillance video?"

"I wish I hadn't."

Another nod. "Carter here tells me you came out to the scene."

"Another sight I wish I could forget."

"Any suggestions?" McCarver asked.

Trask paused for a moment. *Is he testing the guy who really isn't a cop, or is this an honest question?*

"Just a couple," he finally said. "One, once Frank Wilkes and his crime scene guys can tell us what size of sneakers this brute was wearing, I want to see if Lorton or the BOP has any record of releasing someone who fits that profile within the last couple of years."

McCarver nodded again, thoughtfully. "He *could* be a cop-hater fresh out of the DC detention center or the Bureau of Prisons. He could also be a cop-hater who's never been inside."

"I saw one of those posters while I was at the range today," Trask said. "You know, work out today because the cons inside are working out. The thug I saw on that video had been pumping some serious iron somewhere. You don't pull an adult human's head apart without being as strong as a bull."

"Okay," McCarver said. "Makes sense." He looked at Trask. "You said 'a couple.'"

"Your officer's weapon was taken," Trask said. "Are Park Police service weapons test-fired and catalogued in NIBIN?" Trask referred to the National Integrated Ballistics Information Network, a clearinghouse database used to trace bullets to the weapons that fired them.

"Hell, no," McCarver said. "If all the police weapons were catalogued, the most embarrassed people on the planet would be the ATF clowns who run NIBIN, since all the Fast and Furious guns would keep showing up on it." He looked at Trask, scowling. "We're on the same page. I'm worried about that weapon showing up in another attack. I've always had every officer in my district fire their weapons and keep a bullet and casing in the event a gun ever got lost or stolen. We went through Jackie's locker before we went to the autopsy." He reached into his pants pocket, and pulled out a sandwich baggie with a spent round and shell casing inside. "She was a good cop. Followed orders."

"Good," Trask said. "I hope to hell we don't need that, but at least we have it. What kind of pistols do your guys carry?"

"Heckler & Koch P2000s. Forty caliber." McCarver seemed to relax. He managed a half-hearted smile. "Glad you're with us, Jeff. I've heard nothing but good things about you from these two." McCarver nodded toward Carter and Wisniewski. "They told me you were one of those guys who's always thinking 'outside the box,' if you'll pardon the phrase."

"He's never been *inside* the damned box," Wisniewski quipped. He pointed at the taps to Sivella's right. "Are those working, or did Jeff drain 'em before we got here? We were off the clock hours ago."

"Sorry," Sivella said. "What's your pick?" He took a step toward the taps, pausing as he saw Carter responding to his ringing cell phone.

"Whatever Jeff's having. It might smarten me up." Wisniewski took a stool beside Trask, slapping him on the shoulder as he sat down.

"It'll have to wait," Carter said somberly. "We've got another officer down. Seven D. Our guy took some bullets to the head. It doesn't look like he's going to make it."

"Who is it, Dix?" Willie Sivella's face was as serious as Carter's. Sivella had been the district commander of the Seventh District—known as "7D"—in the southeastern area of DC before taking over the police department's Violent Crimes Division.

"Bart Roberts."

"Shit. He has four kids." Sivella threw his towel down on the bar.

Carter nodded. "They dug another round out of his squad car. Forty caliber."

———

Chapter Three

This is wrong on about fourteen different levels.

Trask looked out the rear passenger side window of Carter's Buick as they turned onto Wheeler Road in the Anacostia section of the District of Columbia. Carter was driving. Wisniewski rode shotgun, and McCarver was sitting next to Trask in the back.

I'm going INTO town and it's after dark. I should be home now with Lynn. I'm riding in the back of Dix's car, where countless perps have sat before me. Worst of all, we're going in because not one but TWO cops have died today.

Phil Collins was singing "In the Air Tonight" in Trask's head.

Yeah, there's something coming in the air, and it's not good.

The kaleidoscope of whirling emergency lights firing their beams into the night sky—a collection of the beacons from police cruisers, fire and EMT vehicles, and another ambulance that would go home empty—told him they had reached the spot. He climbed out and followed Carter and the others to where a group of police brass had huddled together near the rear of a body van. Trask glanced inside the open doors and saw two, black low-quarter oxfords, the uniform footwear of the Metropolitan Police Department, protruding from under the small tarp that covered the body. He turned and tried to focus on the conversation that Carter was having with the others, hanging back so as not to inject himself into the mix. It wasn't time yet, not his place. This was a moment reserved for those who had actually patrolled the streets, those who—like their fallen friend—had put themselves in harm's way on every shift.

Trask saw that Carter had turned and nodded in his direction, and a figure stepped from the group toward him.

"Dix tells me you're on this, Colonel," Major Chester Halsey Williams said, extending his hand. "I'm glad to hear that. Good to see you again."

"Not like this, Chet," Trask said, smiling ruefully. Williams was the only cop on the force who addressed Trask by his rank in the Air Force Reserve. Both the men wore service academy class rings on their right hands. Trask's Air Force Academy ring bore a blue topaz in the center. Williams's Annapolis ring also had a blue stone in the center—a sapphire. "I *may* get this case. It depends on the ballistics. We heard this involved a forty caliber, and a service H&K was taken off the Park Police victim at the Lincoln. Her captain over there"—Trask pointed toward McCarver—"had the foresight to have his folks keep some fired rounds in case a weapon was stolen. In any case, I'm very sorry about your officer."

"Damnedest thing." Williams shook his head. "I had the ERT for almost three years, only had one guy get nicked at all. I'm down here for a month and this happens. Just got back from letting his wife—his widow—know. Hardest thing I've ever had to do. In the Corps we wrote letters to the families. Still sucked, but we weren't ringing their doorbells, and it was never as much of an unexpected kick in the crotch. In the desert, you knew your number could be called any day, and way too many were. Here, you'd think it would be different."

Trask nodded. He remembered meeting Williams during the Major's days in command of the ERT. The District's more sensitive politicians had found the usual SWAT label for a police tactical team to be potentially offensive to those who might need swatting, and had chosen to call it an "Emergency Response Team" instead. Even though he'd been named for two admirals by a father who had served as a surface fleet captain, Williams had opted for a commission in the Marines after graduating from the Naval Academy. They'd sent him to Iraq, after which he had volunteered for duty in the Metropolitan Police Department, which had sent him to Anacostia to command 7D.

Trask saw that Frank Wilkes was walking toward them. "Long day for us all, Frank," he said. "Got anything to test?"

"Looks like a good round for matching," Wilkes said, holding an evidence envelope in his left hand. "Headrest slowed it down a little, lodged in the back door. Not too deformed. I heard we might have a sample round for comparison."

Trask nodded toward McCarver, who was still a few feet away, talking to Carter. "See the good captain there. Let me know as soon as you're able to put 'em under a scope. If it's the same gun, I'm in. If not, it goes downstairs to the Superior Court homicide guys."

Wilkes nodded, and headed toward McCarver.

"I hope it's a match," Williams said.

Trask raised an eyebrow. "You do?"

"Yeah. It means you're on both cases, and we have only one cop killer to find."

———

From a third-floor apartment window overlooking Wheeler Road, two men watched the scene below with satisfaction. The younger man, small and wiry, leaned back in a folding chair, his feet pushing against the bottom of the open window sill. An older man, sitting to his left, leaned forward and swept a finger from left to right as if pointing out every police officer in the block below. The older man unconsciously stroked his beard as he spoke.

"See, Ibrahim? It's just like I said. Put one of the pigs down and you get a hundred more swarming in. This is what we call a 'target-rich environment.' You did well tonight. Soon we will all be in the fight. We just need to select the time and place."

———

It was almost midnight when Trask got back to Waldorf. He knew what he'd see when he pushed open the front door, and he lowered his head at the top of the front steps to meet them. The heads of the three rescue mutts ranged in size from the dark, massive, blue-eyed husky mix Boo, to the smaller, tan, Shiba Inu mix Nikki, and finally down to the little mini-schnauzer Tasha. After receiving the usual face bath greeting of eager tongues, Trask stepped inside and hugged Lynn, who was wrapped in her thickest winter bathrobe.

"They missed their daddy," she said, wiping his cheek dry with the edge of her robe before kissing him herself. "I know you've had a rough night. It's all over the news, or was."

Trask glanced past her down into the den on the lower level. The 24-hour news channel had shifted from coverage of the murdered cops to a couple of talking heads who were screaming at each other. Trask pulled Lynn's head to his shoulder and kissed her forehead as he listened for a moment. He recognized one of the program moderator's guests as Aashif Asalati, an Afghan immigrant known to run the most extreme mosque in Washington. His debating opponent for the evening was Amal Saleem, one of the few moderate Muslims to have stepped from the shadows to speak out against the extremists like Asalati, who was using his current TV face time to declare that any American cop, soldier or other infidel who opposed the true law—*sharia*—deserved whatever cruel fate that befell them.

"I guess there's a little hope when one of Allah's faithful isn't totally raving mad and is brave enough to speak out," Trask said.

"You haven't eaten anything, have you?"

"Just a big slice of depression. Watching good people get pulled apart and blown away doesn't do much for an appetite."

"Sit. I'll heat some stew up for you. It's still on the stove."

He sat on the couch in front of the television, and was immediately surrounded by the dogs. Nikki and Tasha took their places on either side of him on the couch, while Boo settled in by lying directly on top of his feet. His eyes followed Lynn as she climbed the stairs toward the kitchen. She'd just turned forty, but looked at least six years younger.

I'm lucky as hell. There aren't many women on the planet who would put up with this lifestyle, or understand it. She does.

After enlisting at seventeen, Lynn Preston Trask had put in twenty years in air force blue herself, the last fourteen as a special agent of the Office of Special Investigations. She'd been able to pass as a younger airman for most of her career, a talent that had enabled her to become one of the service's most successful undercover narcs. She had posed as a two-striper in an orderly room and a new technician fresh from training in a hospital emergency room, whatever was required in order to be accepted in the circles of those interested in supplementing their military pay by participating in the drug trade. Her investigative experience had then resulted in a successful application for an analyst's desk at the Washington Field Office of the FBI.

She knows the job, feels the losses as much as I do.

Lynn reappeared in the doorway to the den, holding a wooden tray with a large bowl on it. Steam and an incredible aroma were both rising from the bowl.

"A little late for something this heavy, isn't it?" she asked.

He shook his head in disagreement, taking the tray and inhaling a mouthful, blowing the steam out to keep from scalding his throat. "Never too late for this. I could eat it for every meal, and snacks, too. I'd just weigh 400 pounds and have cholesterol readings that would set records."

She laughed. "That's why I have you on a strict ration. Once a week. I just didn't know this would be the night—"

"—when all the crazies would converge under the full moon? Neither did I, or I might have called in sick or something."

"I know you better than that. You'd have left to be there earlier." She let him gulp down a few more spoonfuls of the stew. "Who has the cases on the investigative side?"

He finished the bowl, exhaled and sat back into the couch. "Dixon Carter was at the scene at the Lincoln Memorial. Since the victim there was a Park Police officer, her captain—a guy named Nick McCarver—wants to honcho the case, but he's smart enough and flexible enough to want to keep Dix on the investigation, and that means Tim Wisniewski is in, too. Nick and I rode into town in the back of Carter's car. It turns out that McCarver lives about a block away from us. Next street off the parkway."

Lynn leaned forward. Trask read her mind before she asked the question.

"Yes, the Bureau may also get involved, since the offense is a federal one, killing a federal officer in the performance of her duties, in which case it will probably get assigned to your squad."

She nodded. "I love working with my favorite prosecutor. How about the other case?"

"A little more iffy. The victim was an officer in 7D. One of Chet Williams's guys. May or may not be related to the first murder."

"Related?"

Trask saw the scowl on her face. Her mind was already trying to connect dots she hadn't seen yet.

"The Park Police cop's gun, a forty caliber, was taken at the Lincoln. The 7D guy was killed by a forty caliber. Could be a match. Frank Wilkes is working on that now. If it's the same weapon . . ."

"Then we have our own little war on law enforcement, just like Ferguson and New York City." She shook her head. "How the hell did we get to this point?"

"To be determined," Trask said. "When we find the killer, we'll ask him."

"Any leads yet?" she asked.

"Just from the Lincoln: a bloody footprint the size of a small ski, and a surveillance video of what could have been the incredible hulk in a hoodie ripping the victim's head apart."

"Oh my God!"

"Yeah. I don't know what the movie rating is for four levels past triple-X, but what that surveillance cam caught this morning—or I guess it was yesterday by now—is certainly a qualifier."

The cell phone on Trask's belt began playing a customized ringtone. He'd picked the theme from TV's *Law and Order* series to alert him when any cop or agent was calling about a case. He looked at the calling number displayed on the screen.

"What do we have, Frank?"

"Ballistics are back. It's a match, Jeff. Sorry to bother you this late, but I thought you'd want to know."

"You were right, of course. Get some sleep yourself, bud. We're all gonna need some before this is over."

"I'll try. You, too."

"Yeah. Goodnight."

Lynn shook her head. "One murdered cop's gun used to murder another cop." She noticed that her husband was lost in a thought. "Can I help?"

He looked up and smiled. "Not for this. I was just wondering if this could wait until morning before I told Eastman."

"You're right. That's your call to make, when you want to make it."

"I need to think about that. Actually, no I don't. It's too damned late and I need to *not* think about any of this for a few hours."

She leaned forward and kissed him. "Maybe you need a distraction."

He smiled. "Is that my call to make, too? If it is . . ."

She shook her head. "My call, otherwise you'd never leave me alone. I *am*, however, making it tonight, assuming you can think about something other than your next major case."

She turned, dropping the robe behind her, and pointed toward the bedroom without looking back.

———

Chapter Four

At 6:30 a.m., Captain Roger Braswell looked in the mirror and adjusted the black tie so that it fell symmetrically between the black lapels of his uniform coat. It was a uniform recognized only by a few even in the law enforcement community, and even then only by a few of those in the vicinity of Washington, D.C.

Braswell gave himself a rueful shrug as he looked at his reflection. There were millions of citizens in the United States who had never heard of the Uniformed Division of the United States Secret Service. They certainly knew of the plain clothes agents who protected the president, his family, and candidates for that high office. They had also recently heard of the rogue agents who were making the wrong kind of news by refusing to pay their Colombian hookers during an international road trip, but the Uniformed Division? His officers might as well be wearing invisible cloaks.

The agents get the glory, even when they generate the scandals. We operate in the open, but are the most "secret" of the service.

He shook his head. Three of his best men had just applied for transfers to become agents on the protection details. He had trouble keeping the best people on his team because of the virtual anonymity of their jobs. He promised himself to try and talk at least two of them into coming to their senses. Their jobs were more stable, not subject to the whim of some member of the imperial family, and with more time to spend at home with their own families, but . . . the Uniformed Division was simply not why most joined the Secret Service. His guys were going to leave. He'd have to accept and train new officers, as he had done so many times before.

Braswell turned from the mirror and crossed the bedroom to where Becky was still sleeping. He bent over and kissed her forehead. She opened her eyes, smiled, and—as she did every morning—said, "Be careful." He smiled back at her and kissed her again before heading for the garage.

I will. All the evildoers flocking to the Veep's house will have my full attention today.

The drive from Bethesda into the District promised to be the usual, uneventful commute. Braswell figured that he'd be at Number One Observatory Circle, the official residence of the vice president, in twenty minutes or so. It was his team's assigned job to protect Number Two from all those who wished him harm. *As if he's really on anyone's radar.* Braswell punched the preset for his favorite FM oldies station, and the staccato punches of Edwin Starr's "War" blared through the Ford Fusion. Braswell hit the power button on the radio, silencing it.

Never did like that song. Quiet is good for a change.

He headed southeast along Wisconsin Avenue, looking eastward toward the magnificent silhouette of the Washington Cathedral. He had always loved the view.

God still has a home in this godless town. That's a good thing.

He returned his attention to the road, and a flurry of activity to his right caught his eye.

What the hell? Here?

A young tough in a stocking cap was ripping the purse out of the hands of a woman on the sidewalk on the west side of the avenue. Once the victim's bag had been pried from her grasp, the thief started running south, toward the intersection where Cathedral Avenue intersected both Wisconsin and Massachusetts. Braswell gunned the Ford's engine.

He'll run right at the intersection. I can cut him off. A slight smile crossed his face. *Uniformed Division is making an arrest today, boys.*

He swerved right into the intersection, pulling the car into the curb in front of the fleeing felon. Braswell jumped from the driver's seat, his right hand reaching back to his hip for his service weapon. He yelled at the thief to stop, and to his surprise, the perp did. Even more surprising, the guy was smiling at him. Not a friendly smile, but a smirk. Braswell instinctively followed the thief's eyes and turned to look behind him. He saw another man, with a gun of his own pointed at Braswell's head. The explosion of the round from the gun was the last sound Roger Braswell ever heard.

———

Trask got to the scene shortly after 8:30. He pulled his Jeep to the side of the street just outside the barrier tape. He flashed his credentials to a patrolman, and was waved through. Carter and Wisniewski were already comparing notes, standing a few feet away from the Ford straddling the curb.

"Crime scene's just about done." Carter pointed over his shoulder as he saw Trask approaching. "Other side of the car."

Trask circled around the rear of the Ford. He didn't recognize the uniform on the body, but the scene was all too familiar. *Head wound, entry point above right eyebrow. Staring eyes still reflecting the shock of a life's sudden end.* The victim's gun was on the concrete, a couple of inches from his right hand. *The shooter didn't want this gun, or didn't have time to grab it.* Trask saw Carter standing behind him.

"Captain Braswell. Uniformed Division of the Secret Service."

Trask nodded. He had heard of the unit, but had never met any of the officers assigned to it. "Any witnesses have anything helpful to say?"

Wisniewski came around the rear of the Ford. "I've been doing the area canvass, Jeff. We've got two eyewitnesses willing to talk—that is, to say anything intelligent."

"Understood." *Most want to walk, or run, away. If cornered, it's, "I didn't see it happen," or "I don't know," or "I got nuthin' to say."*

"They corroborate," Wisniewski continued. "Perp—small black dude in, of course, a dark-colored hoodie—snatches a purse around the corner on Wisconsin, makes the turn on foot. Captain Braswell, in the Ford, pulls in front of perp to make the stop, then perp's friend—a slightly larger black dude in another hoodie—ambushes Braswell before the captain could raise his own weapon. Perp and shooter then jump in a car—a light-colored Nissan, maybe a Sentra—and head west. Nobody got a plate."

"They left the captain's gun," Trask said.

Maybe it's not related to the murder at the Lincoln, just another skirmish in the new war on cops. No monster here with triple-x large feet.

"That's not all they left," Carter was holding a black purse, and nodding toward a woman standing outside the crime scene tape on the sidewalk. "The snatcher dropped this when the other guy shot Captain Braswell. He could easily have taken it with him, but didn't bother. I'm going to hold onto the purse itself to process for prints, but release the contents to the owner so she can have access to her credit cards, ID, all that."

Trask frowned. "Dix, the captain's car is an unmarked Ford. If this was a staged ambush, how the hell did they know he—?"

"They didn't know." Carter motioned for Trask to follow him.

They walked to the corner. Carter pointed up the street. A marked DC police cruiser was parked on the curb. A single, uniformed patrolman stood next to it, his arms folded as he leaned against the fender.

"Officer Richards." Carter flicked through a small note pad to reach the relevant page. "He was on break and just inside the building getting a snack. There's a little sandwich shop inside, nice big plate glass window for him to see the purse-snatching in progress, only he had to honor the call of nature and didn't see a thing. My guess is that our ambush crew figured he'd see the snatch and come running out to chase the snatcher. The Secret Service guy just happened to be driving by at the same time. He was in uniform, too, so he took the hit instead of Richards."

"Wrong place, last time," observed Wisniewski.

"Was Frank Wilkes here?" Trask asked.

"You know it," Carter nodded. "He'll be ready to match the bullet, once someone at the ME's office digs it out of Captain Braswell's head. If it's in shape to run any decent ballistics, we'll know pretty soon."

Trask nodded.

The slug went into the thickest part of his skull; it could have splintered into several worthless pieces, especially if it was a hollow point. A new job for Kathy Davis, and then—hopefully— more work for Wilkes.

"Any shell casings left around?"

"Not that we could find," Carter said. "Only one shot fired that we know of. Perps could have grabbed it, if they were smart; it could have landed in their clothing, rolled into a sewer grate, been kicked somewhere. At any rate, none found. Our ballistics evidence is limited to whatever's inside the victim's brain."

"Odds are it's a forty-cal."

Trask turned to see Major Chester Halsey Williams standing behind them. *This isn't 7D. Chet's out of his zone, and he's making some real leaps with that guess.*

"I heard the radio traffic," Halsey said. "Had to see if it might be related to the murder of my guy. I'll bet the autopsy ties it up."

"We'll certainly let you know, Chet," Trask said.

"I know." Halsey stared hard at Trask. "I want in, Colonel. Somebody's declared war on everything blue. I know how this works. You and Dix and the bureau feds will have a task force in place by the end of the week. Don't forget me. I've got a man down in this mess."

"That's above my pay grade, Chet," Trask said. "Talk to your chief. If that's the way she wants it played, have her talk to Eastman. Once all the low-level politics are sorted out, we'll see where we are." Trask put on his best poker face.

I hope she thinks you're too indispensable to spare, since you're a district honcho. You're wired pretty tight at the moment.

Williams pointed a finger toward the crime scene. A gurney carrying the body of Captain Roger Braswell was being loaded into a transport van which would take the corpse to the medical examiner. "This isn't right, Jeff. It's not supposed to happen like this." He turned and walked away.

"You sure you want him on the case?" Carter asked in a low voice. "He may be too close to this."

"We're all too close to it, Dix." Trask shook his head. "Anyway, like I said, not my call."

"Yeah." Carter's tone held a good deal of skepticism.

———

Chapter Five

"We can't be sure, given the condition of the slug, but it could very well be related." Trask looked up from the side chair, watching Ross Eastman pace back and forth from his desk to the wall of windows framing his very large corner office. Curtains usually drawn to protect the occupant from the crazies outside had been pulled apart to let in the morning sunlight. "Frank Wilkes was at the autopsy last night. Kathy Davis gave him the bullet—or the pieces of it, anyway—cheap ammo that fragmented when it went through Captain Braswell's skull. Not enough to run ballistics, but it was a forty-cal, and could have come from the same weapon that killed the cop in 7D."

"So we have three dead, with two definitely connected . . ." Eastman began.

"I think it's more accurate to say *probably* connected," Trask cut in. The last thing he wanted was for his boss to say something to the press that he'd have to retract later. "The first victim's weapon *was* used to kill the second victim, but we don't know for sure that the killers were operating together. Bad guy number one could have tossed the Park Police officer's gun in the trash, or could have sold it on the street to another thug, but odds are better, given what seems to be flaring up, that they *are* related. That's something we'll be looking to firm up as the proof starts coming in." He paused. "*If* it starts coming in."

Eastman gave him a sideways glance, still staring out the window. "Can you put your team back together? You've made it all work in the past."

Trask looked up, reflecting before responding. "Most of it. You know that Barry Doroz retired from the Bureau last year."

"How's his replacement? I know you have an inside source of information."

Trask smiled. Lynn had given him steady reports about her new boss, the supervisor of the gang and violent crime squad of the FBI's Washington Field Office, and the replacement for Barry Doroz.

"Supervisory Special Agent Seal is very similar to his predecessor in all aspects other than physical appearance," Trask began. "Barry Doroz was short and kind of nondescript. Richard Seal is a very large, hairy guy. His nickname is 'Grog,' after the character in the old *B.C.* comic strip. Barry Doroz could pass for a dozen different ethnic groups, and could hide in plain sight, which made him the ideal undercover agent, so he knew those ropes. Grog stands out in a crowd. No UC experience, but a lot of police smarts, nevertheless. He was a street cop before the Bureau hired him. Bottom line is that he plays well with others, just like Bear did. Not a micromanager."

"Lynn likes him?" Eastman asked.

"Yeah, and she's usually a good judge of character."

"Agreed. Let's cut to the chase. Could he manage a team including other agencies and cops, and can you work with him?"

"I don't have any reason to think otherwise at the moment, but I haven't seen him do it yet."

Eastman read the hesitation. "Concerns?"

Trask nodded. "Some. The Park Police captain—McCarver—won't be a problem as long as he gets his say in any operational coordination meetings. He's already good with Dixon Carter and Wisniewski being involved. He respects them and knows their homicide experience is a plus. I think he's good with me being on board, too. It's the 7D commander, Chet Williams, who has me worried. He showed up at the scene of the Braswell murder—way outside his turf—and seemed ready to declare war on somebody. I got the feeling he wishes he was back in charge of a tactical unit instead of a district."

"The chief wants him in," Eastman said, referring to the head of Washington's Metropolitan Police Department. "She called me this morning."

"Meaning Chet has been calling her," Trask said, mentally regretting his suggestion to Williams to do just that. "He may be too heated up over losing his man to be making the right decisions on this."

"Which is a situation you will be monitoring for me, and which I will then be prepared to discuss with his chief," Eastman said. "I trust *your* judgment on that."

I wish I did, Trask thought. He nodded. "So . . . Seal and the Bureau chair the committee . . ."

"Seal *and you,*" Eastman corrected him.

"Right. With other members including Carter, Wisniewski, McCarver, Chet Williams . . ."

"And whoever those gentlemen or their superiors wish to designate and bring along from their units to assist," Eastman said. "Secret Service will want a chair at the table as well." He noticed that Trask winced at the thought. "Again, Jeff, concerns?"

"Just this, boss." Trask had learned to use the deferential title when raising any issue to Eastman. "I expect Seal to be a good enough manager to yield to Dixon Carter when it comes to inputs on a multi-victim homicide investigation. I've already seen that Nick McCarver will. I can try and keep Chet Williams in line on that issue, and if he sees progress being made, he might be fine. I just have no feel for how much experience someone from Uniformed Secret Service will have in this kind of case, or whether they'll show up with a capital-sized ego or agenda on their sleeves, trying to take over something they can't handle. We're getting to the point where we may have too many cooks in the kitchen from the beginning."

"Understood. I'll address that with Secret Service before they send their representatives over, keeping in mind that it *was* the commanding officer of one of the vice president's details that was gunned down."

Trask nodded. *Meaning that I should keep that in mind, too.* "Understood. Thanks."

"There's one more thing."

Trask looked up, the question on his face.

"I want you to add one more cook."

The question remained on Trask's face.

Eastman turned back to the window. "I saw what the Zetas case did to you, Jeff. I want you to have some help on this. Someone you can depend on in court, and to cover for you if you need a break."

Trask shrugged. "Okay."

Eastman looked at him in disbelief. "Okay? Just like that? I expected a fight on this."

Trask shook his head, and closed his eyes. "Not this time. Like I said, we may have one, two, or three different cases working here. I'm trying not to approach it with tunnel vision. If it *is* a single conspiracy with all the murders tied together, I'd have no problem working it alone, but since we may have three assassinations related only through a sold pistol and a similar caliber bullet, we may have to hand off the unrelated part or parts to other prosecutors, and carve parts of the investigative team out to follow their own pieces of this mess. At worst, if it *is* all related, I can still hand off a cohesive chunk to an assistant." He looked up at Eastman. "Who'd you have in mind?"

"I didn't. I made it part of your job as my senior litigation counsel to monitor and evaluate the other assistants in their trials. I trust you've been doing that in all your spare time?"

Trask nodded through a half-smile.

"Good. Then you know what you need. You make the pick."

"Any limits on the office division that might be affected?"

Eastman looked puzzled. "I assumed you'd want someone from the federal floor, with a good deal of experience. Are you thinking something else?"

"I may be. If this thing goes where I'm afraid it might, I'll be considering things other than trial experience or expertise."

Eastman returned to his desk and sat behind it. "Explain."

Trask measured his words for a moment, then shrugged. "There's no getting around this. We may be looking at an extension of the war on cops that's popping up all over the country, Ross. Hell, there were even two officers murdered in my sleepy little home town in Mississippi. Whether or not the AG or the president want to admit inflaming it, there's a racial component to all this. Black Lives Matter, the Black Panthers, and other groups are out there publicly calling for police blood every chance they get. You heard the chants on TV: 'Pigs in a blanket, fry 'em like bacon!' Combine that idiocy with the fact that eleven out of twelve jurors in every trial in this district are black, and you get a problem for any totally white prosecution team trying to convict a racially motivated shooter."

Eastman nodded. "You want a black second chair. We have many African-American assistants in the office. Several on the federal side. Good folks with proven track records."

"I know. I want Valerie Fuentes."

The suggestion froze Eastman for a second. "She's brand-new to the felony trial section. Superior Court only, no federal experience. Why her?"

"You know I share the opinion of our normal training regimen that Bob Lassiter had. The whole throw 'em in the pool to sink or swim, seat-of-your-pants philosophy does nothing other than create bad habits. She hasn't had the time to develop them yet."

"We send them to the NAC."

Trask dismissed the notion with a shake of his head. The National Advocacy Center in South Carolina, the training center for the Department of Justice, had some good points. It was not, however, a center where trial tactics were really taught well, or even emphasized.

"It's an academic environment, Ross, and the practical courses are only as good as the instructors who are there for those couple of weeks. I've seen worse, but I've seen a hell of a lot better, too."

"Back to Ms. Fuentes. Why her, and why now? You know that promoting her will cause a lot of squawking among the more senior attorneys in felony trial. They've been waiting for their own promotions to the federal section, some for years."

"You told me I could pick, and I pick her. Tell the jealous competition the truth. Blame me. I've seen her in trial—maybe her only one—and she's got good poise, good instincts, and isn't afraid of defense counsel or the bench. Good prosecutors are as much born as made, and I like what I've seen of her pedigree. Tell the others in line that it's a temporary trial detail. Tell 'em anything. She's my choice."

"You won't like her politics. She's connected. She may be a born prosecutor, but she's also a born liberal Democrat."

"She'll be able to connect to some of our jurors who wouldn't even hear a word I said. If I find out she's too far out in left field to want to prosecute cop shooters, I'll throw her back in the pond. She signed on to prosecute criminals for some reason." Trask took a breath. "By the way, despite what you might think, I changed my own party registration for voting purposes."

Eastman looked stunned. *"You're a Democrat now?"*

"Of course not. Independent."

"I see. Republicans finally go too far right for you?"

"Not exactly." *I could explain, but I won't.*

Eastman shrugged. "Valerie Fuentes it is, then. Now you can do something for me."

Trask's expression didn't change. He had expected to owe a quid for the quo.

"The Secret Service captain's funeral is set for Sunday at Arlington. He was apparently a marine at one time. I can't make it, and as case attorney, you are the natural choice to represent the office for me."

Trask pulled back in surprise. "That fast? I've known other qualified folks who had to wait months for burial in Arlington. How did . . .?" He stopped, answering his own question. "He was the chief of the vice president's protection detail. As you say, connected."

"Exactly."

"I'll be happy to attend for you."

———

The drive from Washington, D.C. to the camp took the usual three hours or so. He didn't really mind the trip as it was a scenic one, taking him west on Interstate 66, then a short distance north on I-81 before turning west again on US 50 into West Virginia. The driver—dark-skinned and bearded— passed the little town of Capon Bridge, drove a few more miles, and then headed south on more rural roads into the hills of the Potomac Highlands and the Allegheny Mountains. He kept the radio off during the drive. The quiet helped him think.

A dirt road off a state highway gave him a completely unauthorized entry into the northernmost section of the George Washington National Forest. He smiled to himself. *No pass required for this entrance.* It was his favorite part of the trip, even though the roads—actually just unpaved trails, built at his direction— were rough and caused the SUV to convey more than an occasional jolt. The roads had been constructed to appear to be *not too* good. Any park ranger stumbling onto the trails would simply conclude that some joyriding ATV drivers had poached some park turf for their enjoyment.

He stopped at a favorite spot. A high curve on a switchback in the trail allowed him to look down at the wild land beneath him. Mountains and ridges stretched in a green canvas as far as he could see. The terrain perfectly suited his purpose, and the fact that the camp had been established on federal land named after the first American president seemed to him to be a perfect irony.

He navigated a few more twists and turns in the road until a check of the odometer caused him to slow the Chevy. *Don't want to miss the gate.* The green streamer was there around the trunk of the pine on the right, a marker only for those who knew to look for it. He pulled to the side of the road.

Two men in camouflage clothing emerged from the trees and appeared to uproot an entire section of undergrowth and shrubs, pulling the living foliage aside to reveal an opening large enough for the car to pull into the forest. A few more yards from the paved road, the grass-covered lane became a dirt road. As he steered the Chevy onto the road, he checked the rear-view mirror to make sure that the concealment strip was being pulled back into place behind him. Seeing that it was, he nodded his approval.

The camp was located on a narrow but level strip of land along the side of a ravine. Several low, sturdy wooden buildings—each painted forest green and with netting and foliage hiding their roof lines—stood in a row on the side of the dirt road. A canopy of green tree branches high above them was more than enough to conceal the camp from the air.

Half a dozen men, all in camo clothing and with automatic weapons slung over their shoulders, approached the Chevy as he pulled it to a stop. He got out of the car, and listened for the sound of the creek flowing behind the row of huts. He smiled, mentally congratulating himself for his selection of the site. It was perfect.

"Any problems with the trip today, *Saaqhib*?" one of the group asked him.

"None, Ibrahim. I got out of the District before all the rats started their commute on sixty-six. If I had waited another hour to leave, the trip would have taken two or three times as long." He nodded toward one of the buildings. "Are the new men ready?"

"Assembled and waiting, as you directed," Ibrahim said, stepping aside to follow him.

He walked to the door of the building and lowered his head to pass through the entrance. The interior of the single-room hut was illuminated by an oil-fueled Coleman lantern on a small table at the front of the room. Five young men, all dark-skinned, sat in folding chairs facing the lantern and another single folding chair. He strode past the seated recruits and took the chair at the front of the hut.

"*As-Salaam-Alaikum.*" The master greeted the recruits in the traditional Islamic greeting. *Peace be upon you.*

"*Wa-Alaikum-Salaam,*" the new men returned the greeting. *And upon you, peace.*

"Welcome to our cause, my friends," he said smiling. He stroked his beard as he spoke. "Soon the injustices that each of you have suffered at the hands of the devils will be revenged. We appreciate the courage it has taken for you to take this first step. That step is one that—for obvious reasons—cannot be reversed. Anyone who tries to retreat from the commitment he has made in coming here . . ." he stroked his beard again, "forfeits his life." He looked the newcomers in the eye, securing a nod of understanding from each before proceeding.

"Most of you will understand the rules I am about to explain from your own past experiences. The devils used a number of tools in the past to identify you, track you, find you, arrest you, and imprison you. It is essential to the success of our mission now that you do without the conveniences that led to your captures, since they also led to the recording of evidence against you. Accordingly, my brothers, you will not use cell phones. You will not use credit cards or debit cards. You will not write home to any family or friends, or contact anyone outside this camp unless directed to do so by myself or your other superiors."

He reached for a glass of water that had been placed on the table beside the lantern, and took a sip.

"We will provide all of your necessities. You will not operate or use vehicles. We will be transporting you to appropriate locations as required. You are not to leave this compound without permission. Is that understood?"

More nods answered him.

"Excellent. Your training begins tomorrow. You will be shown to your quarters. Follow your instructions, and you will all soon be celebrating a great revenge upon those who have oppressed us all in the past."

He nodded to one of the men in camo gear, who motioned the recruits to follow him. The new men filed out the front of the hut. Ibrahim remained behind.

"Are we still on schedule?" he asked.

"The schedule and the plan may be changing, little brother," the bearded man said. "I may have a new scenario in mind for the initial phase of the operation, one with much more impact than the previous one, and with far less opposition. Something came to my attention today as an unexpected benefit from our last probe. I just have to make sure it will be as attractive an option as it now appears."

———

Chapter Six

It was not the first funeral at Arlington that Trask had attended. As with all previous such occasions, he hoped that it would be his last. He felt the usual reverence for the countless souls lying beneath the simple white markers, the heroes who had made the choice to serve and to try to protect their nation.

I salute all of you, gentlemen, he thought. *And ladies. You're outnumbered, but you're here, too, instead of cowering behind some deferment or hiding in a campus "safe zone."*

He shook his head in disbelief, recalling a news broadcast about college students needing therapy because a certain presidential candidate's name had appeared on their campus.

This is a country founded upon freedom of speech. Why run and hide because someone has a different opinion than your own? God forbid they might have taken some chalk and scribbled something you didn't like somewhere. You might have to ask Mommy for a refill on your Adderall. Poor little darlings.

He had driven alone to the ceremony, and he stopped the Jeep when the line of vehicles in the procession pulled to the side of the lane. He saw the freshly dug grave about halfway up the hill, near a stand of trees. As was his habit, he had read through the Arlington history and protocol before the ceremony, not wanting to commit even a minor violation of decorum during the proceedings. He mentally narrated the program as it progressed.

The caisson arrives with the flag-draped coffin. Military members in attendance present arms as the casket team removes the coffin from the caisson. The chaplain leads the way up the hill to the grave site, followed by the casket team. We follow and take our places. The officer-in-charge of the casket team ensures that the flag over the coffin is properly stretched, centered, and level over the coffin. The family is seated next. He saw a woman wearing black, escorted by a Marine officer. *Looks like only a widow this time. No kids. Maybe that's a good thing.*

47

I remember the last time I was here. Poor Juan, the orphan who had enlisted and served before becoming a cop and Dixon Carter's partner. That one was rough on Dix. He had been the only real family Juan had ever known, and he had been the one to accept the flag.

A chaplain stepped forward to perform the service. Trask didn't hear any of it. His eyes instead swept the crowd, looking for anything unusual.

Anyone look out of place? Behaving abnormally? Behaving too normally?

He didn't notice anything, and found himself staring sympathetically at Braswell's widow. He stuck a hand in his shirt pocket, glad to feel the edges of the business card he'd placed there behind the bat phone.

I'll introduce myself after the service.

The chaplain's wrapping up. Here comes the OIC. Time for the presentation of honors.

His gaze returned to Mrs. Braswell.

I hope she's ready for the noise. It shakes some people up. The OIC's asking her to stand now.

Trask heard the officer-in-charge call for the military members to present arms, and placed his right hand over his heart. The seven marines standing to his right—wearing their dress uniforms with rows of medals displayed across their upper left chests—each slammed the bolts of their Garand M1's, chambering a blank round.

I remember drilling with M1's at the Academy for a while. The inspection arms drill was a bitch. Leave your thumb inside that bolt for a microsecond too long, and your white glove would come out with blood on it. Those bolt springs pack a punch.

The firing party elevated the muzzles of their weapons, and upon command, fired in unison. Trask looked again at Braswell's widow. She flinched slightly at the report of the first volley. He noticed no reaction for the second and third.

Strong lady. Impressive. Someone prepared her, and she listened.

The bugler began to play "Taps," and Trask kept his focus on Mrs. Braswell. Her head dropped involuntarily and shook a bit.

It still hasn't sunk in yet. Natural reaction, nothing excessive.

He hated having to do the evaluation, but checked it off.

I don't think the widow Braswell has played any role in this other than becoming a widow. We'll still check the insurance status, but unless she just took out a huge policy on the captain within the last ninety days, she's cleared.

The bugler held the final, mournful note of "Taps" for the appropriate length of time. The OIC waited for the echo to stop before asking the family—Mrs. Braswell—to be seated.

The casket team leader started the folding of the flag. When the colors had been perfectly folded into the regulation triangle, the flag was passed to the OIC and the casket team withdrew. Trask watched the OIC, who turned and presented the flag to the widow.

"*Please accept this flag with the thanks of a grateful nation,*" Trask said to himself. *The vast majority of us are grateful, and we'll do what we can to find those who weren't, who hated your husband enough to assassinate him.*

He noted that Mrs. Braswell accepted the flag with only a nod, but then managed to mouth a silent "thank you" to the officer.

As some friends formed a line to express their condolences, Trask walked to the rear of the queue. He introduced himself, handed her the card, and told her he would be in touch. He promised—as he always did—to give his full attention to the investigation and to the prosecution that he hoped would follow.

She looked him squarely in the eyes. "I plan to hold you to that promise, Mr. Trask."

"Good," he replied. "That always helps, and I'm happy to get a kick in the pants whenever you think I need it. Feel free to call any time."

A slight smile crossed her lips. "That sounds like something Roger would have said." She glanced toward the grave before looking back at Trask. "I think he would have liked you."

———

Trask pulled into the driveway at 8 Amwich Court, Waldorf, Maryland, about two hours later. The three dogs did not greet him when he opened the door.

"They're in here with me," Lynn shouted from the kitchen. "I just got home and was giving them a treat."

The sound of dog biscuits being crunched verified her statement as Trask walked through the door. The dogs rushed to meet him as they finished their snacks.

"I see where I rate," he said, kneeling down to accept the face-licks. "Right behind biscuits." He stood up and gave Lynn a playful lick on the face.

49

"Stop that!" she giggled.

"Oh, they can do it, but I can't?"

"They don't know how to do it right."

He kissed her in the manner of humans. "That better?"

"Yes, thank you."

"And where've you been this Sunday afternoon? I thought you'd be vegging out here, or at least playing in the dirt in the garden."

"I was at work."

"Bureau-style work?"

"Yeah. The Grog called after you left for Arlington to tell me about the task force meeting tomorrow. I already knew about that, of course, since you had told me, but then Dixon Carter called. Frank Wilkes ran down the make and size of that sneaker print from the Lincoln Memorial. A New Balance shoe, size sixteen. I figured I'd try and see if I could do some analysis stuff on that before the meeting—you know, get a head start and have something to contribute. Anyway, I drove in to the office."

"Find anything?"

"I may have," she nodded. "Some good news and some bad news. It wouldn't have taken long, but Mr. Seal was there, too, and kind of complicated my search."

"How so?"

"He's a good guy, but he's a Bureau guy. He insisted that I try plugging the info into ViCAP first. What a waste of time."

Trask nodded. The FBI's Violent Crime Apprehension Program was a notoriously ineffective database. Designed in theory to allow investigators to match violent criminals' *modus operandi* from one case to another, the system required a ridiculous expenditure of time and effort for a search, first for the accessing agency to input data from one case through a mind-numbing plethora of forms, and then for the querying party to wait while the system whirred for hours, searching for a match which inevitably never came. Use of the system had dropped to only about 1,400 of more than 18,000 American law enforcement agencies, and only about one percent of potentially suitable cases were even entered into the database. Lynn had stopped calling it "GIGO—garbage in, garbage out," and now referred to it as "NINO," for "nothing in, nothing out."

"No luck there?" Trask asked, knowing the answer.

"Of course not. We spend $800,000 a year on that crock. I think it may have found matches on a grand total of thirty cases in the last ten years. The damn thing's too fact-specific. If your case doesn't specify Colonel Mustard in the parlor with a rusty sixteen-inch candlestick, it will never show a match, even if it's Col. Mustard in the parlor with some other blunt instrument."

"But you did find something? You said you had *some* good news."

"Yeah, but no thanks to ViCAP. After the Grog left, I ran our sneaker info through ViCLAS—the Violent Criminal Linkage Analysis System. It's the system the Canadian Mounties developed. A lot more flexible, and a lot faster. They plug in data from significant U.S. cases as well as their own."

"You got a hit?"

"Yep. A case from Kansas. Big hulk of a brute raped a stripper outside Kansas City, then tore her apart with his bare hands. The database had some crime scene photos in the case file. Worst thing I've ever seen, and I may not be able to sleep tonight. The vitals on the perp listed a black male, weight of 285 and a size-sixteen shoe. He was released from Lansing, the Kansas State pen, two months before the murder at the Lincoln. Only got a ten-year sentence because the judge thought he might have some mental issues that could improve over time with therapy."

Trask let out a long, slow whistle. "Wow. Helluva job, babe." He kissed her on the forehead. "ID?"

"DeAnthony Barrett. Date of birth nine-eleven, 1985."

"Nine-eleven, huh?"

"Yeah. I caught that, too. You ready for the bad news?"

Trask leaned against a kitchen counter. "Okay."

"Normally, with an identification in hand, I can track just about anybody through our financial systems—you know—credit cards, applications for work, unemployment, all that stuff."

"But . . .?"

"But since his release, our man Barrett has dropped off the face of the earth. I got nothing, and I mean nothing. Very weird. I have no idea where the guy is, or even might be."

Trask kissed her again. "Still a great start. It gives us something."

"Thanks." She paused, looking at him, waiting.

"What? I know that look. It's nothing good."

"When were you going to tell me?" she asked.

He stared back at her. "This is one of those lose-lose situations for me, isn't it? I really have no idea what you mean, but I do have an idea that you don't believe me when I say that."

"You're probably right."

"So when are you going to tell me what I should have told you?"

She scowled at him. "I hear you've picked your co-counsel for these cases."

"Ooooh, so that's it. I have *nominated* someone. The selection isn't final. I haven't even spoken with her about it yet, and she has not accepted the position."

Jeez, there really ARE no secrets in law enforcement, he thought.

"One of the guys on our squad just finished a case with her, and she told him she might be working with you. You really think she'd turn down a job to leap-frog to federal court after only a few months on a superior court felony trial team? You know how rare that is."

"I do."

She's right. I was probably the last one to make the jump, and only then because of Bob Lassiter hand-picking ME.

"So when were you going to tell me?"

"When I made the final decision. I plan on speaking with her tomorrow morning before the first task force meeting. If she passes muster, you'll be introduced to her at the meeting."

"I see. Why this assistant?"

"Well, she's kind of a cross between Halle Berry and Gabrielle Union . . ."

The look on Lynn's face was one of a mock warning.

Good. She almost laughed. Not so much pissed as actually curious.

"We may be smack in the middle of a race war, with the lunatics on one side of the fence targeting police officers whenever possible. If there's even a chance of that, I need a rational black voice coming from our counsel table at trial. It's kind of like that Saleem character on TV the other night. It helps to have a rational Islamic voice in the debate when the nut fringe is calling for a jihad every chance they get."

She nodded. "Makes sense. You've seen her in trial?"

"Only once. She seems to have a lot of natural ability. That ability needs polishing, of course, but with some OJT and lots of late-evening coaching . . ."

He ducked as a box of sandwich bags flew by his head. Lynn reached for her purse and began jingling her car keys.

"Going somewhere?" he asked.

"Back to work."

"At this hour?"

"Yeah. I've got to see if that Canadian database can point me toward a very discreet hit man. One who specializes in pretty prosecutors."

———

Chapter Seven

Aashif Asalati smiled as he watched the exhausted new recruits stumbling back into the camp after their day of drills. Wearing camouflage fatigue trousers and dark T-shirts, the nine dirty, sweating trainees collapsed in place when told by their instructor that they were released until the evening meal.

"A productive day, Ibrahim?" he asked the man in charge of their training.

"Yes, Imam. Conditioning exercises, the obstacle course, some dry-fire practice with the new rifles."

"I see that you came back with one man fewer than when you left this morning."

The younger man nodded. "As you say, still a valuable object lesson for the others."

He pointed up the trail leading into the mountains. An all-terrain vehicle was making its way back toward the camp. The corpse of a man, dressed in the same camouflage pants and a dark T-shirt as the surviving recruits, was slung, uncovered, across the cargo deck of the ATV. The body bounced as the 4X4 hit the ruts and bumps of the path.

"He tried to make a run for it during the first break this morning." Ibrahim looked at his mentor's face, reading the inquiry on it. "It was a quiet kill, as you have instructed us, Imam. Ahmed is very good with his crossbow. No firearms had to be used."

Asalati smiled again, patting the younger man on the shoulder.

"Excellent. We cannot afford to alert any park rangers at this point. As I have said, it is a very good lesson for the other men. Just make sure we have enough of them left." His face grew serious. "You have altered the training to fit the new plan?"

"Yes, as you instructed. And with the dry-fire exercises only—no live ammunition. I was wondering, however, Imam . . . will we have a chance to train with the real rifles before it is time for the operation? These demilitarized blank rifles are older than our usual weapons, and not even our instructors are that familiar with them."

"I cannot promise you that time, Ibrahim. We have the instructions from the *saaqhib.*" Asalati used the Pashto word for 'master,' knowing that his subordinate, a fellow Pashtun, would understand. "The real weapons are difficult to collect, but we are working on that, and on the appropriate ammunition. Our men will have the necessary tools when the time comes. *That* time is also a matter of some concern for now. We first have to find an appropriate solo target to put the rest of our plan into motion. Just keep your team at the ready. We'll need two teams. One will clear the path before the shooting starts, the other team—the one you are training—will have the honor of killing as many as they can target."

"I understand."

Both their gazes shifted toward a huge man walking toward the mess cabin behind them. The man nodded deferentially toward Asalati as he passed.

"He is getting bored, Imam," Ibrahim said. "He can be dangerous when he's bored."

"I know. Tell him to be patient. We will have another mission for him soon, and he will also be useful on the first team that I mentioned to you. His size will help to keep the devils under control until your team can strike. After that . . ." Asalati smiled. "He can work at his own pace with his own prisoners."

Ibrahim nodded. "I understand." He pointed toward the footprints left in the dirt by the passing giant. "We finally found some boots to fit him. That was hard. Size sixteen."

Asalati shifted his gaze toward the mountains around them.

These are much greener than the hills where I was born. So much rainfall here. So many trees, so much foliage. The master chose the location well. The tree canopy hides us from prying eyes.

His eyes moistened.

I wish we had been better able to hide from the Russians.

His mind drifted back decades. He had been born into the Shinwari tribe and the Sunni Muslim faith in a hospital near Jalalabad in Nangarhar province, along the road to Kabul from the legendary Khyber Pass. His family had not been rich, but they had enjoyed enough relative wealth—thanks to the business acumen of his grandfather—to send his father, Amal, to college in Britain as an exchange student.

His father had returned to Afghanistan in the late 1960s to become a fighter pilot in the country's fledgling air force. Further training in the early seventies sent Amal to the United States, where he and his family had been treated to a tour of American bases and courses. There had been air combat courses in New Mexico, management training classes at Keesler Air Force Base in Mississippi on the Gulf of Mexico, and more academic studies at the Air University at Maxwell Air Force Base in Alabama.

It was during this time that young Aashif had first learned English. His initial encounters with Americans had actually been those of a happy childhood. While Amal cautioned his son about the visible excesses of the Americans—seemingly obsessed with material goods and sex—they seemed to be, at worst, *friendly* infidels, and certainly not enemies. He wore jeans and polo shirts, went to the movies with his school friends, and ate pizza. When his family returned to Jalalabad in 1975, Aashif actually missed America.

Everything changed one Christmas Eve. In 1979, emboldened by what they believed was a weak American administration that would never oppose them, the Russians came to Afghanistan. Major Amal Asalati was shot down and killed in a dogfight with a Soviet MiG. Aashif, his mother, and two young sisters fled to a village in the arid foothills of the Safed Koh Mountains, toward the passes that had always been defensible against any occupiers. After all, as the tribal elders always said, even the British invaders had died in the Khyber at the height of their world empire. The Asalatis believed they would be safe there. They did not take into account the ruthlessness of the Russians, or the Hinds.

Enraged by the refusal of the Afghanis to peacefully submit to their new government and their puppet emir, Babrak Karmal, the Russians sent their Mi-24 helicopter gunships—called "Hinds" by the Americans, and "Satan's Chariots" by the rebels—to bomb the villages in the mountains. Flushed into the open by the impacts of Soviet S-8 rockets and 100-kilogram bombs, Aashif watched in horror as the Hinds' machineguns strafed the villagers and refugees, cutting down everyone who moved. A bullet creased his skull, knocking him into darkness, and when he came to hours later, he found his mother's corpse draped over him. His sisters' bodies lay nearby.

That night, as he sat dazed among the lifeless shapes of what had been his family, he felt a hand on his shoulder. The man led him into the hills, and into the ranks of the mujahideen.

Young Aashif's Western clothing was replaced by the loose-fitting *qmis*—a shirt that draped to his knees— and *shalwar*—baggy pants that he tied around his waist with a length of rope. The words he heard most were *"tureh"*—Pashto for "courage"—and *"badal"* ("revenge"). He learned to shoot, to exist on rations that would starve many, to hide and sleep in the daytime, and to move during the darkness of night. He learned the tenets of *pashtunwali*—his tribe's code of conduct. He learned, above all, to hate the Russian invaders.

For a short time, everything came into focus for him. He was to follow the orders of his mujahideen commanders, ambush and fight the Soviets when they came into range, and hide from the helicopters that came to hunt them. He would have stayed in the rebel camps indefinitely, had two horrible events, occurring only hours apart, not intervened.

The first quake in his new normalcy did not come from the Russians, but from his own commander. The man slapped him on the shoulder one day following a successful ambush of a Russian patrol. He was told he had done well, and to come to the commander's tent for a reward. Beaming with pride, he winked at some of the other young rebels who—to his surprise—laughed at him as he followed the man up the hill.

As the commander's tent flap closed behind him, Aashif was shoved against a table. He felt the man's hands reaching around him, undoing the rope that held his *shalwar* secured around his waist. Aashif Asalati's first sexual experience was being raped.

Stunned and reeling from the attack, Aashif staggered from the tent to find his peers snickering. "Now he is a *chai boy*," he heard one of them say. "If he was good, the commander will have him visit again tomorrow." He ran up the hill to hide.

He did not return to camp for the evening meal. He considered not returning at all. He was climbing around a boulder when he saw something beside the rock, half-covered in dust. He picked the object up. It was green, with two wings extending outward from a cylinder with a cap on it. The soft plastic skin of the thing bore a Cyrillic "Y."

He could not have known that the object had been dropped a few nights before by one of the Russian Hinds, or that he was holding a PFM-1 butterfly mine, essentially a hard plastic pouch full of liquid explosives, designed to detonate if subjected to about ten pounds of pressure. When he tossed the mine back down toward the boulder, he did so with more than ten pounds of force.

He had walked far enough away from the rock to avoid being killed by the blast, but the explosion brought gashes and burns to his left leg. The detonation also brought several mujahideen up from the camp. They did what they could for his wounds, and arranged for him to receive the only medical care they had available. He was given a ride in the back of a jeep over the Khyber Pass to a hospital in a refugee camp in Pakistan.

————

"Imam?" Ibrahim asked him. "Will that be all? Is there something else?"

"I'm sorry," Asalati said. "I was distracted. There *is* one more thing for you to do. We need to build a garage—big enough for a car and a truck—and make sure it is completely concealed. And send the big man to me."

————

Chapter Eight

Trask saw her waiting at the door to his office. She was stunning enough in appearance to make him very glad that he had described her to Lynn in appropriate terms.

Five-seven, slim in the right spots, not so slim in the other right spots, with caramel skin and striking gray eyes. I'd be in trouble if I'd said she was anything but incredible. I was hoping for a cup of coffee or two before I started this, but she's early, even earlier than I am.

He smiled and held out his hand.

"Good morning, Val. Jeff Trask."

"Yes, I know. Very nice to meet you."

"You, too. I need some caffeine. How 'bout you?"

"I could do a cup."

"Great. I've got a Keurig inside, or we could go down to the snack bar. What's your preference?"

"I assume that we need to talk, so inside works."

"Good." He smiled as he unlocked the door. "I've got some dark-roast stuff and a few cups that are a little milder."

"Medium-roast if you have it. Cream and sugar, please."

"I do. Have a seat."

The machine poured the coffee and Trask handed her the cup while he started his own.

"Thanks," she said. She sipped the coffee twice. "I have some questions."

Trask finished stirring his mug. "I thought you might. Shoot."

"Why me? There are many more senior assistants downstairs. Some very good ones. Some of them aren't happy, and I've heard them talking."

"So have I. Supposedly, the only reason you were selected is because you're a female, black, and pretty."

"Is any of that true?"

He smiled. "Only partly."

"Partly?" She was scowling.

"Easy," Trask said. "Let me first assure you that I'm going to be completely honest with you about all of this. Then—if you don't like what I have to say—you're free to resume your work downstairs and I'll find somebody else. Deal?"

"Okay."

"Good. It is, of course, true, that you are black, female, and pretty." He studied her face, and saw that she had not taken the remark as a compliment. "Before you assume that I'm trying to make a move on you, let me say that I'm very happily married, and that my wife is a much better shot than I will ever be. Besides, she'll be the analyst assigned on the task force working our cases, so I'll be under constant surveillance. I think the two of you just might get along."

A smile crossed her lips.

"Good again." He smiled back. "However black, female, and pretty you might be, this choice—more than anything else—is about ability. One of the chores Mr. Eastman threw at me as part of this Senior Litigation Counsel gig is to be kind of a scout: identify the best new talent in the office by watching them at trial, and let him know who is ready to move on to bigger and better things when they're needed. I have decided that you're ready, and I know that you're needed."

"I've only had two trials in Superior Court."

"I know. I saw some of the first, and most of the last one. Let me tell you what I saw."

"Okay."

Trask read her face again. The suspicion that had been there before was disappearing.

Good. She's actually interested, open to some constructive criticism. Very good sign.

"First, the good. Lots of it, actually." *She's sitting back, relaxing.* "I've always believed that female attorneys have a harder job than their male counterparts—at least the litigators. Paper-pushers are probably on equal footing. You have been able to 'walk the line' as a female prosecutor already, either because you've studied the matter and figured it out, or because, for you, it's instinctive.

Whichever it is, I don't really care, because both self-awareness and instinct are strong positives. Now what do I mean by 'walking the line?'"

She smiled. "I think what you are referring to is the line between being so 'feminine' that I'd get walked all over by the judge or opposing counsel and being so assertive that I appear to be a bitch."

Trask leaned back and laughed. Hard.

"Precisely. I couldn't have phrased that any better myself. So I take it that, for you, that was a matter of self-reflection and adjustment?"

"I think so."

"Excellent. At any rate, you let the evidence stress your case, and used cold, hard logic as the strong points in your arguments. Regardless of your individual personality as a prosecutor, that approach is never a bad one.

"I was also *very* impressed with your approach to the jury. You never talked down to them. Being condescending can be fatal, especially when jurors are fed the phrase 'presumed innocent' every thirty seconds in our model instructions. Our burden of proof is hard enough to shoulder without the extra weight the courts throw at us. You dealt with the presumption head-on, and explained how your evidence overcame it."

He paused for another sip of his coffee.

"Your examination of your witnesses was also very good. Both prepared *and* instinctive, I'd guess. I told Mr. Eastman that while good prosecutors are more born than they are made, the best have a lot of both in them. Good prep was evident on your questions, no hemming and hawing between them, no 'ums' or 'ahs' used as crutches. Smooth."

"Thanks."

She's relaxing even more. Not defensive.

"Any suggestions for improvement?"

Trask smiled involuntarily. *Good pick, Jeff. She's the one.*

"A couple. Nothing major. Think of them as polishing strokes on an already shining surface."

She smiled back.

"First, in your closing arguments, don't force-feed the jury by telling them what they *must* do, or even what they *should* do. Think of them as the horses in the proverb: you can lead them to water, but you can't *make* them drink it. Even phrases like 'the *evidence* demands' are ones that I try to avoid. Try to use rhetorical questions when you can. They even allow you to be a little sarcastic without being offensive.

"For example: 'Ladies and gentlemen, the defense attacks our witnesses' assertions that it had rained the night before because they were asleep and didn't see it rain, and because no actual weather reports were introduced in evidence. They say that such is merely *circumstantial* evidence. Now, keeping in mind that our burden of proof is beyond any *reasonable* doubt, is it more *reasonable*—given the fact that even the defense witnesses conceded that the streets were wet at the time of the crime—to conclude that rain had occurred during the late evening hours, or to speculate that someone with a very large water truck and sprinkler system, seeing that the lawns on the block looked thirsty, had a benevolent epiphany and decided to donate a few thousand gallons to the residents and their lawns, not worrying for a second about his own water bill?'"

She couldn't help herself and giggled.

"What this approach does," he continued, "is to highlight the reason within your approach, while showing the lack of it on the other side. You've *invited* the horses to drink, and they decided to do so for themselves. Having adopted the conclusion *in their own minds* that you are correct and your opponent is full of what those drinking horses produce after eating, the jurors will hold those conclusions—*their own*—more strongly when they enter the deliberation room, and will even argue your points for you if any *other* juror has any remaining issues with your case."

"You also tied it into the 'reasonable doubt' standard and instruction. Brilliant."

Trask shrugged. "The brilliance is something I can't take credit for. I've had some great teachers. I'm very impressed that you recognized the point."

He smiled at her again, this time raising a finger in a gesture of caution and patience.

"We've discussed the female issue. Now let's talk about the black and pretty. First the 'pretty' part. The majority of our jurors are also female, so not only do you have to walk the female line, you have to—"

"Worry about jealousy. The 'cat-fight' phenomenon."

Trask sat back in his chair and laughed again. "You're hired, assuming you still want the job after we're done talking. Home run on that point. You don't dress to kill in the courtroom, you don't strut the diva in order to avoid alienating the—how do I put this in completely male terms—don't bug the ugly?"

"Oh, my God!" She snickered.

She can laugh about social taboos. Almost home.

"See? You recognized and covered that problem, too. Great. So you have what it takes to do this job. You haven't learned all the bad habits that working in Superior Court can teach you over time, which in theory will let me teach you a few tricks and the *right* way to do things. We just now have to be honest with each other about a couple more things."

"We haven't talked about the 'black' part yet."

"That's next. Let's start with the obvious. I'm not black, never have been, never will be. I'm a white guy from Mississippi assigned to a federal prosecutor job in what a lot of black folks across the country call 'Chocolate City,' given the demographics of the District."

"You're from Mississippi?"

Trask saw the concern flash across her face. Her attempt to pull it back before it became evident failed.

"I am. Home of Ross Barnett, next door to George Wallace, and home—believe it or not—to a whole lot of good people, black *and* white, who actually have no interest in killing each other, despite what the national press would have the rest of the country believe. That is, however, what my former mentor in this office, Bob Lassiter, would have called a 'political infection.' It is something of which I must remain aware, as *you* are aware that you're female and pretty. It also leads me to the details of the case—or cases—at hand."

"The police murders."

"Yes, the police murders. Three to date, cases that are *probably*, but as of yet, not *definitely* related. If the evidence separates them, one or more will be yours to handle alone. If I decide you're right for the team, and you decide you want in, *if the evidence dictates*, we'll handle them all together. That evidence may very well mean that we're looking at racially and/or politically motivated assassinations of law enforcement officials. I've been very candid with you so far. I need a candid response from you on how you would feel about being part of a prosecution team dealing with that sort of case."

She paused, trying to read his face this time. "I have another question for you, first."

"Shoot." Trask didn't flinch.

"How might *your* political views affect the team and the prosecutions?"

"Hopefully, not at all. In my professional philosophy, the only time politics—from any source—are appropriate considerations in a criminal case are when they are injected into the investigation and the resulting prosecution *by the defendant* as a matter of motive. That can happen even when a specified 'hate crime' isn't on the books, or when the case has been indicted as one.

"Politically, I'm a conservative. So what? My oath is to the Constitution. I have no real ethnic allegiances to distract me from that. I celebrate the Fourth of July because I'm an American. I do not celebrate St. Patrick's Day, or Cinco de Mayo, or Kwanzaa, or any other ethnic holiday, because I think that once someone is born or becomes an American, everything else is secondary. Eat some corned beef hash or cornbread; have a beer during Oktoberfest. I don't care. I do all that myself—except for the corned-beef hash, which I think looks and smells like dog food. But aside from knowing that some of my ancestors came across the ocean at some point, I don't know where they came from, or really care. Any clues as to my lineage went up in a courthouse fire in the Carolinas during the Depression. I am, for all practical purposes, an American mutt, and proud to be one."

She looked confused, somewhat taken aback.

"Now. *My* question was, how might *your* political views affect the team and the prosecutions?"

"I'm a liberal by training and philosophy. I have seen police treat minorities unfairly. I've been stopped myself for 'driving while black' in a white neighborhood. I have some sympathy for the Black Lives Matter movement—"

"To what extent?" Trask interrupted. "'Pigs in a blanket, fry 'em like bacon?'"

"No, no. Of course not." She looked back at him, the first hint of confrontation brewing in her eyes. "You don't think that black lives matter?"

"I believe that to be a silly and almost insulting question." He didn't back down from the challenge. "And unless you believe that more than a few bad cops are out there poisoning the well, and unless you refuse to realize that the vast majority of us in law enforcement—hopefully including yourself—are working to protect *all* lives, it's a stupid name for an organization. Do I believe that black lives matter? Of course they do. Do I believe that they matter more than any other kind of human life? Of course *not*. When I see a cop like that psycho in

South Carolina back-shooting someone for no reason at all, my blood boils. But when I see a trumped-up controversy like the Michael Brown thing, I get just as mad. Is that a problem for you?"

She didn't say anything for a moment. When she did speak, her voice was softer, reflective.

"I don't think you can respond to some of the concerns the minority community has in this kind of case."

"Maybe, maybe not. But that's why you're here," Trask responded. "Because I need a prosecutor who can. One who can do so honestly, and who has the same self-awareness of her own possible biases as she does of what *may* be mine, and who won't be afraid to discuss both as the need arises. One who, in the final analysis, may be the more appropriate one to argue these cases to a jury. I'm not saying that I will agree with your politics or perspective; I'm saying that there may be a jury that might. A District of Columbia jury. Maybe an all-black, predominantly female, liberally leaning jury. So I'm looking for a prosecutor who can—despite what may be her own concerns and biases—give these police victims their day in court. Can you do that?"

She sat back and smiled again. "Yes, I think so."

Trask nodded. "Welcome to the federal floor, Val. I'll tell personnel to make the transfer official. We have a task force meeting at the FBI field office at eleven. Come by and we'll walk over together."

———

Asalati felt the cell phone on his belt ring, and he checked the caller ID on the device before answering it. It was the number he expected, the one that no American law enforcement or intelligence agency would have tapped. He wasn't worried about his own phone—an anonymous, pre-paid, disposable piece of crap, suitable only to receive and make calls for a week before being destroyed, discarded, and replaced with another. He was not on paper with the service provider, so as long as he didn't call suspected numbers, the device would mean nothing to anyone who saw its own number.

He walked up the hill into the woods from the compound. *We don't let the men use phones; no need to upset any of them who might resent the double standard.*

"*As-salaam Alaikum*," Asalati said as he answered the call.

"*Wa-Alaikum-Salaam.*"

"Yes, *Saaqhib.*"

"How are things, Aashif?"

"Progressing satisfactorily."

"Excellent. Allah be praised. I have been scouting the route for the revised operation. We will need the car that I mentioned, and a bus."

"I can have the big man get the car. He is getting bored. I told Ibrahim to make the garage big enough for a car and a large truck, so the bus will fit."

"Very good. Hassan is a good fit for the car task. It will give him something to do, and the devils another victim to mourn. I will check on the progress of the garage in a couple of days."

"I understand."

Asalati returned the phone to his pocket. He remembered his first meeting with the man he now referred to as his master, and his own teacher in the faith.

After being wounded by the Russian mine and receiving some initial treatment in a refugee camp on the Pakistani side of the Khyber, Aashif had been transferred to a hospital in the city of Quetta, a pretty city in central west Pakistan known as "Little Paris" for its beauty, and also known as the fruit garden of Pakistan because of the numerous orchards in the area. The hospital treatments for his leg wounds were, however, anything but a thing of beauty. The burns required long, agonizing treatments and surgeries, and he spent months regaining his strength and the full use of the limb.

While his leg healed, he began studying the Qur'an in earnest, trying to find some meaning in the events that had twice wounded him and taken the lives of his family. He lay in the hospital ward reading every night until the lights went out, and often discussed the passages he read with other boys in the room. One suggested that when Aashif got well enough to walk, he would benefit from the teachings of a *mullah* at a nearby school—a *madrassa*. When he was finally able to walk some distance, he found the madrassa and met the teacher, a tall, lanky man with only a closed socket for a right eye. The man introduced himself as Omar.

Asalati began attending the classes offered by Omar, and talked with the other students about his new mentor. Omar had fought the Russians with the mujahideen, and had been wounded four times. One of those wounds had been the loss of his eye to shrapnel from an exploding tank shell, one of the few encounters with a Soviet tank that Omar—who had been an expert with anti-tank weapons—had lost.

Omar's usual lectures consisted of rants against the Russians and any other infidel occupiers of his native Afghanistan. The mullah also, however, had nothing good to say about some of the mujahideen leaders, who he said violated the holy book by engaging in the practice of *bacha bazi*—the rape and sexual abuse of both girls and boys. When Aashif told his teacher that he had been a victim of the practice at the hands of his own commander, the mullah began paying special attention to his new pupil. The lectures in the schoolroom were supplemented by hours of personal instruction, with Omar emphasizing the faith's justification for violence against non-believers.

During their time together, Omar learned that his student had some command of the English language as a result of Aashif's travels with his father.

"That is a blessing, and something that could be of great use to us in the future," Omar told him. "Instead of hiding them, you should continue to develop these skills. Just do not let your contact with the Americans confuse you. We accept America's weapons to use against the Russians for now, but being an enemy of our enemy does not make them our friends. They are *kafirs*—infidels— just like the Russians. They will, in time, try to take our country for themselves, bringing their sinful, godless ways with them."

Omar patted the young Asalati on the shoulder, and stared into Aashif's eyes with his good left eye. He ushered the young man toward the side of the schoolroom.

"Let me share a secret with you. Like you, Aashif, I speak another language. Not English, but Arabic. It has opened doors for me, and I am already working with others to strike our enemies in their economic and political centers. We will strike such a blow that the American devils will never dare to respond, and the world will know the true might and righteousness of our cause. Once we bring America to its knees—and we will—the rest of the world will fall to our jihad."

Omar pointed to a man standing outside the window of the madrassa. He was even taller than Omar himself, and was surrounded by dozens of armed men and others who seemed eager to receive his counsel.

"That, my little brother, is the man we call Osama. Once we take back our own country, we will have a base from which we can influence the world, and Osama will be one of the leaders of our triumphs."

Omar smiled as he saw Aashif's fascination with the scene. "I have someone else for you to meet," the mullah said.

He escorted Aashif to a rear room in the madrassa. A man in Western clothing sat at a desk, studying some documents. He appeared to be in his late thirties, and had the air of an academic. Omar spoke to him initially in Pashto.

"I present Aashif Asalati to you my friend. He may be just the one we've been looking for. I believe you can already communicate with him in the language of the Americans." Turning back to Asalati, Omar said, "This man will be your personal teacher now, Aashif. Follow his instructions. Listen and learn well from your new *saaqhib*. He will help you polish your language skills, and will explain your role in what will be—God willing—a new home and the development of our revolution there."

The man rose and smiled, holding out his hand to Asalati.

Asalati remembered those first words as if he had heard them an hour ago.

"Hello, Aashif," the master had said in English. "How would you like to visit America again?"

By late 1988, the Russians had left Afghanistan, but not before Asalati and his *saaqhib* had returned to the United States, which had been generous enough to grant Aashif resident-alien status as a political refugee. By the mid-nineties, the Taliban had taken the Afghan capital of Kabul, and established the Islamic Emirate of Afghanistan. Leading the Taliban was a tall, lanky, one-eyed figure who his soldiers called "Amir al-Mu'minin"—"Commander of the Faithful." The American intelligence services continued to refer to him as "Mullah Omar."

———

Chapter Nine

The Gang and Violent Crime Squad of the FBI's Washington Field Office had a small conference room, reflecting the reduced role of the Bureau in doing anything but anti-terrorism work in the post 9/11 world. The seventy-five to eighty agents who would have been assigned to investigate street and drug gangs in the 1990s had been reduced to five. Added to that handful were a like number of task force officers or "TFOs," state and local police, or federal agents from other agencies like the ATF—the Bureau of Alcohol, Tobacco and Firearms. The table and twelve chairs in the squad conference area were simply inadequate for the meeting now chaired by Supervisory Special Agent Richard Seal, so he had commandeered the main conference room.

Seal sat at the head of the twenty-foot mahogany table. Trask and his new assistant had taken the seats to Seal's right. Lynn Trask and Nick McCarver of the Park Police sat to Seal's left, and Major Chester Williams, Dixon Carter, and Tim Wisniewski filled out that side of the head of the table. The other agents and TFOs from Seal's squad filled the seats toward the other end. A couple of vacant chairs had been reserved to the right of Trask and Valerie Fuentes. Trask noticed that Lynn had given Val Fuentes a complete visual inspection, and had then given him a raised eyebrow.

"We're just waiting on Secret Service." Seal stated the obvious for the benefit of anyone who wasn't already thinking the same thing.

"Any idea who they're sending?" Trask asked.

"An assistant director named Rosalind Wood," Seal answered.

"Oh, shit." Carter spoke almost involuntarily, shaking his head and rolling his eyes skyward.

"Someone you obviously dated," Wisniewski quipped.

"Hell hasn't frozen over twice," Carter snorted. He saw Trask's eyebrows raised across the table. "She may be a problem, Jeff. She was a political promotion to captain in our department when such promotions had nothing to do with merit. Since then, she got another political promotion, and it damn sure had nothing to do with how she did as a police captain."

"What *did* her promotion 'have to do with?'" Fuentes asked.

Trask noted a defensive chill in Val's tone. Lynn bailed him out before he could intercede.

"Nobody present for now politically promoted. Right, Dix?"

"Of course not." Carter responded calmly. "For all my fellow male neanderthals who might be new to these parties, I can vouch for Lynn Trask as the most capable analyst I've ever worked with. I have not yet had the pleasure of working with AUSA Fuentes, but if Jeff vouches for her, that's good enough for me. As for Roz Wood, her promotion had to do almost solely with the fact that she was a black female, Ms. Fuentes. Being black myself—in case anyone hadn't noticed," he waited for the chuckles to die down, "I have no issue with some applications of affirmative action where they are needed and justified. Sometimes, however, there are those who play the race and gender cards when they're holding nothing else in their hand. I would put Rosalind Wood in that category. She screamed 'discrimination' and threatened to sue the world every time she got passed over for a promotion, and the department finally surrendered and gave in to her. I was unfortunate enough to have to work for her for a few months in 7D before Willie Sivella was appointed to fix everything she had managed to break."

A voice over the office intercom interrupted them. "Mr. Seal, you have a visitor waiting in the lobby."

"Speak of the devil," Seal said. "I'll escort her up." He looked at Carter. "Maybe she's grown into the new job?"

"Benefit of the doubt, for now," Trask echoed the sentiment.

Carter snorted again.

Minutes later, a small black woman in a black Secret Service uniform appeared in the doorway, outlined against the very large frame of Supervisory Special Agent Richard Seal.

Trask saw that she was evidently forcing the smile on her face.

I think her face may crack any second. Looks like it hurts.

He glanced across the table and saw that Lynn had her eyebrows raised again.

Both of our sets of antennae are buzzing. This just HAD to be the one who they sent us— politically connected, too.

Seal made the introductions. Carter was able to smile and say, "We've met," when his turn came, a statement that was returned by Rosalind Wood's icy "Yes, we have."

Once Wood had taken her seat at the table, Seal invited the various agencies to summarize their cases—their losses. McCarver went first, relating the evidence gathered to date regarding the murder of Park Police Officer Jackie Turner at the Lincoln Memorial. Chet Williams discussed the ambush of Patrolman Bart Roberts in Anacostia. Seal then asked Wood if she would like to discuss the killing of Secret Service Captain Roger Braswell.

To the surprise of everyone in the room, with the exception of Dixon Carter, she said, "Of course not."

Trask felt that it was time for him join the discussion, if not to referee it. "And why is that, Director?"

"We weren't even invited to participate in the investigation in time to see the crime scene. Why should we *now* be asked to summarize the evidence that someone else collected?"

"I asked our dispatch to notify Secret Service the minute we identified Captain Braswell as the victim, Roz," Carter said. "I can't help it if your folks didn't get to the scene on time. We had a scene to process and a street to clear, but we were out there for a couple of hours, and would have been happy to brief your agency on the scene."

'Roz,' Trask thought. *Not 'Director Wood.' Great, Dix. That won't help.*

"Thank you so much, *Detective.*" Wood's tone was icy and sarcastic.

"Secret Service lost a great asset, as did the other agencies in this room," Trask said. *I've got to nip this in the bud before it gets worse.* "Because of that loss, we've invited you to participate, and promise to keep you updated on any evidence as it develops. Having said that, Director, there is one distinct difference between your agency's standing in this investigation and the others."

"And what would that be, other than the fact that we lost a captain in the vice president's protection detail as opposed to street cops? You are talking to an assistant director of the Secret Service, Mr. Trask."

"That would be jurisdiction," Trask said calmly. "The loss of the Park Police officer"—*as big a loss to them as your loss*, he thought to himself, *assuming you had actually bothered to meet Braswell*—"occurred at a National Memorial, well within the investigative jurisdiction of the Park Police. The murder of Patrolman Roberts occurred on the streets of Anacostia, and so Metro PD, in the assigned persons of Detectives Carter and Wisniewski, has investigative jurisdiction over that crime. The murder of Captain Braswell also occurred within the District, and within the investigative jurisdiction of the police department. As the assigned AUSAs, Ms. Fuentes and I have prosecutorial jurisdiction over *all* these matters.

"My understanding from the applicable statutes is that Secret Service has investigative jurisdiction only over threats against your protectees, and over counterfeiting, forgery or theft of Treasury checks, some credit card fraud, some telecommunications, identity and computer fraud, and certain other crimes affecting federally insured financial institutions. Even though you have no jurisdiction over murders—even those of your own officers—we will certainly continue to extend the courtesy of inviting your participation in this task force, considering the loss of Captain Braswell. Am I wrong, Director, or do you *have* some investigative jurisdiction over Captain Braswell's murder?"

Wood stared at him angrily, her authority bluff called and exposed. She stood up. "You'll be hearing from the vice president, Mr. Trask, who I'm sure will wonder why some prosecutor—*instead of an investigator*—thinks he can run this task force."

"Please direct him to work through channels, as we will of course do," Trask kept his voice level. "He can direct his remarks to the attorney general, who, if necessary, will speak with the United States Attorney. We hope to see you back at the table."

Wood left the room without saying another word.

"Hasn't changed a bit," Carter muttered.

"Unfortunate," Trask said. "Anyway, we have work to do." He glanced at Seal. "Mind if I outline our side of all this?"

The big man shook his head. "Please."

"Thanks." Trask took a second to collect his thoughts. "We all suspect these attacks are related. We'd be nuts not to approach them in that fashion. There remains, however, the slight chance that they are separate and unrelated incidents. Because of that, we're going to need to compartmentalize the cases, while sharing any evidence that might overlap. That way, we'll be ready to arrest and prosecute separate cases if that's what we develop, or to join them and attack them as a single conspiracy if that's where the evidence takes us. We have a working theory that they're part of an overall conspiracy, but not tunnel vision locking us into that theory and leading us down the wrong path."

He looked around the room and saw no obvious objections, although Chet Williams wasn't smiling.

He'll need to see evidence that convinces him his theory is wrong. We'll have to watch that.

"Because these might be separate prosecutions, and because that contingency might stretch me too thin or even demand that I be in two courtrooms at the same time—an obvious impossibility—I asked Mr. Eastman to allow me to handpick another AUSA to join our little club. Most of you have not met or worked with Val Fuentes."

Trask nodded toward her, and saw that she was making eye contact with everyone at the table.

Good. Confident. No shrinking violet.

"Let me assure you all that while she is relatively new to our office, she got this assignment because of her capabilities in the courtroom, which I have personally observed. I have every confidence that I can break off a piece of this assignment, place it in her capable hands, and know that it will be handled as it should be. If she has any questions, she'll come to me with them. She also knows that if you have a problem with any decision she makes, you will be coming to me. I just ask that you give her a chance first. I think you'll be pleasantly surprised."

Trask looked around the table. "Questions?"

Williams wasted no time. "Whose piece of the pie are you handing off, Colonel?"

"Yours, Chet." Trask's response was just as rapid. He saw Williams shaking his head.

"My reasons are these," Trask continued. "First of all, unlike in the case of your murdered officer, I was on the crime scenes of the other homicides before they were completely processed and cleared. That gives me a head start on those. Second—and I'm going to be blunt, here—I have more experience dealing with multi-agency squawks, so if Dixon Carter and Nick McCarver start throwing haymakers at each other, or if we have to deal any further with the likes of Roz

Wood, I'd rather handle those problems than drop them on Val's shoulders. The shooting of Officer Roberts is a more self-contained homicide. It's a murder of one of DC's finest and will be investigated *by his department*. With your help guiding Val through the ropes, I think she'll do a fine job on the case."

Williams nodded.

Trask read the nod as an unhappy acceptance, for the moment. "Good. I think our analyst has something that might interest us."

He watched the faces around the table as Lynn briefed them on her findings regarding DeAnthony Barrett. Her briefing concluded with a blow-up of his last mug shot displayed on the conference room screen. Copies of the mug shot were distributed to all in attendance.

Carter was the first to respond.

"Great work, as usual, Lynn, but do we have anything linking this guy to our area? He's from Kansas, isn't he?"

"That's the last place anyone could place him, Dix. Like I said, he's dropped off the grid since his release."

Carter shook his head slightly. "So the only thing we've got tying him to the Lincoln Memorial murder is his shoe size—"

"And the fact that he has a propensity for pulling women's heads apart," Lynn reminded him. "Two pretty singular facts."

"Why is he here now?" Carter asked her. "Did your research show any family in this area?"

"No. They're all from Missouri, actually. Just across the line from Kansas in Kansas City, Missouri. The state line splits their metro area."

"If it's him, we need to identify the reason for his move," Carter thought out loud. "That could be big."

"Something to start looking into," Seal said. He looked toward Trask. "Anything more for day one?"

"I think that's where we are, for now. Thanks, Rich."

The walk back across the street to the triple nickel with Val was short, but it was loaded with her questions.

"Throwing me to the wolves with Major Williams? I don't think he likes the idea. You said you'd be honest with me. Could there be some racial bias there? Is he mad at the Black Lives Matter movement for killing his officer?"

"Just give it a shot, Val. Chet's a Naval Academy guy, takes the loss of his officer personally. Meet the Roberts family; work the case. I think you'll be surprised once you know him."

"We'll see. Director Wood was sure a piece of work. Do we need to give Mr. Eastman a heads-up that he might be getting a call from the Secret Service or the vice president?"

Trask smiled. "Good instincts, and good thinking. Ordinarily, his office would be our first stop off the elevator after a meeting like that."

"Ordinarily?"

"Ross Eastman, as good a guy as he is, is also political by nature. If I were to self-report the fact that I had offended a high muckety-muck of the Secret Service—even though I have a dozen witnesses to back up my claim that Roz Wood is a raving idiot—Ross would nevertheless assume that I did *something* in that meeting to justify my *mea culpa* to him. I think we'll wait this time to see if a call actually comes through. If it doesn't, it means that Ms. Wood tried to raise hell with her folks, but they also know she's full of it and didn't want to dirty their hands with another mess of her creation. If she shows up at another meeting without Ross having heard from Secret Service, we'll be able to call her bluff if she starts threatening another power play."

"And if Ross *does* get a call?"

"We will all display shock and righteous indignation that such accusations have been leveled against us."

She laughed. "You're a piece of work, yourself."

"Welcome to multi-agency investigations," he replied. "Is your deck clear for this mess now, or do you have some of your old casework to clean up?"

"One more trial on Thursday," she said. "I'd like to bump some ideas off you, if you have some time."

"I've got a few hundred matters of administrivia to clean up," Trask replied, "but come by after lunch. We'll make time for real work—the important stuff."

———

Chapter Ten

Rusean Short was getting out early. His original sentence for dealing more than five kilograms of cocaine base—"crack" on the streets—had been fourteen years, but the attorney general's "Smart on Crime" initiative had resulted in an adjustment to his sentencing guidelines, and he was being released after serving ten years, his mandatory minimum. He had, after all, not been *convicted* of any violent crimes—his elimination of witnesses had made sure of that—and the offense on his conviction record had been "possession of cocaine with intent to distribute." Accordingly, he fit the new profile of an offender whose sentence was now viewed to be unfairly severe. It had been a 'possession' offense, he was a 'non-violent' offender and he was getting out early.

He sat in the out-processing unit of the prison, listening to the federal probation office's social worker drone on about all the programs available to help him rejoin society and begin a new life as a constructive citizen.

"The Justice Department has instructed us to end the practice of referring to released inmates as 'convicted felons,' 'ex-cons,' or 'criminals,' in the hope that discarding these labels will make it easier for you to re-assimilate into society and the workforce," she said. "You will still have to honestly answer any potential employer's questions about your record—"

"What'll my P.O. call me then? They ain't gonna call me a 'con?' What'll they call me then?"

"Your probation officer will list you as one of his or her supervision clients."

"A client, huh? If I'm a client do I get to fire 'em if I don't like how they're managin' my supervision?"

"You know better than that, Mr. Short. We're just trying to end the use of some troublesome terms to make it easier for you to start over. You know, to remove the stigma, if you will."

"Right, right. The stigma."

"Sign here, please."

The counselor slid the forms forward, realizing that there was little hope of any meaningful dialogue, and preferring just to conclude the process.

"You can collect your things at the next processing station. Good Luck, Mr. Short."

No one was waiting for him outside the gate when it closed and locked behind him. His case was not notorious enough for his release to justify any press coverage. That was fine with him. He was not one of FCI Butner's celebrities. The Federal Correctional Institute at Butner, North Carolina, did have its share of notable personalities. There was Gilberto Orejuela, the former leader of the now defunct Cali Cartel; "Little Nicky" Scarfo, the boss of the Philly mob; and even Bernie Madoff, the scam master of New York City. If one of the big boys had walked through the gate, there would have been TV trucks, maybe even some print media waiting for them. Short smiled. He liked it this way. Rusean Short wanted his new status to be a surprise.

He used his release money to get the necessary bus tickets, and after riding the 25 miles southeastward to Raleigh, he transferred to a bus for Washington. The ride would take a few hours. He didn't care. He was back in loose jeans and a hoodie, not that damned orange one-piece. He promised himself he would never wear anything orange again.

It was after dark when he got off the subway in Anacostia, the southeast section of the District of Columbia. He walked up the sidewalk to the little house he had shared with her before his arrest—the house she'd inherited from her mother, the house for which she had signed the consent-to-search form when the cops gave it to her, the house where they had found his stash of "rock."

That's okay, he told himself. *We been all over that, before the trial and during her visits at Butner. She didn't know my shit was in that closet. If I'd told her, somebody coulda hurt her tryin' to find it. I didn't tell her to protect her, so she didn't protect me by refusin' to consent to the search. She shoulda told 'em to get a warrant, but odds are they already had one. I got snitched out. It's okay. It's all good now. I'm back.*

The front door was locked, so he walked around to the back. The door to the kitchen was open. He stepped inside, expecting to find her cooking supper, or to see her two kids coloring or doing homework at the table. He wondered how tall the girls had gotten. It had been a couple of years since they'd come with their mom to visit him. They weren't his, but he'd promised to help her raise them. He started to call her name, but he heard a sound from the back bedroom, and the words stuck in his throat. The sound he heard was a long, slow moan, and not one caused by pain.

The light in his eyes darkened as his face hardened. He looked back toward the counter, and his eyes found the old cutlery rack. He grabbed the butcher knife from the rack and crept quietly to the bedroom door. He turned the handle slowly, and saw them as the door cracked open. The man was on top of her, inside her, thrusting.

He was in the room with one swift move, making deep thrusts of his own. The first stab went in below her lover's ribs, the second cut his right jugular vein, and the last sound the man made was a pitiful, alarmed gurgle. Short shoved the naked body off the bed and held the knife to her neck.

"Please, please, no," she begged. "No, 'Sean. I didn't know you were out."

"I've been studying." His voice was cold, measured. "If you had been evil in some other fashion, I could have chewed you out, made you sleep on the floor, maybe knocked you around a little. That's what the book says."

"What book, 'Sean?" she whimpered. "What are you talking about?"

"The holy Qur'an," he growled. "The same book that says if you dishonor me with another man, I can have you stoned to death."

"The Qur'an?" she cried. "We ain't Muslims, 'Sean!"

"I am," he said flatly. "I don't have any stones, but I do have this."

He pressed the blade hard into and across her neck, slitting her throat.

"Mama! 'Sean?!" The cries of the girls behind him in the doorway made him turn. They were frozen in shock, still holding schoolbooks, watching the blood pour from their mother's neck across the bed and onto the floor.

He was off the bed as quickly as he had leapt onto it, plunging the blade into the older girl's abdomen while he grabbed the smaller one by the throat. He was fast enough with the knife to prevent any flight or further screams.

He caught his breath and looked down at his clothes.

Shit! I'm covered with blood.

He looked at the naked male body on the floor beside the bed.

He's about my size. Close enough.

He grabbed the man's clothes from a chair across the room, dressed and started to leave, but remembered something. Picking up his blood-soaked jeans from the floor, he plunged his hand into the right front pocket.

Yeah. Good. Still there.

He looked at the business card and read the address for the mosque before walking calmly out the front door.

"Insh'Allah," he said under his breath.

———

Chapter Eleven

Trask looked up from his desk to see the very large figure of Dixon Carter standing in the doorway. He studied the big man's face for a moment before speaking.

"Dixon, you look like hell. What's up?"

"I feel like hell—or, more accurately—like I've just seen another slice of it. We just got back from 7D. Woman and her boyfriend caught in bed by her husband, who just got released from Butner. Both carved up like turkeys. Blood all over hell and gone." Carter paused to collect himself.

Trask waited a few seconds. "What else, Dix?" *What shook you about this one?*

"Two little girls. They were all cut up, too. They apparently walked in on the butchering while it was going on. One lived long enough to tell the first uniform on the scene that it was her stepdaddy, a dude named Rusean Short. I put him inside for crack dealing about a decade ago. The geniuses in your department let him out a few years early, one of those 'Smart on Crime' releases for *non-violent* offenders."

"Jesus." Trask shook his head. "I'm sorry, Dix. We all have bosses, and too many of 'em are idiots. The politicians lobby for a few extra votes and the innocent pay for it with their lives."

"Any way *you* can handle this one if we find Short?" Carter asked. There was a little bit of begging in his deep baritone.

Trask winced as he shook his head. "The revocation on the dope case, sure. The murders? Probably not. Doesn't sound like there's a federal violation there for now, just a heat-of-passion multiple homicide. One of the guys on the Superior Court homicide teams will get it. Sorry."

"Would it make any difference if Short was yelling 'Allahu Akbar' while he was stabbing the little girl?"

Trask whistled and leaned back in his chair. "Possibly. Maybe under a hate-crime theory of some kind, but still pretty iffy. Let me think about that."

Trask stood up and walked to the coat rack mounted on the wall near the door. He removed a navy blazer from a hanger and put it on.

"I have to go over to Superior Court for a while to see how Val's doing on her last trial before she moves up here. Want to come?"

"Sure." Carter's voice sounded flat, his mind still on the crime scene.

They were outside and halfway through Judiciary Square before Carter shook himself out of the crime scene.

"What's Val's case about?"

"The defendant is the girlfriend of a bigtime dope runner," Trask said. "Her boyfriend bumped into some cartel connections while he was driving semi's on the west coast. He started hauling tons of coke for the Mexicans—some of Chapo Guzman's thugs. Boyfriend made lots of drops locally, and on up to Philly and New York. Our local gal was laundering money for him here—making cash deposits, paying his bills, moving money from account to account. She also delivered about half a metric ton of coke for him to his local customers.

"DEA did a deal with the boyfriend to testify against his Mexican suppliers. He cooperates and does fifteen years instead of life. He's held up his end of the bargain, and ID'd everybody who worked with him, including our defendant. He testified against her."

"We're swimming downstream?" Carter asked. "Giving the big fish a break to catch a minnow?"

"For once," Trask said, nodding. "Never easy, and not where we wanted to be. Our defendant was still up to her eyeballs in heavy cocaine distribution. Val did the smart thing by offering her a deal to cooperate against some local customers she was making the coke deliveries to—five years in Lorton—but she told Val to go play with herself. The defendant, Shirley McKnight, never believed her lover was actually going to testify against her. She thought he was as much in love with her as she apparently was with him. She was wrong. She called Val's bluff, but Val wasn't bluffing."

"Still an unattractive case for the jury," Carter noted.

"Absolutely. They have to believe the admitted super-pusher over the poor, jilted girlfriend. Tough case for us to win."

They reached the doors to the courthouse and went in. Carter followed Trask around the usual raucous crowd gathered in the main lobby. They took an escalator to the hallways on the second floor, and went into one of the courtrooms, seeing that the judge's bench was empty and that the parties to the trial were standing around their respective counsel tables.

Valerie Fuentes looked up when they entered the well of the court.

"Recess?" Trask asked.

"Yeah. I'm glad you're here," she said. "The judge just went through the options with her." She nodded in the direction of the defendant, a respectable-looking black woman in her late thirties who was dressed in a taupe skirt and matching jacket. "She's going to testify."

Trask nodded. "Well, then, that will make or break your case. It all depends on your cross." He smiled. "No pressure at all."

"Thanks a lot."

He smiled again. "It's okay, win or lose. We get paid to try the hard ones, too, not just the gift-wrapped ones. I'm proud of you for not running away from this one."

"Any suggestions for the cross?"

"Just a couple. Keep it short, keep it safe, and listen."

"*Listen?*" A bewildered expression was on her face.

"Yep. Relax and listen. Don't put extra pressure on yourself by trying to trap her into one of those Perry Mason movie confessions. They almost never happen. Listen to her answers. She may give you something that has nothing to do with the elements of the offense charged, but which will still show the jury who she really is. Listen for anything that doesn't fit, that doesn't make sense, that defies logic. You know your evidence and your case. Take your time as you *listen* to her testimony. Only write something down if it smells fishy. You'll know it when you hear it—even if nobody else does—because you know all the evidence. Okay?"

"I guess so."

Trask looked past her to see that the courtroom clerk and court reporter were taking their seats on either side of the judge's bench. He nodded toward the front of the room. "You're about to resume. Relax. You'll be fine."

She turned and walked back toward her table as Trask and Carter retreated into the spectator section and stood in front of one of the pews while the court was called to order.

"What do you really think?" Carter whispered as they took their seats.

"Cross of a defendant is the hardest part of trial work," Trask whispered back. "We'll see how it goes."

They watched as Shirley McKnight, playing her best victim role, explained to the jury that she had believed her boyfriend, one Wilton Everson, when he told her that he was a legitimate trucker who owned his trucks, was making good money, and just needed to have several different accounts open because he tracked his customers through those different accounts. He had told her that some of his customers paid him in cash, which was why he had money on hand all the time.

McKnight's defense counsel asked her to explain why she had made some large cash deposits into accounts she shared with Everson. She answered that while she frequently made small deposits—a few hundred dollars—from cash he left with her to cover his local bills, she also transferred funds from her own account at another bank into Everson's account because he had told her to feel free to use some of his money for improvement projects on her home. The commingling of funds allowed her to write one check instead of two.

"It was his way of paying me back for helping him," she explained.

Her direct testimony concluded with what Trask expected: the absolute denial that anything she had done was in any way connected with drug trafficking, at least as far as she knew. Trask and Carter gave each other a knowing glance. Right out of the defense script.

"Cross-examination, Ms. Fuentes?" the judge asked.

Carter looked at Trask again, an eyebrow raised.

Trask shrugged. "I didn't hear much to work with, Dix, but I don't know the case," he whispered. "Val does."

"Ms. McKnight." Val nodded to the defendant who was sitting in the witness stand. The defendant returned the nod without speaking.

"You have testified that several of the larger deposits that you made into Mr. Everson's accounts were actually just transfers from your own accounts at another bank, correct?"

"Yes. That's what I said." McKnight seemed inconvenienced by the requirement to respond.

Not the best demeanor on the stand for a criminal defendant, Trask thought. *Either her counsel didn't coach her enough, or she didn't listen to him.* He looked to his right at Carter, who raised an eyebrow. *Dix caught it, too. He could probably do my job with a little practice. Glad I don't have to do his.*

"Exhibits 201, 204, 211, 212, 217, and 222 are all deposits of between $8,500 and $9,800. Those deposit slips are already admitted into evidence," Val continued. "What does the term 'structuring' mean to you, Ms. McKnight?"

"It doesn't mean anything to me."

"So you're telling us that you—at the time you made all these deposits—were *completely unaware* that the Internal Revenue Service requires a bank to report all deposits of $10,000 or more? You did not know that they have to file what is called a 'suspicious activity report' or 'SAR?'"

"I didn't know anything about that."

Good start, Val. No way to lose on those questions. No wiggle room for her to explain it away.

"You do admit that Exhibit 211 shows that you deposited $9,200 on July 11 of last year, and that you deposited an additional $8,750 into the same account on the very next day, as is shown by Exhibit 212?"

"If that's what the slips say, I guess that happened."

"So you deposited a total of almost $18,000 over two days, but split the deposit into two amounts, each under $10,000, is that correct?"

"Like I said, if that's what the slips say. I really don't recall."

Good job. She's quibbling now, with way too much attitude. The jury doesn't like it. Trask saw that Val was taking another look at the first exhibit she had referenced. *What did you find, Val?*

"Ms. McKnight, where did you get the funds for the money that you deposited on July 11?" Val asked. "The $9,200?"

The defendant shook her head in disgust. She answered more slowly, as if speaking to a child.

"Like I said before, I got it from my own account at another bank. I put it with his money because I had a lot of rehab projects going on at my house, and he told me I could use some of his cash. That way I only had to write one check."

"Which bank did you withdraw the money from?"

"I don't remember. I had money in three banks at the time."

"At any rate, we have no withdrawal slip in evidence to support your claim, do we?"

"I suppose not."

No objection yet, Val. Leave it there. Defense might be yelling about shifting the burden of proof if you push it any further. She has no burden to produce any evidence.

Val nodded, staring knowingly at Shirley McKnight.

"Did your bank give you a cashier's check to deposit into Mr. Everson's bank?"

McKnight shifted in her chair. "I don't remember."

She's nervous. What did you see on that deposit slip, Val?

"Do you remember that this deposit on July 11, Exhibit 211, was all in cash?"

McKnight was squirming again. "I said I didn't remember. I made lots of transfers and deposits."

"Maybe this will help refresh your recollection." Val stepped to a notebook computer at her counsel table and pushed a button. Exhibit 211 came up on several television screens in the courtroom. There was a screen for the judge, the court clerk, each counsel table, and a large one at the end of the jury box.

"I think we may have missed this earlier, Ms. McKnight," Val said. "Could you please read the small print at the bottom of the deposit slip?"

"I can't read it."

Sure you can, Trask thought. *You just don't want to read it. She's got you. You're toast.*

"The exhibit has been admitted into evidence, Ms. Fuentes," the judge said. "You may read it for the jury and the record."

"Thank you, your honor." Val zoomed the computer frame so that the small print was now large on all the screens. "Nine-thousand, two-hundred dollars in cash, all in twenty dollar bills."

Val turned back to the defendant.

"Is it your testimony, Ms. McKnight, that instead of giving you a cashier's check to transfer, your own bank—apparently having no concern for your safety or the lining holding your pocketbook together—presented you with four-hundred and sixty twenty dollar bills to carry to your car?"

The defendant shifted positions again in her chair. "The bank said that was all they had that day."

Trask almost fell out of the pew. He looked at Carter, who was trying hard not to laugh, a task made more difficult by the fact that several jurors had already lost the same struggle, and were snickering loudly.

"I tell her not to expect a Perry Mason moment, so she generates one," Trask whispered.

"I never saw Perry do *that*," Carter chuckled. "This case is over."

"At least for now," Trask said, nodding toward the front of the courtroom. The judge, unable to control the laughter from the jury, was declaring a recess for an hour. Val waited until the jury cleared the courtroom before coming back to talk with them.

"What do you think?" she asked.

"I think your verdict will be a quick one," Trask said. "After your defendant's visit to the Andrew Jackson National Bank—the one that only stocks twenties—she lost any credibility she may have had with your jurors."

Val laughed. "That's pretty good. Can I use it in my closing argument?"

"Be my guest. I don't think you even have to *make* a close after that, but the rules of court require one. It should be confident and brief."

"Will do. Thanks for the help."

"When your conviction comes in—and I agree it will be a quick conviction—why not meet us at the FOP for a quick drink and dinner?" Carter asked.

She hesitated. "I don't know—"

"It *is* customary," Trask noted. He nodded toward the prosecution counsel table in the center of the courtroom. A pretty brunette detective in civilian clothes was waving at him behind Val's back. "Make sure and bring your lead witness."

"We'll save a place for you," Carter said. "Done deal."

She smiled and nodded. "Okay."

"Go take another look at your notes," Trask instructed. "Remember, confident and brief. The jury is with you. Any time they laugh with you, or at your opposition, you've got them."

She smiled and headed back toward her table.

Forty-five miles from Richmond, Virginia, Asalati peered through a set of binoculars as he sat in the driver's seat of a Ford pickup. He watched as a large truck approached the row of huge casks just inside the fence line. A crane-like structure opened the top of one of the storage silos. Moments later, an arm lowered the cargo into the cask, and the top was closed.

"It is just as you said, *Saaqhib*. Minimal security, and very accessible. We could easily hit them during the transfer into the casks. How much material will we require?"

The other man, sitting in the passenger seat of the truck cab, did not answer immediately. Instead, he held out his hand, palm up. Asalati obediently removed the binocular strap from around his neck and handed the set to his superior. The older man took in the scene for a moment. When he spoke, it was if he was thinking out loud, repeating what he had studied, now that he had visual confirmation.

"Not that much, my friend. Those are spent rods. They've been cooling for a while, but remain highly potent. The half-life of that material is still thousands of years, even after losing eighty percent of its strength in the tanks. They're putting it in dry storage now. The water will be pumped out of the cask momentarily."

"Why not just take one of the casks while there is no security present?" Asalati asked.

His mentor snorted. "Do you have a truck that can lift and transport over a hundred tons?"

"I am sorry, *Saaqhib*. I did not know."

"I have been doing much research, my friend. I see no way around a tactical assault in order to acquire this ingredient. That is why your first team's project is so critical. If successful, it will divert virtually every resource at our enemy's disposal back toward their capital."

"It is a good plan, and the diversion alone will be a worthwhile endeavor."

The older man returned the binoculars. His tone was conciliatory. "I'm glad that you agree. I have always valued your opinion."

"Thank you, *Saaqhib*. Have you selected the other target yet?"

"Yes. His death will attract the attention of both the police and the enemy's military, and will concentrate hundreds of them in the target area. I expect that we will be able to conduct that phase of the operation very shortly."

Asalati nodded. "The big man is ready and eager to get started. It will be good to have him occupied again."

The older man chuckled. "The infidels have a saying, my friend. 'Idle hands are the devil's playground.' The devils will soon find that they themselves are the playground, and that Hassan's strong hands will be anything but idle."

———

Chapter Twelve

"Here they come now."

Trask stood up from the table and waved. Val's eyes found him and she and the pretty brunette headed toward the table. Trask, Carter, and Tim Wisniewski had been waiting at the Fraternal Order of Police dining room for about fifteen minutes.

"Must have had to touch up their faces," Carter remarked.

Trask held his thumbs up, a question on his face for the new arrivals.

Val smiled. "Guilty. The jury was only out for forty minutes," she shouted across the room.

Several cops and agents in the dining room applauded at her announcement. Both women were beaming now.

As she reached the table, Val attempted to introduce her case detective to the others.

"Miranda Rhodes, this is Detective Tim—"

Before she could finish her sentence, Wisniewski pulled Rhodes close, wrapped her in a passionate embrace, and kissed her full on the lips for several seconds. He finally released her, and held out his right hand to Valerie Fuentes, who shook her head and retreated.

"Uh, I don't think so—" She looked down and saw that Trask and Carter were doubled over, laughing.

Trask waved her back to the table.

"Val, let *me* introduce *you* to Tim Wisniewski and his fiancée, Randi Rhodes."

Fuentes turned toward Rhodes, her hands extended and palms skyward. "*Jesus*, Randi, you could have told me before we got here!"

"What fun would that have been?" Carter boomed, still chuckling. "We're all old friends here. Randi has done some work with this gang of thieves before, back when she was a rookie patrol officer, and before she got her detective's shield."

Rhodes nodded. "I still miss working with you guys." She patted Val on the back. "You're a lucky lady to be joining this club. I don't think I ever learned so much in such a short period of time as when we were all chasing the Zetas together." She giggled. "Sorry about the joke, Val. As you can see, I got some fringe benefits out of the deal."

Randi looked at Trask. "Where's Lynn? I was hoping she'd be here, too."

Trask shrugged. "She had to head home and keep the one and only Boo on her feeding schedule." He saw the question on Val's face. "Our big dog is diabetic. She has to eat and get her insulin injections at a certain time."

"That's a shame," Randi said. "I really wanted to see her. It's been months."

Trask saw that Val was still trying to put all the pieces together. He started to explain further, but was waved off by Carter.

"Have a seat, ladies," he said. "I'll fill Val in on the history."

They sat down as a waitress approached and passed out menus. After they ordered, Carter resumed.

"Once upon a time, I was the training officer for a good rookie cop named Sam, and years later, Sam became the training officer for a good rookie cop named Randi." Carter winked at Rhodes across the table. "Sam and Randi did some good street-cop work, and noticed that a truck with Texas plates was dropping some packages to a Tennis Club south of Capitol Hill. That turned into an investigation into heroin trafficking by a Mexican cartel, which got all of us involved in a federal task force, and unfortunately got Sam and a bunch of innocent bystanders blown up by a truck bomb at a convenience store. My old boss agreed to let Randi work with us after she lost her partner. She did a helluva job, and Jeff here did *his* usual helluva job, and the cartel chief is now on death row."

"Your old boss?" Val asked.

"Willie Sivella," Trask explained. "A Metro PD legend, former chief of the Violent Crimes division, and a kind of Yoda to the DC law enforcement community. He bore the cross of being the immediate superior to one Detective Sergeant Dixon Carter for a couple of decades."

"How's Willie doing?" Randi asked. "I'd love to see *him* again, too."

"Loves his new job," Carter said. "Happy as I've ever seen him, but still plugged in to everything that happens in this town. Just as involved, but with none of the pressure."

"Maybe I can meet him sometime," Val mused. "What's his new job?"

Trask caught a nod from Carter, and took his cell phone out of the clip on his belt. He waited for the phone to ring.

"Hi, babe. Want to meet us at the FOP East in about ninety minutes? We'll finish eating and head that way. Randi and Tim are with us and she wants to catch up. Great. See you there."

He looked at Val. "The whole team is reassembling for you."

"But I—"

"We'll give you a ride back later, counselor," Carter assured her. "And at least one of us will be sober enough to do the driving. Are you parked in a safe spot somewhere?"

"No, I take the Metro to work."

"Good. Another done deal, then, and worth your time, too." Trask said. "The best thing you can do in this job is network with the best people." He pushed his chair back and stood. "I have a toast to make."

They all raised their glasses.

"To Valerie and Randi. Congratulations on a great win, to great wins to come, and to the teamwork that produces them."

"To teamwork," they echoed.

Trask pulled his chair back up to the table. "Everybody dig in. We have somewhere to be after dinner."

———

Valerie Fuentes sat in the passenger seat of Dixon Carter's green Buick, an unmarked car he had used on the job for several years. She was initially quiet as they drove eastward from the District through southern Maryland, but then decided to break the ice.

"So, Detective Carter—"

"No, no, no. It's 'Dixon,' or just 'Dix,' or even 'D.C.' We won't be having time for formalities. We're gonna be very busy."

"'Dixon,' then. Married? Family in town? What's your story outside the job?"

"Not much of one, I'm afraid." Carter had a brief debate with himself on how deep to go with his response. *Oh, what the hell. Jeff vouched for her.*

"I got divorced a couple of years back. No kids."

She waited for a moment. "Was it the job that came between you, if you don't mind me prying a little?"

"It played a role, but I keep playing all the scenes over in my head, and in the final analysis, no, I don't think that it was the job. I think she just got tired of me."

"How many years?"

"Twenty plus."

"I'm sorry. That's a long time."

"Yeah. Apparently too long."

She turned and watched the big man as he drove.

"Why do you say she got tired of you?"

He thought for a moment. "What kind of music do you listen to?"

She laughed. "Mostly hip-hop, some top forty, some R&B. Why?"

"Our friend Trask says that the world runs on a soundtrack, and that there's a song that answers every question. He would have answered your last question with an old Righteous Brothers' tune: 'You've Lost That Lovin' Feelin'.' You know it?"

"I've heard it. I like most of my soul brown-eyed, not blue-eyed."

"I see." Carter gave her a glance. "Anyway, there's a line in there about the gal starting to criticize every little thing her man tried to do. That's a pretty telling thing. We guys are simple creatures to keep happy, but when a man's girlfriend or wife refuses to be happy—or more importantly—won't let him make her happy, the ship is leaving port. Everything he tries to do is wrong, or at least she can find something wrong with it. Nothing cuts a man down more than that. Little, trivial things turn into mountains. Things that weren't even worth a comment before turn into major arguments.

"At the time we were going through all that, I lost a partner. He was murdered by one of our targets. Maybe I wasn't in the mood to put up with all the little battles she wanted to get into. I don't know. At any rate, I had some pretty major things to deal with on my own, and it probably made her feel like I was ignoring her when all the passive-aggressive nonsense started happening."

He paused.

"It's all water under the bridge now. She just moved out and left. I got the papers in the mail. Signed 'em and mailed 'em back to her."

"I see." She took a pause of her own. "How long before you start dating again?"

"I'm not in a rush. If the one gal who I thought was perfect for me turned out to be a disaster, I'm not sure I trust myself to know the difference between another problem and the solution. For now, I'm married to the job. How 'bout yourself? Relationship?"

"Just me and the law and some social work."

"The law has been enough for me," Carter responded. "If I see a social worker on the jury panel, I always advise the prosecutor to get rid of them."

His remark drew nothing but silence.

"No more questions?" Carter asked after several minutes.

"Hundreds. I just don't know where to start."

"That's natural. It would be unnatural, however, if I started answering them before you asked them. I might even guess wrong about a couple of them."

She smiled. "Okay, then. Do you think Jeff Trask really asked me to join this team because he trusts me and believes in my ability? I was way down the line for promotion before he pulled me out of Superior Court."

Carter nodded. "A reasonable question, but the last time you should ask it of anyone, including yourself. Jeff is the most mission-oriented person I've ever met. If he had *any* doubts about your ability, you wouldn't be here."

She waited a moment before asking the next question.

"Do you believe in *him* that much?"

Carter pulled the Buick to the side of the road and stopped. He looked her in the eyes before speaking.

"Why did you ask me that?"

She did not drop her gaze before answering.

"It just hasn't been my practice to have that much faith in white people before. I'm surprised to see how close you two appear to be, especially since he's from Mississippi."

Carter nodded. "I thought that might be it, especially with some of your *social work* in town."

"You have a problem with that?"

"I do, actually."

"Why?" She was pulling back now, her body language defensive. "You disagree with the Black Lives movement?"

"Completely. Do you think that makes me less black?"

"It might."

Carter nodded patiently. He wasn't going to get into a shouting match with her.

"You would agree, would you not, that the main issue with racial prejudice as *you* know it is someone judging you only from the color of the skin on your face?"

"Of course," she answered.

"So why is it fair of you to judge Jeff Trask by the color of his skin, or even by his birthplace, since he had no choice whatsoever in advance of either issue?"

"That's not the same thing."

"Why isn't it?"

"There are two-hundred years of history in this country to explain why it's not."

"You don't look that old to me."

"Excuse me?" She looked incredulous.

"I'm a lot older than you are, and I was never a slave, was never whipped by an overseer, and I don't see any shackles on you, either. What I see is an impressive young lady with a law degree and a damned good job. I really don't think Jeff Trask or his daddy ever owned a plantation, and the history I know says that slavery was abolished a century-and-a-half ago. What I *do* know about Trask is that he saved my neck on more than one occasion by putting his own on the line, and that's good enough for me. You can learn from history—as I believe that Jeff Trask and a lot of other good people have—or you can let it define you as a victim for the rest of your life. I believe you're bigger than that, and so does Jeff. I believe that *all* lives matter, that it isn't heresy to say so, and if I had to push one color to the top above the others, it would be blue."

"Blue?"

"Police officers, Val. Law enforcement personnel. The guys and gals who push their own priorities to the rear when other people—black, white, yellow, red, whatever—are threatened. When some of your BLM friends are out there shooting us because of the uniforms on our backs, I have a lot of trouble seeing them as victims. Racism isn't just a one-way street, you know."

He started the car and pulled back onto the road.

She was silent for another few minutes.

"One more question," she said.

"Shoot." His tone was even, and patient.

"Why, out of all the murders we're looking into, did he give me the one on Officer Roberts? I think Major Williams has a problem with me—maybe even a racial problem—and he wishes that Jeff had kept that case for himself. If Trask believes in me so much, why did he throw me into *that* case."

Carter smiled and shook his head. "Maybe he thought it would be the easiest one for you to handle, given some of your volunteer work."

"Easiest?" she asked. "Why would he think that the killing of a white cop—maybe by someone who has a *history* that gives him a reason to hate white cops—would be the *easiest* for me to prosecute?"

"He wouldn't." Carter kept his eyes on the road. "But Bart Roberts was black, and his wife and all their little kids are just as black as we are. Despite that, Chet Williams still wanted the best prosecutor in town on his case because he cared more than you may ever know about *his* officer. His *black* officer. Like I was trying to tell you: for those of us on the job, *all* lives matter, but if there are any who matter more than the others, it's the *blue* ones. Whatever color is *under* the badge doesn't matter."

———

Trask turned on his bar stool when he heard the door swing open behind him. Carter saw him and headed toward the vacant stool to Trask's right. Val followed, and the sweep of her eyes told Trask she was looking for something. Willie Sivella saw it, too.

"Ladies' room is toward the back on the left," he said, pointing.

She smiled and nodded, heading that way. Sivella handed Carter a cold bottle of Corona Light, earning a nod of appreciation.

"Interesting ride?" Trask asked. "Did she pass your inspection?"

"She'll be fine," Carter answered. "Might need a minor attitude adjustment, but that should come with experience. Bright girl, and like we saw, a lot of talent in the courtroom."

Trask nodded and turned to Lynn, who was sitting on the stool to his left. He was about to ask if she needed another beer when the door to the bar swung open again, and Tim Wisniewski and Randi Rhodes entered. Randi rushed straight toward Lynn.

"Here she is!" Randi said, wrapping Lynn in a hug. "We missed you at dinner. I haven't seen you in months!"

As the women caught up, Wisniewski stood between Trask and Carter, a hand on each of their shoulders. "This seems familiar," he said, looking at Sivella across the bar. "I think I have you to blame for it."

"Blame me all you want," Willie shot back at him, smiling. "I give you the best senior partner and the best prosecutor in the District to work with, and you get engaged to the prettiest cop on the force. I don't think you got too much of a raw deal."

Before Wisniewski could respond, Val appeared behind Carter.

"And this must be the new star of the courthouse," Sivella said, extending his hand across the bar. "Willie Sivella, Ms. Fuentes. Welcome to the Beverly."

"I see you've been talking to Jeff," Val said, shaking Sivella's hand and shooting an accusing glance toward Trask.

"Nope," Trask said, shaking his head. "I haven't said a word, other than to tell Willie you'd be showing up. I told you he was still plugged in."

"That I am," Sivella said smiling. "If you haven't figured it out already, Val, you soon will," he said, raising an instructing finger in the air. "The way to any boss is often through his secretary, and the same thing is often true of judges and their staffs. You gain the trust of the courtroom clerks and court reporters, and the judges follow suit. I know 'em all, and the clerk for Judge Potter called and told me that they were all betting against you today until you cross-examined the defendant. Very nice work. You are now a legend."

"It's just one case," she said. "It doesn't make a career."

"See? Modest, too." Trask shrugged. "Does she get your seal of approval, Willie?"

"Only one more block to check," Sivella said. He gave Val the once over, squinting like a pirate. "What are you drinking, young lady? It's on the house."

"Crown on the rocks," she replied.

Sivella turned back to Trask. "The block is checked. She's welcome here at any time, with or without you. I'll get that drink."

He stepped to the rear of the rectangular bar and pulled a bottle of Crown Royal off a shelf. It gave Val time to whisper in Carter's ear.

"He was your *commander*?" she asked.

"Don't let appearances fool you," Carter whispered back. "Willie never missed anything, whether it concerned the bad guys or the good ones. That's why he was so good at putting teams together. I even found a tracking device he'd slapped under *my* car once when he thought I might be outrunning him a little."

"I heard that, and I did that," Sivella admitted, returning with Val's drink. "Don't let Dix drag you down with him, Val. He can go rogue from time to time."

"I'll watch for that," she said, smiling. "Thanks for the warning."

They were interrupted by the ringtones of multiple cell phones going off simultaneously. Carter and Trask both reached for their belts. They headed for different corners of the building, away from the clamor at the bar. Carter was the first to speak when they returned.

"We have another officer down, in southeast again. Another one of Chet Williams's guys. Neck snapped like a twig. Description isn't conclusive, but it may match the big Barrett guy, the one from the murder at the Lincoln."

"I got that, too," Trask said. "Frank Wilkes is on the crime scene already. One more thing, Dix. Frank said the big guy had an accomplice, and that they got away in the officer's patrol car."

"They took the *marked unit*?" Willie Sivella asked, wincing.

"Apparently," Trask said. "Wilkes said the first guys on the scene grabbed witnesses who saw it make one turn, but after that the patrol unit seemed to just disappear."

"That all just smells very, very wrong," Sivella said, shaking his head. "Did you get a name on our victim?"

"You'll know as soon as we do, Willie," Trask said. "Or maybe before."

"I'll head back into town," Carter said. "You coming, Jeff?"

Trask started to rise, but had a second thought and sat back on his stool.

"Not this time, Dix. Val needs a ride back anyway. She can go with you to the scene and brief me tomorrow. Stay safe."

———

Chapter Thirteen

Val was waiting in the hallway by his office when Trask arrived.

"Come on in, and fill me in," he said, unlocking the door.

He started to make their coffee while she sat in front of his desk, pulling a small notebook from her briefcase.

"We got to the crime scene about ninety minutes after the incident. Dix contacted the officers and crime scene guys on the scene, and this is what he was able to piece together. He said he'd have the relevant reports to us later today.

"Basically, the patrol officer, a guy named Dorian Thompson, had pulled to the side of the road to check on what appeared to be a stalled vehicle. When he got out of his cruiser, a very large black male popped from behind the cruiser, surprised the officer as he was looking into the other car, and broke his neck by grabbing and twisting his head. Another, smaller black male then jumped into the police car after the big guy got into the first vehicle, and both cars left the area in a hurry."

"Witnesses?" Trask asked.

"One bystander across the street who said he got a look at the killer's face. No one got the plates of the other car."

"That shouldn't matter if the dead officer was following his protocol," Trask said, thinking out loud. "He should have radioed that information to dispatch before he got out of his cruiser. Dixon Carter will probably be checking that angle already. Odds are it was stolen anyhow."

"Should we be showing a photo of Barrett to the witness?" Val asked.

"Not a single photo," Trask said. "Tell Dix we need a spread—six photos of similar suspects, same race, facial hair if there was any—or some defense counsel will be moving to suppress the identification because of suggestivity—you know, that we suggested that the guy in the photo was the killer. If the witness picks Barrett out of the photo array, we'll get an arrest warrant for him."

"It looks like another planned ambush," Val said.

"Yeah. The war on cops continues. Was the body still on the scene when you got there?"

"I'm afraid so. It was covered at first, but the tarp fell off when I saw them load it into the body van that arrived to take him to the morgue. Pretty gruesome."

Trask studied her face. "I know this is your first time to be on-scene for a homicide. You okay?"

"I think so. I wanted to thank you for trusting me to handle it for you."

"It wasn't for me, Val. It was for you, for the victim, and for all of us. You needed the experience, and the case needs your focus. As for the trust, you're right about that, and you're welcome."

That other phone in Trask's shirt pocket started to vibrate. He pulled it out and held it to his ear.

"Hello, Julia. What's up?"

"Mr. Eastman would like to see you and Ms. Fuentes as soon as possible," the secretary said.

"Val's in my office now. We'll be right there."

Eastman was standing by Julia's desk when they walked into the outer room. He waved them into his office and closed the door behind them. The United States Attorney motioned for them to sit before walking to his desk and taking his own chair.

"I hear we lost another officer last night?" he asked.

"Yeah," Trask nodded as he spoke. "I'm starting to lose count."

"This one is related to the others?"

Trask looked toward Val, deferring the question to her.

"According to one of the witnesses at the scene, the killer from the Lincoln Memorial murder may be good for this one as well. Same size, anyway, and the method of the homicide seems to point in his direction."

"I want your full attention devoted to it, but tomorrow. I'm assuming your investigators are already on all of this?"

Trask was frowning. "They are, of course, but why do you say *tomorrow*, Ross?"

"Because I have to send everyone in the office to a new, mandatory, department-wide training program. They have some slots open in the first group this afternoon at Main Justice, and I figured it would be better to get this out of the way for both of you, rather than have it interrupt something more important later. The AG was adamant about having everybody check the box. No exceptions. Is there anything case-related that demands your presence today?"

Trask hesitated before answering. "In all candor, nothing that can't wait for us. What kind of training is this, Ross?"

"Race relations. Diversity sensitivity."

"*Oh for God's sake!*" Trask was angry, and on his feet.

"Calm down, Jeff." Eastman was standing now, too, his hands up.

"Really, Ross? DOJ didn't vet their people enough before they hired us all? They really think they've got a bunch of racists working as federal prosecutors? What a bunch of happy horseshit. The political optics strike again and override real working considerations."

"Here's the room number." Eastman offered a piece of paper to Trask. "Be there at 1:00. Get it out of the way and then you can concentrate on the investigation. This wasn't my idea, Jeff. I think it's pretty silly, too, but just check the square and move on. I'm sure you saw stuff like this in your Air Force days."

"Yeah. I did," Trask said, heading for the door. "It was stupid as hell then, too. If somebody's still dumb enough to be a closet bigot in this day and age, you're not going to talk them out of a lifetime of prejudice in an afternoon of hand-holding."

Val shrugged, took the note from Eastman's hand, and followed Trask out of the office.

——————

The classroom at the Department of Justice's main building had been arranged with a circle of twelve chairs in the center. Trask had a sinking sense of *deja vu* as he followed Val into the room and sat next to her in one of the vacant seats.

105

I've seen all this before. Just like the old Social Actions program in the Air Force. Probably just as effective, too. Mandatory thinking. Always works. As if.

A couple of last-minute arrivals took their seats about five minutes late, completing the circle of "students" for the seminar. Trask couldn't help glancing noticeably at his watch.

Damn civilians. In the military, we at least started and finished this farce on time.

"Good afternoon, everyone."

A very short, pudgy guy in an ill-fitting suit stepped to the center of the room. The sleeves on the suit coat swallowed the man's hands completely anytime that he dropped his arms to his side.

You knew you'd find your size on the rack, did you? Trask thought to himself. *That five-nine coat really hangs well on your five-five frame.*

"My name is Richard Hornsby. I am a clinical social worker with the United States Bureau of Prisons. Welcome to the Justice Department's diversity seminar. The purpose of this program is to make us all aware of the value that each of us brings to the department's mission, a mission enhanced by the individual backgrounds that we all bring to the table. This department, as we all know, is charged with the *fair and impartial* enforcement of the laws of the United States. It is only possible to fully perform that mission if we also realize the harmful impact of any prejudices that we may be bringing to the table. Recent events in the news have called into question whether our department personnel—and some of our state and local partner agencies—are doing all that we can to minimize the impact of some of these prejudicial viewpoints—"

Trask shot a look at Val which suggested that if Richard Hornsby started saying, "Black Lives Matter," Mr. Hornsby might witness at least one walkout from his seminar. Val's look back begged Trask to take it easy.

"With that in mind," Hornsby continued, "I want to try something. All of us here today, being DOJ employees, probably do our best every day to make sure that we treat all of our co-workers and everyone else with the dignity and respect they deserve. Some of us may, however, still have some feelings about some other groups in our society that may hold us back, to some degree, in dealing with those persons with complete fairness—"

I can't believe this! Trask thought. *It's the same old USAF Social Actions drill they put us through years ago. I've had twenty years to think about what I should—or should not have said—then.*

"So what we're going to do as an initial exercise," Hornsby continued, "is to search our souls a little, and then to admit to the group what we honestly feel might hold us back a bit in our dealings with some of our co-workers or members of the public. In other words, you might not be *totally* biased against someone because of his or her background—his or her race, color, religion, sexual orientation—but if there's something there that even makes you uncomfortable, that's what we want to admit and then discuss."

And you've got a canned presentation for all the obvious bigotries, don't you? Trask thought. *Blacks, Asians, Hispanics, Jews, Muslims, Native-Americans, LGBT's. Curveball coming at you, Richard. Let's see how you handle it.*

"Let's start with you, can we, Ms.—?" Hornsby was looking at Val.

"Fuentes."

Great choice, Hornsby old man. Two diversity blocks checked with your first choice of a black female. If she follows your lead, that persuades everybody else to play the game, right?

"Fuentes. Thank you, Ms. Fuentes. Are there any uncomfortable feelings that you find yourself dealing with in your interactions with others?"

Val squirmed uncomfortably in her seat.

"It really is okay. We *all* have biases, to a degree," Hornsby said in his most comforting social worker voice.

"Well," Val collected herself. "I do have to admit a little distrust—at least initially—of some white people. I don't think it's so much a racial bias as much as it is a reaction to what has happened historically to people of color at the hands of some whites."

"No one can deny that history, can they?" Hornsby asked the group.

Trask saw what he thought were a couple of raised eyebrows, but the eyebrow-raisers were smart enough to keep their mouths shut.

"So tell us, Ms. Fuentes; how do you deal with these feelings when you feel them bubbling up to the surface?" Hornsby walked around the group like a game show host, stepping backward as if he were giving Val additional space for her answer.

"Lately, actually, I've been questioning the validity of those feelings," Val said. "It was recently pointed out to me that no one—white, black, brown, red or yellow—had any control over the circumstances of their birth, and that much of the history in this country that is regrettable is over a century old now. I've also realized that I have personally been granted many opportunities by my superiors because I've earned them, and not because of or in spite of my color. I think I'll always be on the lookout for prejudice, but maybe I'm not as ready now to presume it's always there. I think I'm more ready to give everyone the benefit of the doubt, at least for starters."

"*Excellent*, Ms. Fuentes." Hornsby was beaming, his class off to a fine start.

Trask thought that if he were back in high school, he'd be making a gagging motion behind the teacher's back.

"Let's just keep going around the circle, shall we?" Hornsby turned his gaze to Trask. "What is your name, sir, and what do you do in the department?"

"Jeff Trask. I'm the Senior Litigation Counsel for the U.S. Attorney's office in the District."

"I see, and that certainly implies that you have several years behind you of prosecuting some serious cases, doesn't it?"

"Several years, yes."

"Well, I'm sure, Mr. Trask, that with all that experience behind you, you've taken whatever steps you could to minimize any improper biases that you may have felt along the way, haven't you?"

"I hope so."

"Good, good."

You're dancing on egg-shells a little there, Richard. Don't be afraid. Go to the lesson plan; ask the question.

"Even with that being the case, Mr. Trask, are there some groups that you find yourself being a little more suspicious of than others? Considerations that might impact your feelings when picking a jury, for example?"

"We don't pick juries anymore, Mr. Hornsby," Trask said. "We eliminate those who would be disasters, and we get stuck with the rest."

A chorus of snickers broke out around the circle of students. Hornsby laughed politely with the rest of them, an artificial little cackle designed to show that he was one of the common people.

"What about African-Americans on your juries, Mr. Trask?" the instructor asked when the chuckling stopped.

"What about them?" Trask shot back.

"Do you think twice about not 'eliminating' them—not striking them—from your juries?"

"If I tried to strike all the black jurors, we'd never have trials in this town, Richard. The population is ninety percent black. I'm much more likely to be suspicious of white people on our panels."

More giggles from the peanut gallery. Good.

"Oh, and why is that?"

Got your attention there, didn't I, Hornsby? You don't know why, but it sounded like it might be wrong, so you just had to ask.

"*Not* because of their race, but because of the professions that residency in D.C. usually indicates for whites. They could be lobbyists, politicians or their staff members, priests—"

"And might you have something against priests?"

Another lure, another little fishy.

"Certainly not as people, Richard, but as jurors, I might certainly have a problem with them. If they don't think it is appropriate for them to judge their fellow man, then they can't do the job as jurors, because that's what juries do. If they're all about rehabilitation—like *social workers*—well, there's a place for that, but not in a jury box. A trial is about guilt or innocence. Sentencing and treatment come later. Of course, there is an additional question I ask if a juror tells me that he's a priest."

"And that is?"

"What order he's from. If he's a Dominican or Franciscan, I take a note and strike him. If he's a Jesuit, I point to the jury box and tell him to have a seat. I find Jesuits to be a lot more about reality and discipline. That's the result of study, not so much of any prejudice."

The circle was collectively snickering again, causing Hornsby to attempt to get back on point.

"So, Mr. Trask, you're just *unwilling* to admit to any biases as a result of ethnic factors?"

Now you played your trump card, didn't you, Richard. The old UNWILLING question. One you think is a win/win for you, and a loser for me.

Trask hung his head for a few seconds, then looked up as if he'd just had an epiphany. "There is one group that I must admit to having some issues with; I wasn't going to admit it until I heard this courageous young lady speak up—"

He nodded toward Val, who rolled her eyes and appeared to be on the verge of having a gag reflex of her own.

"And which group is that?" Hornsby interjected.

You're thumbing through that file of canned responses already, aren't you? Trask thought, suppressing a smile.

"Lapps," Trask said.

"Excuse me?" Hornsby blurted out.

"You know, Laplanders. Saami folks from the north of Scandinavia. Lapps."

"And what gives you reason to have issues with Lapps?" Hornsby tried walking around the circle again, smiling knowingly at those sitting around him.

"Well," Trask mused, "Name a great painting painted by a Lapp. Name a great concerto composed by a Lapp. Name a great book written by a Lapp. Hell, name a Lapp, for that matter. You can't, can you? These people follow reindeer around all year, eating them, wearing their hides, and on occasion drinking their urine. They're so nondescript, the freakin' Russians don't care if they come and go across their border. They don't even bother to check them since the only thing the Lapps apparently care about is reindeer."

The circle erupted into roars as the other prisoners of the seminar followed the parody. Hornsby was, however, suddenly very serious.

"You think this program is a joke, Mr. Trask?"

"Oh no, not at all, Richard. I was trying to use some humor to point out some stereotypical bigotry—you know, the kind that's much more overt than the kind you showed us earlier."

"*Excuse* me?!"

"You know, when you asked Ms. Fuentes here to expound on her biases without asking her what she did for our good old DOJ. Had you bothered to ask her, she would have told you that—*like myself*—she is a federal prosecutor for the District of Columbia. It did not—for *some* reason—occur to you to ask her the same occupational questions you asked me. Why was that? Did you assume that because she was a young, black female, she had to be an administrative staffer somewhere?"

Hornsby's face was now red. Trask didn't know the percentages of anger and embarrassment that made up the combination, but he was sure both were present.

"I see. Is there anything else we should know about the Lapps that offend you, Mr. Trask?" the instructor inquired, a bit of a sneer now crossing his face.

"Well, there is one more thing," Trask responded. "They *are* all ridiculously short."

————

"Are you proud of yourself?" Ross Eastman asked, glaring across his desk.

"Did they check the square for me?" Trask asked.

"What?" Eastman scowled as he leaned forward.

"Did I complete the training, get a certificate, all that stuff?"

"Oh good God!" Eastman stood up, exasperated. "I ask you to just get through an afternoon, and you get sent to the principal's office, and I get a call from the AG."

"It *is* my first time since high school," Trask responded.

"*What?!*" Eastman demanded.

"To get sent to the principal's office. Twenty-five years is a pretty clean run for my permanent record, don't you think?"

Eastman put his hands on his desk and shook his drooping head.

"They sure don't want you to repeat the course, so—yes, I think you checked the square."

"Val, too?"

"Yes, Val, too. They had the impression that the two of you were some kind of tag team."

"We are. Great. Back to work then. Thanks, Ross."

Eastman shook his head and made a shooing motion with his hand.

Trask winked as he walked past Julia's desk. He motioned to Val, who was sitting across the room. "Let's go."

"Not back to Main Justice, I hope," she said, wide-eyed.

"Nope, they signed off on both of us. We're now officially fair and balanced. Let's go talk to some cops."

————

Chapter Fourteen

Aashif Asalati watched approvingly as the police cruiser backed out of the rear of the truck and down the ramp. His men pulled the car into its slot in the new garage at the camp. Both bays in the new building sat beneath roofs covered with camouflage and foliage, making them as invisible from the air as the rest of the buildings in the facility. The huge driver of the truck approached Asalati, a half-smile on his face.

"Piece of cake. The cop never saw me coming. Quiet kill, and we have our police car."

"Excellent work, Hassan," Asalati said. "The other car?"

"We pulled off on one of the exits and ditched it. Ibrahim rode back with me in the truck. No witnesses."

"Good. Go get some food and rest. You have served us well today."

Asalati felt the cell phone vibrating in his pocket. He walked up the hill to a point where his reception would be better, and where the rest of the camp could not see him. He pushed the contact icon and returned the call listed as missed on his screen.

"Yes, *Saaqhib*?"

"The mission was successful, Aashif?"

"Completely. Hassan was able to kill the policeman without using a weapon, and we have the cruiser in the garage. The stolen car was abandoned off the interstate. No complications."

"Very good. I received several shipments today. The uniforms are complete, and the rifles and ammunition are here as well. I will have them delivered to you soon. Are the men ready?"

"They drill every day, *Saaqhib*. They should be."

"Make sure of it, my friend. All the eyes of the world will be on them soon. How about the bus?"

"Painted and ready. We studied the photos carefully. It should pass without any questions. Hassan is ready for the next assignment, *Saaqhib.*"

"Tell him the target has been chosen. Send him my way with a driver."

———

"The witness on the scene couldn't make the pick from the photo spread?" Richard Seal asked, directing the question to Dixon Carter, who was sitting to Seal's left at the conference table.

"Afraid not," Carter said. "He looked at Barrett's mug shot long and hard, but couldn't make a conclusive ID. The last photo we had of Barrett is a few years old, and time can make a difference."

"No warrant for now, then," Trask said. "Not that we'd know where to look if we got one. Anything on the cars?"

"Virginia troopers found the stolen car abandoned off of I-66 west of the beltway," Wisniewski said. "Same plates that Officer Thompson had radioed in, anyway. Nobody saw it get dropped. We're having it printed, just in case."

"Ideas, Jeff? Val?" Seal asked.

"We'll wait on the fingerprint results, of course, just in case we get lucky," Trask said. "I'm interested in everyone's thoughts on why the cruiser got snatched."

"It can't be good, whatever it is," Carter noted. "Serial attacks on our people, and now they have a vehicle that will let them get close without raising suspicion. They could even leave the thing on the street with a trunk full of explosives. I've got lots of bad dreams running through my head."

"How fast was the initial response to the scene?" Trask inquired. "First officers on site?"

"Not as bad as it could have been," Carter said, "especially given the fact that 7D had the tires slashed on eight of its cruisers about an hour before the attack. At any rate, I don't think we missed anything from getting there when we did. The uniforms who were first to respond did a decent job with the witness canvass."

"Was disabling your cruisers related, Chet?" Trask looked across the conference table at Major Williams.

"I don't think so," Williams said. "We think that a couple of young banger wannabes just got brave and destructive. At least they took it out on our tires and not our guys this time. I'm getting sick of these family notifications."

"Any objection to Val taking this one, since she was on the scene and is already working with you on Officer Roberts's murder?" Trask asked Williams.

"None. She's been great." Williams nodded in Val's direction.

Trask thought he saw a smile crossing her face.

"Good. Chet, any electronic tracking devices on your stolen cruiser that would help us locate it?"

"Not that one, unfortunately. Older unit, the kind we usually get in 7D. HQ and Georgetown usually get all the new toys. It did have a number painted on the roof, but by the time we got a chopper airborne, the car had disappeared. No sign of it. We put a bulletin out to let everybody know not to trust the unit or its driver until further notice, but who knows how or when we'll see it again."

"Chet, if the same perp got your man that got my officer, I'd appreciate anything you get in the way of information," Nick McCarver said. "You have my guarantee that if I get anything first, you'll get it within five minutes."

"Done," Williams agreed.

Seal, at the head of the table, was looking at notes he'd jotted on a pad. "Lynn, assuming that we're on the right page in thinking that this Barrett character is in town, have we come up with *anything* else that might give us a location on him?"

"Sorry, boss. Nothing. I've hit all my indices at least five times. No credit card usage, mail, new accounts, nothing."

"We'll put his face out to everybody as a person of interest, then," Seal said. "Do not stop, just notify us. Maybe we'll have some observant guy or gal on the street spot him and at least get an area to watch."

"Couldn't hurt." Carter was pushing back from the table.

Trask smiled.

Dixon has unofficially closed the meeting.

"I guess that's it for now," Seal said.

Motion seconded. We're adjourned for now.

———

Trask sat on his usual stool at the Beverly, nursing his usual Michelob Ultra. He looked up at the TV mounted inside the corner of the bar. The two Muslim talking heads were going at it again, the moderate Saleem condemning the extreme Asalati.

"You and your kind have poisoned the minds of young Muslims everywhere with your garbage, Aashif. Islam is a religion of peace. I am surprised and extremely disappointed that the authorities here have not yet arrested you."

"And you and *your* kind are weak, and are traitors to the prophet. Look at the crime and moral decay around us. Only a strong and decisive law like *sharia* could be expected to save this sickening society from itself. In time, it will happen. The authorities here have nothing to arrest me *for*, since I do not advocate a violent overthrow of the American government. I do not have to do so. Time is on the side of the true Islam. The acts of our martyrs across the globe are the products of their own heroic choices, following the true religion. In time, the entire world will choose our faith."

The news anchor, seated next to Saleem in the studio, turned to his guest as the camera shot of Asalati disappeared from the screen.

"Imam Saleem, how can there be two such divergent viewpoints coming from the same faith, and how can moderates like yourself combat the influence that radicals like Asalati seem to have over your young men across the globe?"

"There are passages in the holy book that those like Asalati emphasize to the exclusion of all others. Read as a whole, it is my belief that our Qur'an teaches love and tolerance, not hatred and jihad."

"You have written in some news publications about the influence that Asalati and others are having in American prisons."

"Yes, I have. We of the *true* faith refer to it as 'prison Islam.' The false teachers of our faith tap into the anger and hatred that your prisoners—and especially young black males—feel for your society as a whole. I have volunteered, and have been vetted by your Bureau of Prisons to serve as a Muslim guest clergyman in order to try and counter some of these false teachings, and I am happy to be on the president's advisory council on religion and matters of faith.

"I go into the prisons and jails to teach our real faith. Information and education are our best weapons, but those like Asalati are finding audiences behind bars far too often. They also list themselves as spiritual advisors, and if an inmate puts an Asalati on a visitor's list, the current BOP regulations make us powerless to restrict what the inmate may hear from him or another extremist in a private counseling session."

Willie Sivella pressed a button on the remote, changing the channel.

"Time for some sports," Willie said. "This is supposed to be a bar, after all, and I'm sick of listening to that crap. The race-baiters are at war with cops all over the country, and the whole country is at war with jihadis, even though the clowns in charge won't admit it."

"Thanks for the channel switch, Willie," Trask said. "I've had enough stress for one day."

"Let's do this, then," Sivella said, clicking the remote and turning off the TV. He walked to the other side of the bar where a huge CD jukebox commanded a medium-sized dance floor. He pushed two buttons and Percy Faith's "Theme from A Summer Place" filled the room.

Trask smiled. "Better, thanks. Won't be too long now. We just have to get to spring first. It's been a long winter."

"Too damn long, and a sad one, with all the good guys biting the dust. I just have a bad feeling that it might get worse before it gets better. You said it yourself. We have nothing to go on yet on all these local cop-killings, and I don't think those bastards are going to go down without a fight."

"Neither will we," Trask said, downing the last sip of his beer. "Got to head home, Commander. Lynn will have supper waiting for me. I just needed a minute or two to clear my head. Thanks."

"Anytime. Give Lynn my best."

At 12:32 a.m., Willie Sivella gathered the trash from the evening's business and tied a square knot in the twist-ties on the top of the large, dark trash bag. He glanced out the front door to the parking lot.

No cars, no customers. Won't hurt to close half an hour early tonight. A smile broke out across his weathered face. *It's good being your own boss.*

He stepped out of the back door to The Beverly, locking the door behind him. He hauled the trash bag over to the dumpster located along the back wall, flipped the lid open, and tossed the bag in. The lid creaked loudly as he lowered it back into place.

I really do have to oil that noisy thing tomorrow. Kathy will have my ass for not doing it already.

He looked down and fumbled for the car keys in his front pocket, turning toward his car as he did so. His eyes saw a huge set of feet facing his own.

The big man's hands closed hard around Sivella's neck, spinning him around, twisting him and choking the air from his brain. He reached instinctively for the aircraft-grade aluminum tactical pen in the front of the pouch on his belt. His left hand found it, and he jammed the steel point of the pen hard into his attacker's thigh.

The big man grunted in pain, and released Sivella long enough to allow him to spin toward his assailant. Sivella's right hand found the subcompact pistol in his pants pocket, and he pulled the weapon, drawing a bead on the massive figure in front of him. Before he could pull the trigger, however, the big man's partner, positioned behind Sivella, fired his own gun. Sivella dropped to the ground, blood pouring from the wound in his head.

"Let's go, Hassan," the smaller man said. "I'll drive."

The big man nodded, stumbling toward the compact hidden on the other side of Sivella's SUV. He lost his balance as he shifted his weight onto his injured left leg, and braced himself on Sivella's car.

"Wrap it with this," the driver said, handing Hassan an ace wrap from the car's glove compartment. "It'll stop the bleeding until we get back to camp. Doesn't look like he got your artery. You'll be okay. We got the job done."

"Hurts like hell."

"Puncture wounds. Yours will heal up soon enough. His won't."

Chapter Fifteen

"Dix won't be in today," Wisniewski said. "He's just too torn up."

Trask nodded. "Understandable. First Juan Ramirez, now this. Willie was retired, for God's sake. His end of watch was vertical—he was alive. It's not supposed to happen like this."

Richard Seal's cell phone buzzed on the table. He picked it up and just said, "Yes?" before listening intently for several minutes. "That's something definite, at least. Call me back when you get the DNA. Thanks."

He looked at the others sitting around the table.

"We finally have something concrete. Lynn was square on. It was Barrett. His bloody handprint on Willie's truck left good prints for the palm and two fingers. We have 100 percent confidence in the ID. The Maryland forensic guys are checking the blood for a DNA match, so we should have a second confirmation when that comes back, as long as it's Barrett's blood. If it was Willie's, then we still have Barrett's prints."

"My bet's on Willie," Nick McCarver offered. "I mean that it's Barrett's blood. I can't see Willie Sivella going down without getting in one good lick. I talked to one of the guys on scene and he said that Willie at least got his gun out. They found a tac pen beside his body, too."

"Anyone heard from Kathy?" Lynn asked.

"Dix had gone by their place when he heard about Willie," Wisniewski said. "He told me when he called that it hadn't really hit her yet. At least it will be the Baltimore Medical Examiner who'll have to do the work, and she won't have Willie lying in a locker in the morgue behind her own office."

"The Commonwealth of Maryland will have a warrant for Barrett's arrest sometime today," Trask said. "It won't be a DC case unless and until we can tie it to our murders here, and even then we'll have to have some sort of federal connection to charge it. At any rate, I talked to the District Attorney this morning. The prints were enough for him to move on the warrant."

"This sucks," Wisniewski complained. "Can't we handle this, since we're all federally deputized? We all knew Willie. He was one of us."

"That's the problem with pushing too hard on this, Tim." Trask shook his head. "If we make a power play to try and take the investigation, we'll appear to be too close to the case, and if we're honest with ourselves, we probably are. The U.S. Attorney for Maryland and Ross Eastman aren't exactly the best of friends. They've had some jurisdictional squawks on other cases in the past. It's a county matter for now, and we risk bringing in our federal friends in Baltimore if we complain too much. They could even conflict us out with Main Justice, and end up with *all* the murders if we get disqualified.

"I think our best approach for now is to let Rich continue to use his connections in the Maryland State Police to keep us informed, and we'll see if we can work the info on this side of the river. Nobody knows where Barrett's hiding anyway. He could be in our district, or in Maryland, or Virginia. We just know he's somewhere close."

"And probably good for the murders of at least three of our own," Chet Williams added. "Nick's officer Turner, my guy Dorian Thompson, and now Willie."

"And Willie was part of the story of every one of us," Wisniewski noted, boiling. "If I see Barrett and he makes *half* a funny move, I'm not bothering to ask him twice to hit the pavement, or to let that brute get within twenty feet of me."

"Not our case for now, Tim," Trask reminded him, "and I wouldn't be saying anything that could end up hurting myself in an investigation later. We've all got motives to want to put this creep down. Let's not give ammo to an internal affairs or inspector general scalp-hunter. Play it by the book, and then throw the book at Barrett when we get him, hopefully alive."

"Anybody know about the arrangements yet?" Lynn asked. She saw a curious look or two around the table. "Sorry, the funeral."

"Yeah." Wisniewski was composed again. "Willie had a purple heart from 'Nam, and like Major Williams, he was a marine before he was a cop. Dix told me that Kathy made a couple of calls. Arlington told her they could handle a funeral with full honors late next week. It seems like everybody in three states knew Willie, and they were more than willing to get him on the schedule."

"Arlington again." Trask shook his head. "Beautiful place. I'm starting to hate it."

———

Dixon Carter watched as the crime scene processors pulled the last yards of yellow tape from around the Beverly. Once the last vehicle pulled away from the rear parking lot and passed him, he started the Buick and pulled past the rear of the building, stopping on the back corner where no passing cars would see his car from the highway.

The Maryland state police are pretty good. Probably didn't miss anything. It happened out back here, so I don't need to get inside, not for now at least.

He walked the rear perimeter of the building.

Two sets of tire tracks here. The wider ones would have been Willie's SUV, the smaller ones the perp's car. Bad guy—or guys—parked over here. Willie wouldn't have noticed it from the back door. Looks like they took an impression of the perp's tires. Thorough job, but probably a waste of time. Probably a hot car, dumped somewhere. I told 'em to process Willie's ride, so they put it on a flatbed tow. I'll get it and return it to Kathy tomorrow.

He stopped in his tracks as he rounded the spot where the SUV had been parked.

She sure as hell doesn't need to see that.

A circle of dried blood had formed a dark stain in the dust where Sivella had fallen in the unpaved area behind the building. Some edges of the stain had been disturbed, indicating that samples had been taken by the crime scene techs.

Carter knelt down and stared at the dirt.

Maybe they found a shell casing, maybe the bullet lodged in your skull, boss. I hope that hard head of yours didn't mess the slug up too much. I'll clean this up for you so Kathy doesn't have to deal with it.

He went to the wooden storage closet next to the small dumpster on the side of the building, and took out the rusty shovel, large plastic dust pan, and rake he'd seen Willie using to clean up trash after a busy evening, when the front lot overflowed and customers pulled behind the bar. He dug the shovel into the hardpack to dislodge the discolored dirt, raked it into the pan, then walked to the back of the cleared area and tossed the stained soil into the weeds. Returning to the shallow hole, he loosened the dirt around it, and raked the area until it was level and uniform in color.

He stood looking at the rear of the building for anything else that could either speak to him or call for his attention. There were no sounds, no voices speaking to him, only silence.

Jeff would be conjuring up Simon and Garfunkel right now, wouldn't he, boss? Maybe he'll have some ideas, some more leads to follow. Give us time. We'll do the job.

He backed the Buick up and drove over the raked area, his own tire tracks making the dirt over the hole that he'd filled look even more normal.

———

Asalati nodded with approval as he watched the seven men go through the manual of arms for the fifty-third time that day.

"That will do, Ibrahim. Just make sure the discipline is evident and perfect. No movements at all while at attention or parade rest."

"We have studied the films repeatedly, Imam," Ibrahim assured him. "The uniforms have been tailored and cleaned. The shoes are polished and spotless. The medals just arrived, and we will put them on tonight. The decals on the bus are dry as well. We will be ready tomorrow."

"Excellent," Asalati said. "Where is the other team?"

"At the garage. They are changing the number on the top of the police car so that it will not be recognized from the air, as you directed."

Asalati nodded again and crossed the camp to the two-bay garage. Two of his men were working with a stencil and black paint, converting the "13" on the roof of the police cruiser to an "18."

It will still be an unlucky number for you tomorrow, soldiers of Satan, he thought to himself.

He reversed his steps, walking past the camouflaged barracks. The door to the large, single room was open, and he could see several men inside cutting their hair close, and shaving their bodies.

Good, my friends. It is good to be clean when one meets the prophet, as several of you may do tomorrow.

He climbed the hill on the northwest side of the camp to the spot where he knew he'd have the best cell service.

"All is ready, Saaqhib. God be praised. Tomorrow will be a day of glory."

———

"I thought I'd find you here," Val said, sitting down beside Trask on the raised concrete curbing.

"You know what's ironic?" Trask didn't look at her, staring instead at one of the lions head statues that stood watch over the National Law Enforcement Officers Memorial. "Willie deserves his name here as much as any of the others, but since he wasn't on duty when he was murdered, he doesn't qualify. I plan on raising that with the memorial's board to see if they'll make an exception. They did it for Bob Lassiter. He's the only prosecutor on these walls, for now. "

"Would it help if we find a murder motive related to his status as a retired officer?"

Trask shrugged. "Sure couldn't hurt. You have something on that?"

She shook her head. "No, not yet. Just thinking. It just doesn't feel random."

"You're right about that. It doesn't, and it's not."

"Okay, do *you* have something on that?" she asked.

"No, not yet." Trask stood up and motioned for her to follow him back to the office. "But we will."

———

Chapter Sixteen

"It's very good of you to drive, Chet," Trask said as he took his seat in the shotgun chair.

He turned and looked toward the back of the Toyota Sequoia, seeing Val and Lynn in the third row. The large figures of Dixon Carter and Tim Wisniewski took up what would have been the seats for three normal-sized people in the second row.

"No problem," Williams said. "I've been to too many of these things, and the guards at Arlington probably know my car by now. If they don't, they'll just check all our IDs at the gate. They'll wave us around any traffic once they see them. We used to have window decals issued by DOD, but they ramped up the security after that shooting at the Navy Yard. All the bases are supposed to be checking IDs now."

"Your marine reserve ID plus a police badge probably carries some weight at a marine's funeral service," Carter said. "I doubt if our man Barrett will be stupid enough to show his face at the cemetery, but stranger things have happened. We'll keep our eyes open; otherwise, we'll all be there for Willie."

No one in the car spoke, but several heads nodded in agreement.

"We'll be early enough to watch folks arriving," Williams said as they headed northwest along the George Washington Memorial Parkway. "We'll beat the rush, too. With all the motorcade and well-wishers in attendance today, the place will be packed. There's a scheduled procession all the way from our HQ to the gravesite. Motorcycles, marked units from at least three states, pipes, the works."

"Ross Eastman and Rich Seal will be in a car in the procession. Nick McCarver's driving another one. They'll meet us at the grave," Trask said, looking toward the Pentagon as they passed the huge building on their left.

125

"Spend much time in there, Jeff?" Carter asked.

"Thankfully, no," Trask answered. "I feel about as comfortable in *that* puzzle palace as I do at Main Justice. Some good people, of course, but too many political animals kissing butts and stabbing backs for my taste."

"Happens in every headquarters," Williams agreed. "I never had much use for them either. The best commanders have always been the ones who could break out of their little circle of yes-men to talk to the guys in the field and get the truth before they made any final decisions."

"Like Willie," Lynn chimed in from the back.

"Yeah, like Willie," Trask and Wisniewski said, almost in unison.

Williams made the turn into the main gate at the Arlington National Cemetery, and—as predicted—was waved into the park by a soldier at the gate who then snapped to attention and saluted. Williams began steering the Sequoia slowly along the roads winding through the lawns lined with thousands of markers honoring the nation's fallen heroes.

Trask turned again toward the back of the vehicle and saw that Val was silently staring, mouth slightly open, at the sight.

"First time here, Val?" he asked.

She nodded, but remained quiet.

"Marines are here, first on the field," Williams said, pointing to a dark-blue bus pulled to one side of the road. He pulled the Sequoia past the bus and parked.

Trask waited until Carter and Wisniewski were out of the back door. He held the door open and helped Lynn and Val climb down from the step rail before meeting Williams at the back of the Sequoia.

"That's different," Williams said, pointing to the license plate under the white decal on the front of the bus: the Eagle Globe and Anchor insignia of the U.S. Marine Corps.

"Virginia plates," Trask noted. "I thought all the ceremonial vehicles for the Marine Barracks were at the motorpool at Anacostia now."

"They are," Williams said. "All I've seen before is the blue government tags. Must be a new acquisition. Maybe they haven't had time to change the plates yet."

Williams pointed up a slight rise. More than a hundred folding chairs had been neatly lined up facing a freshly dug grave. Several yards in front of the chairs, eight men stood in the ceremonial dress uniform of the Marine Corps. Seven of the men were at parade rest, their M-I Garand rifles held at their right sides, the rifle butts resting on the ground.

"Firing party is here," Williams said, "but I don't see the body bearers. They usually ride out on the same bus from 8th and I."

8th and I Streets. Home of the Marine Barracks, Trask recalled. He remembered watching a video of the body bearers of Company B during a tour of the installation. The bearers were huge marines selected for their size, strength, and stamina. They lifted weights for hours a day so that six of them could carry the caskets of their fallen comrades—for hundreds of yards if necessary—from the hearses to the gravesites at Arlington or other places of burial.

"I'm getting a bad feeling about some of this, Colonel," Williams said.

He called me 'Colonel' again. That's never good.

"What's wrong, Chet?"

"I don't know yet. Let's go up and have a chat with the chief of the firing party."

Trask followed in Williams's footsteps as they walked up the hill. The marine wearing what Trask would have called sergeant's stripes came to attention as Williams approached him. Williams held out his identification card, showing the marine that he held the rank of major in the Marine Corps Reserve. The man examined the card, then snapped a salute. Trask noted that the man's wrist was not straight, but held at a slight angle during the salute. He scanned the uniforms of the armed men, taking in the dark blue tunics trimmed in red, the sharply creased white trousers, and the rows of medals worn on the upper left of the tunics. He saw the same decoration on two of the marines, and a cold shiver ran down his back.

"At ease," Williams said to the marine in charge of the detail, motioning toward Trask. "This is Colonel Trask of the Air Force Reserve. We were just wondering where the body bearers were. Haven't they been riding out with the firing parties?"

"Not anymore, sir. New procedure," the man explained. "They will be arriving shortly by separate transport."

"I see," Williams said calmly. "New procedure," he repeated. "Your men look great today. We're glad to have them here. We're friends of the marine who we're burying today. Do him proud, gentlemen."

"Thank you, sir." The marine snapped to and gave another salute.

Williams turned and started back down the hill, Trask at his side.

"Did you see the medals, Chet?" Trask asked.

"Yeah. Let's get back to the others. I want to call the barracks."

At the Sequoia, Williams took his cell phone from a pocket, walked behind the marines' bus while giving it another inspection, and dialed a number from memory. Trask heard him ask for Company B. After a short conversation, Williams returned to the others.

"The company clerk told me that the firing party and body bearers left half an hour ago in the same vehicle," Williams said. "A bus with motor pool plates."

———

The dark-blue marine motor coach carrying the members of the firing party and the body bearer detail pulled to the right lane of the roadway of the George Washington Memorial Parkway, and took an exit just north of the Reagan National Airport.

"Why are we pulling off?" the ranking marine asked the driver, a Navy enlisted man.

The driver jerked a thumb rearward and shrugged at the same time. The marine turned to see a marked police unit, lights circling, following the bus.

"What the hell?" The marine stepped to the front door of the bus. "We weren't speeding, and that's a DC squad car. We're in Virginia. He's out of his jurisdiction."

The bus pulled to the side of the road, the police cruiser following it to a stop.

"What the hell is he waiting for?" the marine asked, checking his watch and the bus's side mirror as the officer in the driver's seat of the police cruiser appeared to be making a phone call. "This clown is going to make us late for the service!"

The uniformed cop approached the door of the bus on foot. The marine stepped forward as the door swung open, surprised to see the police officer's gun in his hand. The shot hit the marine square in the chest, and as his body fell onto the stairs inside the door, a second bullet passed him, striking the bus driver. A very large man who had followed the one dressed as a police officer then grabbed the dead marine's body and pulled it out of the bus onto the ground. He jumped onto the stairs and quickly rolled two hand grenades down the aisle of the bus.

———

"Those are not real marines up there," Williams said quietly. "We have to act before hundreds of innocent people get here to become targets. If they have live ammo, there are eight rounds in each of those clips, and they may be carrying spare magazines. A thirty-caliber rifle round can do a lot of damage at close range."

"You're the TAC guy, Chet," Carter said, referring to the Major's recent assignment as chief of the police tactical unit. "What's your plan?"

"Who's armed here?" Williams asked.

Carter and Wisniewski raised their hands, as did Trask and Lynn.

"Sig 226 service weapons, sixteen rounds each," Williams nodded toward Carter and Wisniewski. "What are you carrying, Colonel?" he asked Trask.

"Sig P-239. Eight plus one in the chamber," Trask replied.

Carter chuckled. "Didn't like the marshals' Glock?"

"Not particularly."

"Lynn?" Williams asked.

"My subcompact .45," she said. "Seven rounds."

"Val, stay here," Williams ordered. "Behind the bus." He saw her start to protest. "Just do it."

He took another look up the hill.

"Nobody draws or exposes their weapon until I give the word or those bogus marines up there start shooting. Dix and Lynn take the right, Jeff and Tim take the left. We'll have about the same amount of ammo on each side. Try to look nonchalant until we get close. Watch your fields of fire. We want a crossfire from each side without shooting at each other. I've already talked to the head goon up there. If we can get the draw on them, maybe we can take this down the easy way."

He looked around at the faces of his irregular command.

"Okay, let's do this."

Lynn followed Trask a short way behind Williams, whispering as they walked.

"Are you sure they're not marines?" she asked.

"Check the medals," he said.

She looked hard at the men dressed as marines as they got closer.

"Oh, shit!" she said under her breath.

"Stay behind Dix if you can, babe," Trask said. "I love you."

"I love you, too."

She split off to follow Carter.

Williams smiled as he approached the detail chief, who again popped to attention and saluted.

"At ease, again," Williams said. "I just have one unusual request. I haven't handled an M-1 since we drilled with them at Annapolis. I know you just have blanks in them, and I don't want to fire one, but I wanted to ask—since there's so much time before the services begin—if I could check and see if I remembered the mechanism on that rifle. Would that be possible?"

"That's highly unusual, Major," the man responded.

From twenty feet to the side, Trask watched the face of the detail chief as the man stared at Williams from under the white wheel hat. The fake marine seemed to be considering some options.

Sirens began blaring in the distance. Trask wanted to turn but couldn't. He noticed that one set seemed to be coming from the east.

That will be the cycles or units in front of Willie's procession.

The sound of another siren seemed to be coming from the south.

I think that's an ambulance or fire truck. May have been an accident on the parkway.

Trask looked at the 'marine' in front of Williams. The man's demeanor changed suddenly, relaxing.

"Major, I don't see any harm in letting you see one of the guns."

Trask remembered the drills he'd heard from *real* marines, and a certain movie scene: *'This is my rifle, this is my gun—'*

Those sure as hell are not real marines!

The two men in front of him screamed at almost the same time.

Williams yelled for his people to draw, the command coming just soon enough for them to bring their weapons on target before the man dressed as a marine shouted, "Allahu Akbar!"

The bogus marines tried to shoulder their rifles and fire as Trask and the others emptied their pistols into their ranks. Three of the wounded terrorists managed to get a shot off before falling. To his horror, Trask saw one of them point his rifle at Chet Williams before firing. Williams fell in front of him and did not move.

When the shooting stopped, Trask spun around, looking for Lynn. Her eyes found his, telling him that she had not been hit. He turned back and rushed to where Chet Williams was lying. Carter was already kneeling beside the fallen major.

"He's gone, Jeff."

Trask stood up again, checking his pistol. He dumped the empty magazine into his left hand and pulled a second, loaded one from his pants pocket. Jamming it into the weapon, he racked a round, and began walking up and down the line of fallen imposters.

"Shooting the wounded?" Carter was behind him, a conscience in the fury.

"No." Trask glanced toward the body of Chet Williams. "But I'd like to." He kicked one of the rifles out of reach of a surviving terrorist who was still moving, moaning, and coughing up blood.

An additional chorus of closer sirens now joined the others in the distance.

"Better give me your gun, Jeff," Carter said. "Unload it first."

"Dammit, Dix, I'm not planning on shooting anybody else today."

"I know that," Carter said. "They'll take everyone's. Tim's, mine, Lynn's too. Evidence and ballistics. You still have the Glock at home?"

"Yeah, and a spare Sig."

"Good. Start thinking about the statement you're going to make, unless you plan on lawyering up."

Trask shook his head. "I never really liked lawyers."

Chapter Seventeen

"First of all, I'd like to thank you all for sparing the country, my office, and the District from what surely would have been even more of an unspeakable tragedy."

Ross Eastman, the United States Attorney for the District of Columbia, had descended from his tower of power to meet with the task force in its conference room at the FBI field office.

"I would further like to thank you for sparing the lives of the chief of police, the mayor, and most probably myself. We would have all been sitting in the front row when that order to 'fire' came, and I'm quite sure those rifles would have been pointed at us.

"All that having been said, I'm afraid there are some unfortunate consequences in addition to the tragic loss of Major Williams." Eastman looked across the conference table at Trask. "Jeff, the Department has instructed me to remove you from this investigation."

Dixon Carter snorted in disgust. "He didn't do anything but help save lives, Ross. We couldn't have stopped those bastards without Jeff and Lynn."

"I'm not saying that he *did* anything wrong, Dix." Eastman held up both hands, first in a gesture of caution, then turning them over in a sign of helpless resignation. "The fact is, however, that the only surviving member of the attack at Arlington had two bullets in him that were fired from Jeff's pistol. There's a clear conflict of interest in having him remain on the case. I have no doubt that the Virginia authorities will clear all of you of any wrongdoing, but Jeff's not a cop who can be returned to duty in this matter. He's a prosecutor, and I have to replace him."

"It's okay, Dix. He's right," Trask said. "I'm just sorry that my head shot missed. Chet might still be with us."

"Where does this leave us with charges on this survivor, this Rusean Short?" Richard Seal asked.

"I'm not out of the room *yet*," Trask said. He looked at Eastman, an eyebrow raised.

"Go ahead and explain," Eastman said, conceding the fact.

"Since the shootout happened in Arlington—in Virginia—our federal authorities in Alexandria have venue over the murder of Chet Williams, who was deputized, and therefore a federal officer in the performance of his duties. We were, after all, at Arlington both to attend the funeral *and* to see if anyone connected to Willie's murder and the other police assassinations showed up. Ballistics says it was Short's rifle bullet that killed Chet. The slug miraculously stuck in his body after hitting a couple of ribs, even though it was fired at close range. It appears to have ricocheted off something fairly hard—maybe Chet's belt buckle, which had a good nick in it. In addition, I saw Short fire the shot from about fifteen feet away. Between the ballistics match and my testimony, we can easily prove that Short was the killer.

"We also have the local—I mean non-federal for court purposes—murders here in the District of Short's wife and step-daughters. They'll be tried in Superior Court instead of federal district court. Even if we don't have a death penalty to apply in Superior Court for the triple-homicide because of the limitations in the D.C. Code, the District of Virginia can use those murders as aggravators to justify a capital punishment certification under *federal* law, *if* the Department approves it. A Virginia jury is much more likely to vote for death than a D.C. panel, so we have that going for us."

"Why the hell *wouldn't* DOJ approve the death penalty in this case?" Nick McCarver asked. "Four people dead, including a couple of kids and a police officer, and that isn't enough?"

Eastman looked down at the table.

"I'll take that, too, Ross," Trask said. "Since I'm off the case anyway, I'll answer the question. Don't worry. I'll answer it in here, but not in public."

"Go ahead again," Eastman said.

"Dix put Short inside on a drug beef years ago," Trask said. "He should have still been serving the sentence, but the AG and the president put him on their 'Smart On Crime' early release list as a *non-violent* offender. They'll be embarrassed enough when the press connects the dots without having the story getting perpetual headlines because of all the death penalty litigation. I think the odds of them doing the right thing here—"

"Are about the same as them doing the right thing with Fast and Furious, the Clinton email mess, the IRS targeting scandal, and the Ferguson riots," Carter interjected. "So . . . We lose Jeff, Chet's killer doesn't get what he deserves, and we get who or what as Jeff's replacement?"

"You keep Val," Eastman said. "We all agree that she's proven herself, and Jeff can advise her from behind the curtain if necessary. And—to the extent that the death penalty package remains open as an option—Jeff can help draft the indictment and the supporting package with the Virginia team. He's done it before. My counterpart in Alexandria has already told me that he wants Jeff going to the capital committee meeting with his guys. If the committee members have any doubt as to what happened in the cemetery, we have a witness. If the Department wants to disqualify him from helping to prosecute the case because he was there, they can damn sure listen to him describe what happened for the same reason: *because he was there*. At least they can't disapprove the request for capital certification because of any uncertainty of evidence."

"*What kind* of committee?" McCarver asked.

"The Department has a committee that meets to review any request from a United States Attorney's office seeking to impose the death penalty," Trask explained. "It's not up to the United States Attorney. We had to go through it in the Zetas case. They evaluate the evidence, make sure it fits the statute, and look at every aggravating and mitigating factor before giving the request for the death penalty certification a thumbs-up or down."

"Who sits on the committee?" McCarver leaned back in his chair, arms folded.

"Mostly some career attorneys at Main Justice, Nick," Trask said. "The group usually includes some experienced guys or gals from out in the field—at offices like our own. Actual prosecutors. They all meet and discuss the case, listen to the prosecutors *and* the defense counsel on the case, then make the recommendation."

"To whom? Who makes the final call?"

Trask felt a rueful smile cross his face. "The new attorney general."

"Shit." McCarver shook his head, pushed away from the table, stood up, and left the room.

"Anybody else?" Eastman asked after a moment.

"He'll be okay," Carter said. "He just hasn't had as much experience in dealing with . . . Jeff, what was that term that Bob Lassiter liked to use?"

"Politibrats."

"Yeah." Carter nodded. "Nick doesn't have the experience dealing with *those* that the rest of us have."

"Thanks, Dixon," Eastman said sarcastically. "Point taken."

"That's it for now." Seal adjourned the meeting. He held his hand out to Eastman. "Thanks for coming, Ross."

Eastman nodded. He saw that Trask and Val were leaving the room.

"Jeff."

Trask turned. "Yes, sir?"

"Wait up outside. There's something else."

Eastman joined them as they crossed the street back to their own offices.

"Just Jeff for a moment, Val," he said, waving her on toward the triple-nickel. "I didn't want to do this in there," he said, handing Trask an envelope. "I was also instructed by the Department to deliver this to you."

Trask stopped on the sidewalk and ripped the envelope open. He looked up at Eastman with a scowl on his face.

"A Congressional subpoena?"

"I'm afraid so. Senate Committee on Homeland Security and Governmental Affairs. Some of them want to praise you as a hero, and some want to use you for an anti-gun campaign. One thing you can be sure of is that both sides will want to use you as a pawn. The official line is that they want to investigate the events at Arlington."

"Wonderful. Am I the only one?"

"No. Dix and Tim Wisniewski will be getting theirs from Rich Seal. Lynn, too. I looked at the appearance schedule. You're last. I think the other cases that you and Lynn have been involved in will probably come up. If you want counsel for your appearance—"

"I don't."

"You know what they say—"

"Yeah. I'll have a fool for a client. Me."

Asalati pointed to the satellite image on the laptop.

"I think we could still go in *here, Saaqhib.*"

"No, Aashif. I have to cancel that phase of the operation for now. The events at Arlington were disastrous for us. It could have been just a coincidence that our martyrs were discovered so early, but we cannot assume that. We must assume instead that we may have a leak. If that is the case, then our other plan would be subject to an ambush. I cannot risk two very public failures in such short succession."

"We *did* kill seven of the marines on the bus. I understand your concerns, *Saaqhib,* but we have planned this thoroughly. We could go up Kentucky Springs Road here, take the exit onto Haley Drive, and ditch our vehicles here before the road turns to the east. That way, the guards at the entrance would never see us. We would be into the woods south of the security gate and information center, out of sight. We then turn north and east, remaining in the woods just west of the utility clearing, here, and—"

"I am sorry, my friend. My decision is final. If there *has* been a leak, our soldiers could be trapped as they cross the clearing. The damned drones the Americans use are so quick and quiet. We would never hear or see them coming until it was too late. There may be ground sensors in these woods near the storage casks as well. A ground operation would take too much time for success to be guaranteed. We had hoped for mass casualties at Arlington, followed by some of our people escaping, and a massive manhunt drawing the enemy's resources away from the other target area, but my plan has failed."

The older man patted Asalati on the shoulder.

"Do not worry. Time is on our side, and none of this failure falls at your feet. Your men were ready and well-trained. I obviously overlooked some details that may have given us away. We will not know until we talk to the new man, Rasheed, the survivor. What is his status?"

"Hospitalized under heavy guard. The news reports that he was hit three times. Two shots fired by the lawyer, Trask, and one by a policeman. Getting past the guards to speak with him will be almost impossible."

"Still, it must be done. Does he know to ask for an imam if he regains consciousness?"

"He does."

"Then that will be our opportunity, but it should not be you, Aashif. They will be watching you too closely. Send one of our associates, and have him report back to us."

"It will be done, *Saaqhib*."

"Good. What was this lawyer—the one called Trask—doing at Arlington with a gun?"

"I do not know. We are trying to determine that. He seems to be well known in their Department of Justice.

We will ask our contacts."

"As will I."

Asalati looked at the laptop screen again.

"Look, *Saaqhib*. There is no fence *here*. No barrier of any kind. It would not take an attack team, and if we could open all the casks at once—"

Asalati's mentor grabbed him on the shoulder with a firm grip, staring hard into his eyes.

"Are you sure, Aashif? You are very valuable to us. Are you volunteering?"

Asalati stood up and nodded, returning the older man's gaze.

"We could guarantee that there would be no security leaks. Only you and I would have to know. It would be the ultimate honor for me, *Saaqhib*."

The older man nodded. "Very well. In the meantime, send Hassan to stay with me. We can keep him hidden. The enemy's police have put his face all over the television. We do not want him to be recognized."

———

Val sat in the chair facing Trask's desk, sipping her coffee, waiting for him to speak. He didn't, so she did.

"It's obvious that I have *my* hands full, now," she said. "What's next for you, other than answering my questions as they come up?"

"Getting ready for my very first Senate hearing, and helping the Virginia guys with their capital case submission. Also helping Lynn with her appearance at the Senate."

"She didn't need much help at Arlington. How many of those guys did she take down?"

Trask chuckled. "Three, but that was operational—in the field. She has ice water for blood if she's undercover or in an emergency, but she's always hated testifying. When I was prepping her for the courts-martial back in our Air Force days, she'd take a break and I'd find her chain-smoking and hiding behind a soda machine. Once she hit the witness stand she did fine, but the anticipation of all the cross-examination drove her crazy. That was with a single defense counsel to worry about. Now she's facing a whole committee of senators and their staff wienies. She'll be okay once it starts, but I'm not sure *I'll* survive the wait."

"That's a couple of weeks off yet. What about your time here in the office? What's on your plate?"

"Twiddling my thumbs. Ross doesn't want me doing anything case-related other than answering all your questions, and you haven't had that many for me to answer. Maybe I can find some off-the-record games to play on the desktop."

"I'll stop in and keep you posted."

"Thanks. Call ahead to see if I'm in a critical phase on a timed game of Minesweeper or something. I wouldn't want you breaking my concentration."

She laughed. "Will do. The boys at the task force say hello."

"Hello back at 'em. I hope to be back in the game after the dean takes me off double-secret probation."

"What?"

"*Animal House.* The movie."

"Never saw it."

"You should. It has some black people in it."

She laughed again. "That'll get your probation extended. You might have to repeat the training at Main Justice."

"Only if you rat me out."

"Not a chance. I'm actually getting used to you."

"Thanks for letting me know he was awake," the tall man with a mustache said as he approached the guards.

"No sweat." One of the uniformed officers held the door open to the hospital room, glancing down at his watch. "How long do you think you'll need?"

"Just a few minutes. Anyone else been in since he came to?"

"Nope. We called you first, as requested."

"Great. Thanks again."

The tall man entered the room and closed the door. The other figure in the room lay on the hospital bed, his arms handcuffed to the rails on either side of the bed.

"Good morning, Mr. Short," the tall man said as he pulled two syringes from his jacket pocket.

"That's not my name. It's Rasheed. Rasheed Mohammed. Who the fuck are you, anyway?"

"Not important, Mr. Short. Your prints say that your name is Rusean Short, so I'll go with that. I doubt that you've been to the courthouse to register an official name change."

"My imam changed my name. That's all I have to do."

"Whatever you say, Mr. Short. Anyhow, in light of your apparent conversion, I have a couple of different paths we can take here."

He walked over to an IV line which led from a bottle of fluid down into the arm of the man in the bed. He took one of the syringes and inserted it into an injection port, then pushed the plunger.

"What is that shit?" Short demanded. "Who *are* you?"

"Just someone with some questions, Mr. Short. The fluid in that first needle comes from a formula we borrowed from our Russian friends. You'll be giving me some answers in no time. Depending on those answers, we may or may not be using the second syringe. Let's just say it could contain anything from cyanide to pork gravy. You'd hate either one. If you're cooperative, I'll keep it. I can always come back if you don't tell me the truth."

"*What?!*" Short squirmed on the bed, jerking his arms hard against the cuffs and rails before giving up. "I want an imam!" he yelled. "I may be dying here. I ain't tellin' you shit! I know my rights!"

"As far as I'm concerned, Mr. Short. You gave up all your rights at Arlington."

Short suddenly relaxed and appeared groggy. He tried to protest, but felt himself slipping into a fog.

"Attaboy," the tall man said, smiling. "Now, let's chat a bit."

———

Chapter Eighteen

Trask didn't leave the house in Waldorf until 9:00 a.m. He didn't have to. Eastman had put him on flex time, so there was no need to fight the rush-hour traffic into the District. *No court appearances means flexible. No job to do means totally flexible.*

He took his time making the drive as well. It was an early, warm spring morning, and every plant and tree in sight seemed to be blooming. The bugs were back, and more than a couple met their demise by splatting into the Jeep's windshield on the Indian Head Highway.

"Sometimes you're the windshield, sometimes you're the bug," he sang to himself.

Good tune, Mr. Knopfler.

He switched the radio on. Spring fever had also hit the DJ on the oldies station, and the Rascals' "A Beautiful Morning" made Trask think of turning around and just kissing the whole day off.

No can do today, he remembered. *Capital Crimes Committee meeting at 11:00 on Rusean Short.*

He had spent the last week with the AUSAs in Alexandria, fine-tuning their submission to the committee. The facts of the offense had been written in detail, both concerning the murder of Chet Williams and the almost certain association that Short had with the murder of the marines on the bus. The most technical aspect of the written package had, as usual, concerned the applicability—or the lack thereof—of each aggravating and mitigating factor listed under Title 18, United States Code, Section 3592, the statute in the federal code governing procedure in capital charging and sentencing procedures. The prosecutors would highlight the evidence supporting the aggravators, the appointed defense lawyers would argue that mitigating factors were present, and the jury would weigh all the evidence. Since death was a possibility, the taxpayers would foot the bill for at least two qualified attorneys to represent Short.

Trask mentally worked his way down the applicable checklists again.

Aggravators. Yes, the death occurred during the commission of another crime. In this case, those other crimes include the terroristic attempted murder of scores of others, and the conspiracy which resulted in the deaths of the marines on that bus that got blown to hell. No, he doesn't have a prior conviction for an offense involving a firearm. No, he doesn't have a prior that he got life or death for; that's the one for lifers or death-row murderers who've already killed so they have nothing to lose by doing it again, whether the victim is another inmate or a careless guard.

He does *have two or more convictions for other serious offenses, meaning felonies, and counting the dope case Dix hit him with, even though the prez and the AG didn't consider them serious enough to justify serving the sentence imposed. Yes, there was a grave risk of death to other persons. Hell, there was a risk of death to other persons at a GRAVE. Bad pun, Jeff. Pocket that one; no gallows humor today. Oops, there's another one.*

Heinous, cruel or depraved method of killing? No, the murder here was 'humanely' committed by blowing a hole in Chet Williams with a 30-06 round. I'd love to meet the moron who came up with that gem when they drafted the law. Still, Chet wasn't tortured; he died instantly, or within seconds, at least.

Procurement of the offense by payment? No. Some jihadist promised Short that he would earn a few dozen virgins for committing the offense. I never understood that one. Being in any room—much less a bedroom—with that many virgins couldn't really be fun, and just think of all the chatter and giggling. Pecuniary gain from the offense. Nope. Same answer, and how would you put a value on those virgins anyway?

Substantial planning and premeditation. Hell, yes. By somebody, *anyway. Gotta find that guy. When we do, we win. It ain't Short, however.*

Two felony drug convictions? He has three, counting Dix's case. Nothing that qualified as a kingpin case, though. Those separate aggravators don't apply.

Vulnerability of victim? Not applicable. Chet wasn't infirm, or old, or a child. He was a cop trying to do his job. Seems to be open season on those.

Subsection (14). Yep. Chet was a deputized federal officer and a law enforcement officer engaged in the performance of his duties. We'll argue that one hard. It's important, damn it all.

Prior child molestations? No, he didn't molest his step-daughters; he merely slit their little throats. What a system. Lewis Carroll would be impressed.

Multiple killings or attempted killings? Oh, yeah. Both. And many.

He shifted gears to the probable defense mitigators.

What are they going to argue?

Impaired capacity doesn't seem to fit. He wasn't drunk or on dope at the time. The hospital toxicology screen came back clean. Probably one of the few times in his free life that our man Short was NOT on something.

Duress? Maybe. The imams and Allah made me do it. Wonder what our politically correct committee would do with that one.

Minor participant in the offense? Hell, no. He's the shooter, and wanted to shoot more.

Other equally culpable defendants who aren't punishable by death? Not any in custody at least. Not yet. We were able to summarily dispatch a few others at Arlington. I thought I heard some cheers out there from some of the ghosts.

He paused, feeling the tears well up in his eyes.

Sorry, Chet. I should have shot at the head first, while he was still upright. I went center-mass in all the fury of the thing.

What else? No prior criminal record? No chance in hell. He has a sheet as long as LeBron James's arm.

Severe mental or emotional disturbance? Oh, yeah. We'll hear that, whether there's evidence to support it or not. We call this one the "Full Employment for Defense Psychiatrists Act." They'll always find something, or at least make it up.

Nothing else fits, which means that there WILL be something else from out of left field, something creative from the minds of the abolitionists, most of which can be boiled down to "It's not fair," or "It's not civilized." OOhh. And . . . he's black, came from a broken home, a bad neighborhood, and had no opportunities to become anything other than who he is. AND he only shot a cop. Maybe we'll just call this the Black Lives Matter mitigator. What would Val say about that now?

Weigh 'em all together and let the grand committee make the call. If the aggravators substantially outweigh the mitigators, they're supposed to give us the green light. No side bets, please. That would be unseemly. Will the politibrats do the right thing? Admit their error in releasing the thug to kill repeatedly? Admit that he became a murdering, radical Islamic terrorist?

He looked out all the Jeep's windows, turning his head from one side to the other.

Nope. No pigs flying today, folks.

Trask left Main Justice and took the Metro from the Federal Triangle Station to Judiciary Square. When he returned to the daylight from the subway system's escalator, he felt that other phone in his shirt pocket vibrating.

"Does he want an update on the meeting, Julia?" he asked as he answered the call.

"You guessed it. Val's already in his office."

"Five minutes. I just got off the Metro."

"See ya."

———

He waved as he passed her desk. The door to Eastman's office was open.

"So, how'd it go?" Eastman asked.

"Like I was in the Soviet navy," Trask replied.

Eastman winced. "I knew this wasn't going to be easy. Explain please."

Trask sat down in a chair next to Val.

"How's your day going?" he asked her.

"*Jeff!*" Eastman actually growled a little.

Val snickered.

"Don't encourage him," Eastman warned. He turned back to Trask. "*Russian navy?*"

"*Soviet* navy," Trask corrected. "Actually, it might apply to the current Russian navy as well, but I'm not sure. At any rate, if you've studied any military history, or just read or seen *The Hunt for Red October*, you know that someone in the Soviet navy always had to serve two masters. The first would be his operational, military commander. In my case, that is the role played by yourself, as the United States Attorney, and by your counterpart in Alexandria, Mr. Henry, who—like yourself—ordered me to ride into battle and try to secure a capital punishment certification from the committee that issues such certifications. I—and *my* counterparts from Alexandria—attempted to perform that mission."

"The second master?" Eastman asked. "As if I want the answer," he said under his breath.

"The second master on any Soviet naval vessel was the political commissar, who could often override the orders of the operational military commanders if he—the commissar—felt that they would run counter to the goals of the party or the revolution, depending on which label they were using at the time. In this case, I *met* the commissar, but I'm not sure I caught his name, *if* he actually gave it."

"Just tell me what happened, please." Eastman had his head in his hands, which were now resting on his desk.

"We were ushered into the same little conference room where we had the meeting for the Zetas case. Most of the players were the same, at least for the Capital Crimes Unit career guys. We—the prosecutors and the enemies of the republic—"

"He means the defense attorneys," Val said.

"Thank you," Eastman said sarcastically.

"We laid out our respective positions on all the aggravating and mitigating factors. The career committee guys were—in my humble opinion and despite the embarrassment that Rusean Short poses for the administration—strongly leaning toward certifying Mr. Short for the sentence that he so clearly deserves, having murdered five, attempted to murder dozens more, and conspired to kill God knows *how* many others. Their questions posed to us were reasonable, and the defense assertions were outrageous, and met with the contempt that those assertions merited."

"However . . ." Eastman assisted with the transition.

"However," Trask nodded as he continued, "the vote changed dramatically when the political commissar entered the room."

"Describe him, please, since you didn't catch his name," Eastman instructed.

"Certainly. He was blond, bespectacled, and appeared to be fresh out of high school. I mean law school, of course."

Eastman put his head down on the desk again.

"At any rate, after possibly mumbling his name—"

"Which you didn't catch," Eastman muttered between his hands on the desk.

"Exactly. He then announced that he was from 'the head office.'"

Eastman's head came up from the desk. "The 'head office?'"

"Correct. I'm sure you can imagine my confusion, Ross. I—like you—have been around the bowels of that building many times over the past few years. I've seen job titles like 'Second Deputy Assistant to the Associate Attorney General for Blah, Blah, Blah,' 'Service Dog to the Principal Gofer for Blah, Blah, and Blah,' but I do not *once* recall seeing 'Head Office' on any door or nameplate. Like I said, imagine my confusion. I was, therefore, forced to deduce that by 'Head Office,' the commissar meant the new attorney general. You know, the one who had the meeting on the tarmac with the husband of the target of an investigation."

"A fair assumption." Eastman's head was back down.

"The committee then adjourned to vote, and shortly thereafter, informed us all that there would be no capital certification in this matter."

"Thanks for getting to that so succinctly," Eastman said, raising his head to take a long breath. He looked at Val.

"Since we have no death penalty leverage, Ms. Fuentes, I suggest you prepare for trial. The defendant will have nothing to lose by rolling the dice in both our trial and in the one in Virginia. If he pleads guilty, he gets life. If he goes to trial and loses, he gets life. If he wins at trial—juries have done stupid things in the past—he walks. At least we get two bites at the apple. If he loses either case, it's life."

Val nodded. "If I may be excused, I have work to do."

Eastman nodded, dismissing her. After she was out of the room, he turned back to Trask.

"Are you ready for the Senate hearing on Monday?"

"As ready as I can be."

"The Department wants to assign counsel for you."

"No." Trask paused. "Make that '*Hell, no.*' After today, I'd probably start throwing elbows at them, especially if that junior commissar showed up again. That's assuming he's even an attorney."

"I'll inform them of your decision, perhaps not in those words."

"I appreciate that."

"I can't protect you if this goes wrong."

"I know. I appreciate your concern. I really do."

"Jeff, if you criticize the AG, or the Department, or the president in the middle of a public senate inquiry, you could be fired. The AG wanted to keep you under wraps and claim executive privilege, but his staff couldn't find a justification for it since you were responding to an attack and not initiating any official action."

"Funny, that hasn't stopped them from claiming the privilege before."

"*Dammit*, that's exactly what I'm talking about. That'll get you fired if you testify that way."

"You know I won't. I wouldn't have lasted this long if it weren't for your understanding and my own recognition of the proper time and place to be me, or to don my official courtroom demeanor."

"I hope you remember that. If you don't, if this *does* go badly, what will you do? Where will you go?"

"America, if I can find it. I hear that it's still out there, somewhere."

———

Chapter Nineteen

"I'm sure you've done your homework, as usual," Eastman said as he watched Trask pace back and forth across the carpet in the waiting room.

"What I could. If the questioning sticks to the events at Arlington, as it should, then I'm completely comfortable. If they start coming at me from outer space, then I'll just have to do the best I can."

"At least you have a friend sitting in the chairman's seat," Eastman offered.

"Once upon a time, maybe," Trask said shaking his head. "Now I'm not so sure."

"Why do you say that?"

"The last time I saw the good senator from Georgia, the Honorable Sherwin 'Digger' Graves was in my office trying to chew my ass. He blamed me for the death of his mentor, Hugh Heidelberg."

"But you found the guy that gave Heidelberg's daughter the heroin that killed her!"

"Right. His buddy, Senator Anderson. Heidelberg blew him away on the floor of that hearing room in there, and then ate the gun himself. Graves blames me for all that, or at least he did."

"What did you do when he came to your office?"

"I basically told him he was full of crap and tossed him out."

"Wonderful," Eastman said. "Now, I'm not sure I want to watch this."

"Neither am I," Trask said. "But it's not like I have a choice."

A page entered the room after knocking on the door.

"Mr. Trask, they're ready for you."

Trask nodded and followed the young man into the room, taking a chair at the center of the table facing the raised, circular row of overstuffed leather chairs, chairs that were vacant but waiting behind the nameplates of the senators who would occupy them in moments. Most of the staffers were already in place in chairs of their own behind the senators' seats. Trask noticed that there was no shortage of television cameras in the room, and that all of those cameras seemed to be pointed at his face.

The senators began filing in, with Chairman Graves entering the room last. Graves took the center seat, and smiled warmly at Trask as he gaveled the hearing to order.

Trask mentally reviewed his notes on each of the senators he'd be facing.

Digger Graves, chairman. Republican from Georgia. My second chair in fourteen courtsmartial years ago when I was riding the JAG circuit for the USAF. Former chief sycophant to old Hugh Heidelberg, and who blamed me for HH's suicide. Now he's grinning at me like it never even happened.

"In the interest of candor, ladies and gentlemen, I must acknowledge that Jeff Trask and I go back a few years," Graves said, still smiling. "In fact, Jeff taught me a lot about trial work. It was my pleasure to serve as his assistant prosecutor in several Air Force courts-martial when we were both on active duty. Now we're both still in the reserves. The Department of Justice had big plans for Jeff, and I must humbly thank the people of Georgia for having some plans of their own for me."

The other senators responded with smiles of their own, some nodding, and some good-natured laughter.

Trask looked up at all the smiling faces.

"Sometimes they don't tell the truth." "Smiling Faces." The Undisputed Truth—a hit in 1971, I think. Very prophetic. They look like a school of sharks up there. Settle down, self. Remember all those coaching sessions you gave to your own witnesses. Follow your own advice.

"Welcome, Jeff." Graves was still smiling.

"Thank you, senator," Trask smiled back, as genuinely as he could.

Don't be combative unless it's required. Control the exchange. If anyone is going to lose control, make it these high-and-mighty ones.

"As you certainly know, Jeff, we've already had the pleasure this morning of hearing from the others who were with you at that tragic event at Arlington, including Detectives Carter and Wisniewski, and even your lovely wife. I'd like to be the first on this committee to personally thank you and those other heroes for taking the swift action that you *all* took to spare us from any further loss of life. I believe that you deserve the thanks of the nation, and I'm proud to call you my friend."

With that, Graves rose and began a standing ovation which was joined by all members of the Republican majority, and even a couple of senators on the minority, Democrat side of the dais.

"Thank you very much," Trask heard himself saying. *Is it all going to be this painless? I have re-election value as a friend of the Senator, photo op to follow?*

When the applause died down, Graves did have some questions.

"Do you have an opening statement for us?" he asked.

"No, Senator." *I thought that might put you off guard, actually. I know you expected one.* "I'd be happy to answer any questions the committee might have, of course."

You folks are going to tell me where this is going before I put my big feet in my bigger mouth. I'm not going to trap myself.

"Fine," Graves said, the smile returning to his face to mask a flash of confusion. "The other witnesses have indicated to us that you were out in front with Major Williams before the shooting started, and that you might have some more insight as to why Major Williams—or maybe it was you—why either or both of you were able to recognize that these terrorists posing as a funeral firing party were not who they seemed to be. Can you explain that for us, please?"

"Certainly." *Still using run-on sentences for questions, Digger? I tried to train that out of you. So much for my teaching ability.* "Actually, most of the critical observations came from Major Williams. As a former marine himself, he certainly had the foundation to make those observations."

"He was an Annapolis graduate, and you attended the Air Force Academy."

"That's correct, Senator." *Your inside knowledge will certainly impress at least a couple of viewers.* "Chet's first observation was that the bus that transported this firing party to Arlington had the wrong license plates. Buses used by the companies at the Marine Barracks at 8th and I Streets come from the motor pool at Joint Base Anacostia, and they have government plates. The bus we saw at Arlington had standard Virginia license plates. Chet even called the Marine Barracks at 8th and I to see if they had sent both the firing party and the body bearers in the same bus, as usual. He was told that both details were en route in a coach from the Anacostia motor pool. We knew that *that* bus would have government plates, and we didn't see the body bearers on the scene.

"The second thing that both of us noticed was that every member of the firing party—that's the term we use for the marines, sailors, or soldiers who fire the twenty-one-gun salute at a military funeral—were all minority members. That in itself was not conclusive, as our military is probably the greatest melting pot in our society, but it was the first time that either of us had seen a firing party that was composed *entirely* of minority members.

"One of the *biggest* giveaways was the fact that two of the marines were wearing medals that they could not have possibly earned. Those were unmistakable, because the dress uniforms used for these ceremonies by the Marine Corps include rows of full medals, not the narrower rows of ribbons that you and I wore on our class-A uniforms for court."

Trask smiled back at Graves, who nodded and grinned back. *I'll be your pawn today, Digger, and even throw you some cred, if I can get out of here with my scalp.*

"Finally, there was a statement made by the terrorist posing as the detail chief, which let both of us know that he was an imposter. Chet Williams, who was in charge on the scene because of his experience as a marine officer and as a former commander of the District of Columbia Police Department's tactical unit, then told the rest of us to draw our weapons. When we did so, the fake detail chief yelled, 'Allahu Akbar!' and the other terrorists tried to raise their rifles to fire. Three of them were able to get shots off. One round went screaming by my head. Another unfortunately killed Major Williams. He was the real hero out there. The rest of us followed his lead."

"Thank you, Mr. Trask," Graves said. "That's all I have for this round of questions. I may have a few more later. The chair recognizes the ranking minority member, Senator Manke."

"Thank you, Mr. Chairman." Senator Manke smiled at Trask. "My congratulations also."

Trask nodded.

Rick Manke, Democrat from Massachusetts. New heir to the Teddy Kennedy seat, with presidential ambitions of his own. Thinks he's the smartest guy in any room; gets overconfident and sloppy with his facts as a result of his arrogance.

Trask looked at the smile on the face of his new interrogator.

That's not the same kind of smile that I got from Digger. I held back some aces, senator, if you really want to dance.

"I do have a couple of caveats to my congratulations, Mr. Trask." The senator's smile was gone now. "This isn't the first shooting you've been involved in, is it?"

"Actually, it is, Senator. I hope it's my last. It wasn't much fun."

Manke frowned, reaching for a note passed to him across his shoulder by a staffer.

"You were the prosecutor in the Demetrius Reid case a few years ago, were you not?"

"I assisted Robert Lassiter in that prosecution."

"And Mr. Reid was killed before that case went to trial?"

"Mr. Reid killed *himself* by charging at the judge—and at me—in the courtroom, Senator. That happened *during* his trial, not before it. His head crashed into the judge's bench and he died on the scene from traumatic brain injuries."

"I thought there was gunfire involved in some fashion." Manke asked the question smugly, as if he had inside knowledge and was being misled by Trask's answers.

"Mr. Reid had hired a hitman to assassinate Mr. Lassiter. Mr. Lassiter was shot and killed by the assassin after the trial, and the assassin was then shot and killed as he tried to flee the scene."

"So *you* never shot anyone that day?"

"I did not. I was not armed at any time during that trial."

Pretty sloppy research by your staff, Senator. I bet you'll have a talk with them later, and you'll be really pissed when you find that you could have asked me who killed the bad guy. It was Tim Wisniewski and Lynn, and they were at Arlington with me, thank God. You might have made a small point with that, but I'm not volunteering it.

"I have no more questions for Mr. Trask at the moment," Manke said. He swiveled around in his chair, scowling and whispering at the staffer.

"Senator O'Neal?" Graves yielded to the ranking republican member.

Thomas O'Neal, Republican from Alabama. Used to be pretty sharp, now getting way up there in years. Hates the current administration. We have that in common.

"Thank you, Mr. Chairman. Mr. Trask, I'd like to concentrate for a few minutes on the surviving terrorist who is now in custody. As I understand it, he is under guard at a local hospital, is that correct?"

"That's correct, Senator. His name is Rusean Short."

"Am I also correct in stating that Mr. Short was one of the inmates who received an early release from the president's administration, including the past and present attorneys general, as part of this so-called 'Smart on Crime' initiative?"

"That is also correct, Senator."

So THIS is where the politics are going to kick in. Buckle up.

"And am I also correct in stating that—prior to his killing Major Williams at Arlington—this Rusean Short killed four other people in the District of Columbia?"

"He has not been tried or convicted for those homicides yet, Senator, but—if I may anticipate your next question—there is evidence placing him at the scene of those murders, and one of the victims—a little girl—identified him as her killer before she died."

"Thank you, Mr. Trask. Finally, am I correct in stating that—if it were not for the so-called 'Smart on Crime' initiative—Rusean Short would still be in prison, and at least four—make that five—innocent people would still be alive today?"

"I believe that to be accurate."

"And this is all *despite* assurances from the Justice Department that all those being released were supposedly non-violent drug offenders who might have been guilty of only simple possession offenses?"

"If I might, sir, the system is rigged to support that fiction."

"Explain that, please."

"Certainly. For several years now, the courts have required federal prosecutors to file a criminal case cover sheet at the same time when we file an indictment. For drug offenses, there are categories or codes for distribution, manufacture, or possession. It is the *possession* codes that are problematic, in that there are *no* separate codes for what we call PWID offenses—possession with intent to distribute.

"The typical federal drug prosecution is the result of an investigation that probably included three-to-five undercover buys from the defendant or his organization. These buys are usually for relatively small amounts of drugs. In a cocaine case, it might be for an 'eight-ball,' the street term for an eighth of an ounce. Following those undercover buys—during which a surveillance team is watching the defendant and tailing him back to his house or stash house—we get a search warrant for his house and try to recover the main supply stash of drugs. When we find the stash, we charge the defendant with possession of *that* amount of drugs with intent to distribute: PWID. He may also be charged with distribution offenses for the lesser amounts, but that's not always the case.

"At any rate, since we are required to take guilty pleas—if offered—to the most serious, readily provable offense, and since the most serious offense is the one citing the highest weight of drugs, the typical case involves a guilty plea to a charge of possession with intent to distribute. It could be three, five, fifty, or even five hundred kilograms of cocaine. The defendant pleads to that, because we insist that he plead to the more serious offense, and the weight drives the sentence. Quite often, we even *drop* the distribution charges as part of the plea bargain."

"That doesn't make the defendant just a drug *possessor*, does it?" Senator O'Neal asked.

"No, Senator. The defendant is a serious, big-time, dope *pusher*—maybe even a kingpin—wreaking havoc on the community around him, but his court code for the count of conviction reads 'possession,' and makes it seem like he was just smoking a joint of grass in his car. It is *that* fiction that the administration has used to justify the release of several hundred very dangerous drug pushers as non-violent offenders who were convicted only of drug-possession offenses. In fact, they are often the final targets of major investigations. If you look at the summary sheets handed out by Main Justice listing the violations committed by those whose sentences are being reduced, the vast majority of them were convicted for PWID offenses."

"Thank you."

Graves looked to his right at the next Democrat in line. He was never happy to do so, as he was looking at his political nemesis, Senator Claire Moore of Illinois. "Senator Moore."

"Thank you, Mr. Chairman."

Senator Moore, a very large black woman, pulled herself as close to her microphone as the space available to her person would allow.

Claire Moore, Democrat from the south side of Chicago. An infamous race-baiter. Any event put in motion by a person who is not "of color" is racially motivated. All people of color are victims who can do nothing for themselves without massive assistance and intervention from their guardian angels in government.

"May I assume from your last answers and comments, Mr. Trask, that you are a Republican? I hope that the question does not offend you."

"It does not offend me at all, Senator, since—if I *were* a Republican it might be some evidence of bias. We explore the issue of bias in almost all of our trials, so the question does not offend me in the least."

"Gooood. I'm happy to hear that."

"I am not, however, a Republican."

"*You're not?*" Moore was now trying unsuccessfully to swivel in her own chair to glare at a staffer. Her girth completely prevented the attempted movement.

"In all fairness, I used to be," Trask said. "No need to be angry with your research team. I am now a registered independent."

"Please do tell us then what it was that convinced you to leave the Republican Party." Moore smiled for the first time.

Graves's gavel came down with a bang.

"Senator Moore, that question is improper and outside the scope of this hearing unless it had something to do with the issues properly before us, which are the events at Arlington, and the early release of Rusean Short."

He smiled again at Trask.

"Mr. Trask, does your change in voting status have *anything* to do with those issues?"

"Actually, it does, Mr. Chairman."

Graves sat back in his chair, stung by the response. He was not smiling anymore.

"Why thank you, Mr. Trask," Senator Moore smiled widely—and disingenuously—at Graves. "Please tell us about that."

Fine, lady. Neither one of you will like it.

"One of the reasons that I changed my voting registration was the support for the 'Smart On Crime' initiative by several prominent members of the Republican Party, some of whom call themselves 'conservatives.' Several Republican senators supported the program thinking only of money—the costs of incarceration—or minority votes, and not of the victims of the criminals they were releasing back to the streets. In my opinion, and in the opinion of the majority of federal prosecutors who work criminal cases, this initiative is one of the most ill-conceived in the history of the Justice Department. We knew it would eventually lead to upticks in violent crime, as it has, *especially in minority neighborhoods.* That opinion was made known to both this Congress and to the Justice Department by several groups, including the Association of Assistant United States Attorneys, an organization made up of federal prosecutors like myself."

"So you and your group substituted your judgment for the combined judgment of this Congress, the president, and your boss, the attorney general, is that it?"

Moore tried to lean back in her chair, feeling very satisfied with her question. There wasn't room. One of her staffers patted her on the shoulder.

Trask took a deep breath to calm himself.

"I think that a more accurate characterization, Senator, is that this body and the others you mentioned decided to substitute *their* judgment for the judgment of the prosecutors and investigators who collected the evidence against these criminals, for the judgment of the *grand juries* who heard that evidence and returned the indictments, for the judgment of the *trial juries* who heard that evidence and returned unanimous verdicts of guilty, for the judgment of the *trial judges* who also heard that evidence and who fashioned appropriate sentences, and for the judgment of the *appellate courts* who heard the defense appeals of those convictions and sentences and who *upheld* those verdicts and sentences.

"Those folks got close to the evidence in each individual case, Senator. Up close and personal. They heard from witnesses—*most often from minority neighborhoods*—who were dodging bullets as the dope dealers shot it out with each other. Some lost loved ones in those fights. In many cases, these were people who were brave enough to risk life and limb to testify, or to give evidence to us in confidence, hoping that we would help them take their neighborhoods back. Now their demons are coming home to them. Those demons—like Rusean Short—are coming home *early* because someone thought it might mean a vote or two in their next primary or general election race. I can't support *any* party that stands for that. Not the party that proposed it, and not the party that did nothing to stop it."

Trask sat back. He could hear the heavy sigh released by Ross Eastman, sitting behind him.

Sorry, boss. They asked; I answered.

Moore changed her attack.

"Listening to your earlier answers, I got the impression that one reason you all decided to shoot these people was that none of them were white."

Trask paused again to control his temper.

"Then you misunderstood my answer, Senator. I said that the fact that there were no whites on the detail was unusual. I never said that that was why we had to fire our weapons."

"Then there was something about the *medals* they were wearing? You shot these people because they were wearing the *wrong medals?*"

"Of course not. A combination of facts that we—Major Williams and I—noted, convinced us that the firing party was not made up of real marines."

"And how did these *medals* tell you that?"

"Anyone who has spent any length of time in the military, Senator"—*and I know you never have*—"learns to look at those rows of decorations. They can tell you a lot about the service member wearing them—where they've been, what they've done. Two of the young men in that line were wearing Vietnam service medals."

"And how in heaven's name did you know that they shouldn't have been wearing those medals? Maybe they served in Vietnam!"

Moore got another pat on her shoulder from the staffer.

Trask shot a look at Senator John Delancey, the next republican in line, who was spinning in *his* chair so as not to laugh out loud.

He knows. He was a warthog pilot in the desert. He'll enjoy this.

"Senator Moore, we knew they were not Vietnam veterans because they appeared to be in their twenties, and the war in Vietnam ended in the mid-seventies, before they were born."

The senator was flustered. She tried again to turn back to the staffer, who wasn't patting her on the shoulder any more.

"*Anything else, Mr. Trask?*"

Moore was hot now, having been embarrassed by her own questions.

"You decided to shoot these people and deny them the due process of court hearings because they weren't white and were wearing the wrong medals. Anything else?"

"Yes, Senator," Trask responded calmly.

He remembered what he'd told his own trial witnesses.

Let the other attorney lose his cool; keep yours. The one losing control loses the jury.

"As I believe at least one of the other witnesses told you this morning, Major Williams had a conversation with the fake detail chief. Major Williams told us to draw, and then the detail chief yelled, 'Allahu Akbar!,' at which point the other terrorists started raising their rifles to aim and fire."

Come on out of the weeds, little fish; follow the lure, take the bait. This will be fun.

"Did you hear the conversation between Major Williams and this man?"

That's it; now bite so I can set your hook.

"Yes, Senator, I did."

"What could this man have said to Major Williams—and you—that justified your drawing your guns on these people? You're a prosecutor, Mr. Trask, not an executioner! They were entitled to their days in court!"

"Senator, Major Williams asked to inspect one of the firing party's rifles. His thinking was that if those rifles contained only blank rounds—as they would for a funeral detail firing a twenty-one-gun salute into the air—then there might be a lot of confusion going on, but perhaps nothing more. If the rounds were live, we would know that these were not real marines, but people with killing on their minds. The detail chief then told him to go ahead and look at one of the '*guns*'—"

"So he agreed to let you inspect the gun, and you still started shooting!"

"Senator, no true marine would have said, 'Look at the gun.' To a marine, a 'gun' is an artillery piece, or something else, if you've seen *Full Metal Jacket*. A rifle is something completely different."

Trask noticed that Senator Delancey had turned around, facing his staff again, and appeared to be laughing hard.

"You're not making any sense," Moore declared. "A gun is a gun."

"Not to a marine, Senator. At any rate, the terrorist yelled what he yelled, they tried to shoot, they had live ammunition, and we opened fire."

"Senator, your time has expired," Graves said, turning back to the next Republican in line. "Senator Delancey."

"I'd like to thank you for your candid answers today, Mr. Trask," Delancey said. "That took guts, and I'm sure it won't put you in line for any promotions any time soon. I want you to call my office if you suffer any professional retribution as a result of your remarks. I think there are those on both sides of the proverbial aisle who needed to hear them. I have long believed that the extended sentences imposed on many of these criminals were the main factor in our violent crime rates dropping over the last couple of decades."

"Thank you, sir. I agree."

"I'll be happy to explain that movie scene to Senator Moore later, Mr. Trask. I believe you were referring to the lines, 'This is my rifle, this is my gun,' and the ones that followed." Delancey chuckled a little.

"I was."

This is my rifle, this is my gun. This is for fighting, this is for fun.

"I'd like to get back to the facts of this matter. As I understand it, this funeral at Arlington was to be for one of our retired police commanders in the District of Columbia?"

"Yes, Willie Sivella. He was both a retired police officer and a former marine."

"There's no such thing as a 'former marine,' Mr. Trask. Once a marine, always a marine. Do you believe that Mr. Sivella was targeted in such a manner as to set these other events in motion?"

"I do, Senator. We have evidence from the scene of the Sivella murder linking it to several other recent murders of police and federal officers. It is my belief that he was killed because someone knew that his death would result in a full-honors ceremony at Arlington. He was entitled to one as a Purple Heart recipient. The terrorists we encountered at the cemetery were part of a much larger conspiracy. They murdered another District officer and stole his patrol car, used that cruiser to stop and then attack the real ceremonial detail on their bus, and then more members of that terrorist cell showed up at Arlington instead, ready to kill both military and police officials who would have been in place to honor Willie Sivella."

"I understand. I'd like to thank you and the others from preventing those additional murders. In light of your answer, are we correct in having reason to believe that there are several members of this terrorist cell still at large?"

Trask nodded. "Yes, sir."

"I have one other question for you, in light of your previous answers, Mr. Trask."

Delancey took his glasses off and polished them for a moment. He finished, put them back on, and leaned forward.

"In light of what you seem to believe are improper, politically motivated actions by the current heads of your department—if I can put those words in your mouth—would you have any recommendations—as an *independent* professional—as to how we could stop such errors from recurring?"

The question made Trask pause. He was surprised, but not caught off guard. It was something he'd been thinking about for months.

"I do, Senator. I'm not sure yet how to implement my suggestion, but I think it *could* solve the issue of the political decisions which I believe are improperly affecting our prosecutions within the Department of Justice. It might also remove the need for special prosecutors which might occur when conflicts of interest are alleged against the attorney general, who is one of the members of the president's cabinet."

"Such as when the AG meets in a private plane with the subject of an investigation?" Delancey asked pointedly.

"That could be such a case," Trask agreed. "I would strongly recommend *removing* the position of attorney general and the entire Department of Justice from the presidential cabinet. Make it an independent appointment much like the director of the FBI—with a term of years overlapping presidential terms and not subject to renewal. If the AG is supposed to be the chief *law enforcement* officer of the nation—the country's conscience—then take the job out from under the thumb of any president who would try to make it anything else."

"Would that have been your opinion prior to the actions of *this* administration?" Delancey asked.

"It would. I was a history major, Senator. I've served both in the military and in civilian federal service. Whether we're talking about John Mitchell under Nixon, Ms. Reno under Clinton, Alberto Gonzalez under President Bush, or Mr. Holder or the current attorney general, the prosecutors in this department have suffered under a long series of political operatives posing as our chief federal prosecutors. We've had the Saturday Night Massacre, Waco and Ruby Ridge, the Elián Gonzalez mess, a purge of United States Attorneys for political reasons, Fast and Furious, and now the Clinton emails and that meeting on the tarmac that you referenced.

"We would all have benefitted from being led by real career prosecutors who wanted simply to enforce the laws that you in Congress pass, and to do the right thing. Thankfully, there have been some exceptions, like Judge Mukasey and a couple of others. But looking back, there aren't more than two or three attorneys general with whom I'd like to share a beer."

———

Chapter Twenty

The tall man with the mustache adjusted the straps on his camouflage backpack as he spoke in a voice just above a whisper. The dozen members of his team—all heavily armed and outfitted with night-vision sights and scopes—huddled close.

"The punk in the hospital said the camp was in the mountains, and that it was heavily concealed. That's about all he knew that he could cough up, and that Russian juice I used on him is pretty persuasive. I had the tech boys do a sweep from one of the low-orbit infrared satellites, and the heat signatures we got at this point seemed to fit. The camp had to be close enough for the bad guys to travel to Arlington in short order. They could make it from here in three hours or less. Seems to fit the bill. We have GPS coordinates about one click out from our position. Later satellite sweeps say that it's still active."

One of the other men checked a cell phone, then nodded toward the tall man without speaking.

"The president has cleared the op," the tall man said, returning the other man's nod. "But this is without attribution, gents. We get caught or smoked, it's all on us. The folks on top never heard of us. We win, the president suffers no further embarrassment for having a terrorist training camp this close to the capital. We lose, odds are another clean-up team follows us in to finish the job and bury all the bodies, including ours. Quiet kills if possible. We don't want anyone hearing explosions out here and coming to check out the situation. Everybody in?"

All heads nodded. Affirmative.

"Everybody ready? Good. Let's go."

They made as quick a march of the distance as they could, given the moonless night and rugged terrain. The mile took them a slow forty minutes to cover, rolling every boot step slowly to minimize noise as they navigated toward the coordinates.

As the point man topped a ridge, the patrol halted at his signal. Moments later, a muffled grunt and choking noise told them that the first sentry had succumbed to the point's knife. He came slowly back down the ridge.

"I think that was the only guard on this side of the perimeter, boss," he said to the tall man. "First third of a triangle. Two of 'em seem to be on the rim of the ridge behind what looks like a row of huts with camo'd roofs. They're about 270 and 25 degrees from my point up there, if you marked me at 180. If we sweep the ridge, we'll have all the high ground and can work downhill."

The tall man selected two of the team to work in each direction.

"Stay out of sight beneath the ridge line until you take 'em out," he said. "One quick flash when we're good to go. The rest of us will space out in front of and on the flanks of the huts. Odds are they're asleep. Let's make that a permanent condition. Good luck."

His operators fanned out, and the tall man, accompanied by a single, much shorter team member, crouched low until they reached the top of the ridge overlooking the camp. They saw the body of the dead sentry a few feet away.

"Tony's a hell of a point," the tall man said. "Former Navy Seal. Bet you never saw this kind of stuff in the Bureau."

"No. Other kinds of ops, some just as dicey, but never quite like this."

"You watch the right; I'll take the left. Let me know if you see our little firefly flicker."

"Right."

Fifteen minutes passed before the shorter man said, "Confirmed."

Two minutes later, the tall man got the signal from the left. He raised a small radio to his lips and ordered, "Move, move, move!"

The team swept down on the unsuspecting camp, their carbines quietly spitting through sound suppressors. The all-clear came fourteen minutes after the attack began.

"Everybody okay?" the tall man asked as he came through the center of the perimeter.

"No KIAs on our side, one wounded," the point man said as he appeared from the darkness. "We have nine enemy dead, boss, plus the three on guard duty."

"Who got hit? What kind of wound?"

"Patterson got hit in the shoulder with a damned crossbow bolt while he was taking out one of the sentries. He's pretty ripped up, but he'll make it. No arteries clipped."

"That's different. Give him some meds. We have one of our docs ready to meet us at the rendezvous point. Can't take him to a hospital. That's too freakin' weird even for West Virginia."

"Clean up?" the point asked him.

"We have enough of a clearing here for a chopper. Patterson and the bodies go out on the first bird. We'll want to print the enemy KIAs before we dispose of 'em. Can't risk attention with a fire, and it's too dry to contain it anyway. Old George Washington would be pissed at us if we burned down his whole forest. The buildings will have to be left standing. Just clean 'em out before we leave. We may get some intel from the process. The park rangers will just think it's a hell of an illegal hunting lodge when they finally find the place."

———

"At least we don't have to go back to Arlington," Eastman said. "Chet Williams had left instructions with his family to have him buried at Annapolis."

"Pretty place," Trask commented. "Chet loved his time at Canoe U."

He looked across the desk at Eastman, who was leaning back in the big leather chair as he always did before delivering bad news.

"Ross, are we here to discuss Chet's funeral, or mine?"

"Do you want to stay with DOJ?" Eastman asked him.

"It's been my dream job to this point," Trask responded. "Not always a good dream, especially lately. Do I actually have options?"

"Limited, but yes—believe it or not—you do." Eastman leaned forward and rested his elbows on the desk. "The AG wanted to fire you. Senator Moore wanted several pieces of your ass. You know that she and the president are very close. Your friend Graves didn't step up to defend you after the hearing, much to nobody's surprise.

"On the other hand, that mess at Arlington, coupled with the televised senate hearing, has made you enough of a celebrity that the administration knows it would have PR hell to pay if they canned you now. Your new friend Senator Delancey was ready to call for new hearings, and to pay the Dems back for what they did to Attorney General Gonzalez when he fired all those U.S. Attorneys for not kissing his ring hard enough.

"All that might *still* not have been enough to save your professional bacon, but I was told by a little birdy I know in the White House that someone in the president's inner circle went to bat to keep your paycheck coming."

"I have no idea who that could be," Trask said, frowning.

"He goes on TV frequently to sing the praises of those who fight Islamic extremists," Eastman said. "But he's a believer in Allah himself. I'm talking about Amal Saleem."

"You're kidding."

"Not one bit. But here's the rub, Jeff. If you want to stay on, you'll be reassigned. You're going to the JTTF."

"The Joint Terrorism Task Force? Wonderful." Trask felt his head drop as he spoke. "I'll never see a courtroom or real cops again. I'll just read intel reports, comment on how terrible and scary the situation is, and hand the paper over to somebody else to read so they can see and agree how terrible and scary the situation is. Everything's so classified you can't risk revealing it in a courtroom, so you're never in trial, never even arresting anybody."

He looked up.

"Any other way I can pay my mortgage, or is that it?"

"That's the only door that's open for now," Eastman said, "And it's barely cracked. Imam Saleem apparently thinks you'd be an asset over there, since you've already proven yourself to be a big bad terrorist fighter."

He walked out from behind his desk and sat next to Trask on another chair.

"Give it some time, Jeff. Let the noise die down. When I can, I'll bring you back to your old job. You're too valuable to me and this office to let you rot in a SCIF for too long. Take some time off, and report to the JTTF when you're ready."

"I'll think about it. Val may need some coaching on the Rusean Short thing before I take the leave."

"She won't."

"Why is that?"

"Rich Seal just called a few minutes ago. Short's dead."

"What happened? I thought they were upgrading his condition?"

"He apparently took a turn for the worse last night and died of his wounds. It looks like you got a capital sentence for him despite that committee vote."

Trask reached into his shirt pocket for the cell phone.

"I assume you'll want this back?"

Eastman smiled. "Nope. Hang onto it. I may still need to reach you from time to time."

"They won't allow it in the SCIF. No phones or anything else that could photograph or download all those scary secrets."

"Hang onto it. It will be one way I can still hang onto you. That's an order."

———

"I am terribly sorry, Imam." The younger man bowed his head as he spoke to Asalati.

"As am I, Ibrahim. I understand there was nothing you could do."

"They did not check the entrance to the road where I was posted. I do not think they knew it was there. They came in from the rear of the camp. I ran back to the ridge, where the road dropped into the camp, and saw them shooting our people. They hit the camp from all sides. I wanted to fight them, but I thought that you and the *saaqhib* needed to know, so that you would not travel to the camp and be caught."

"I understand. You did the right thing. Did anyone else get out with you?"

"No, Imam. I believe that I alone survived."

"Then the rest of our martyrs will dine with the prophet tonight, and their beds will be full in heaven. Were you followed?"

"No. I took hours to leave the national forest on foot. I saw no one behind me. We had the car parked in the back of a store near the interstate. I came straight here. No other cars followed me on the roads."

"That is good. Go upstairs, Ibrahim. There is a guest room. Clean up and get some rest."

"Thank you, Imam."

Asalati watched Ibrahim as he climbed the stairs. When the younger man closed the door to the bedroom, his imam pulled the cell phone from his belt and hit the button for the only contact in the device's memory.

"I regret to tell you that the camp has been wiped out, *Saaqhib*. The only survivor is Ibrahim. He is here now."

"How is it that he is the only survivor?"

"He says that he was at the camp entrance, and was not discovered by the attackers. They hit the camp from the high ridge to the northwest."

"You do not find his survival to be suspicious?"

"That is why I called you, *Saaqhib*. I do."

"First the disaster at Arlington, now this. Ibrahim was involved in the training of our teams at Arlington, and now he mysteriously survives this attack. We cannot risk being wrong about him, Aashif."

"I understand."

"I will send Hassan to pick him up. Ibrahim regards Hassan as a friend."

"He is upstairs preparing to sleep."

"Let him sleep then. Hassan can do it there. It is regrettable, as Ibrahim seemed to be very committed to our cause. We simply cannot afford to take any chances."

"It is Allah's will. It will be done."

"It always will be, Aashif. Thank you for calling."

———

Chapter Twenty-One

Trask put both his cell phones—the android one from his belt and the bat phone from his pocket—into the small wall locker he'd been assigned, then stepped up to the keypad outside the door to the SCIF.

Sensitive Compartmented Information Facility. So sensitive I'm not even in the triple-nickel anymore. At least I'm just across the street if I need something from the old office. I miss my Keurig already.

The JTTF was located in the same building—the FBI's Washington Field Office at 601 4th Street, N.W.—as the task force where Lynn, Val, Carter, and the rest were still trying to find DeAnthony Barrett, now known to his friends as "Hassan." The JTTF was behind very secure walls on another floor. Trask was replacing another attorney who was leaving the Department of Justice.

Never got an explanation for that. Maybe he read too many scary reports and couldn't take it anymore. Maybe he got bored to death. Maybe he got a raise somewhere else. Maybe someone will tell me. Ross just told me to report to the new squad supervisor. At least we'll both learn the ropes together.

He entered the code into the keypad beside the door, and heard the electronic locks whir to permit his entrance.

The first cubicle he came to was actually on the side of the hallway when he entered. The squad's administrator smiled at him across the counter.

"Mr. Trask? Go on in. Squad 16. The acting supervisor's expecting you. First door on the left."

Trask nodded and walked a few feet down the hallway before making the turn into the squad supervisor's office. Before entering, he glanced at the nameplate.

Adam Hill?

He didn't recognize the name.

When he saw the figure sitting at the desk, he *did* recognize the face, and he froze.

"You have got to be shittin' me," he said as he looked at the grinning face of Barry Doroz.

Doroz, a short, olive-skinned man with a happy, round face, stood and walked around the desk to shake Trask's hand.

"Old Bureau guys never die," Doroz said. "We just retire and return. The old federal double-dip: a pension *and* a paycheck. I'm a retired agent turned special civilian contractor. I'm just the acting squad supervisor for now, just warming the seat as usual. They have to have a *real* agent supervising the squad on paper. Main guy's on leave for a few weeks."

"How long have you been here?" Trask asked. "I'm always in and out of this building, and I haven't even seen you around the parking lot. Besides, I know you turned down a couple of these JTTF jobs while you were still a 'real agent.'"

"I've been back about a week now," Doroz said. "Retirement was boring the hell out of me, so when they called and offered me this gig, I finally took the plunge. The money's good and I sure haven't been bored lately. Sit down and let's catch up."

Trask took a seat in front of the desk. Doroz sat on the front of the desk instead of behind it.

"Eastman knew you were here, didn't he?" Trask asked.

"Of course he did. He needed a place to hide you for a while, after our friendly Imam Saleem intervened for you with the White House."

"So that really happened?"

"It did. We actually have a code name for the imam here. He's one of our sources. We call him Scorpion."

Trask rolled his eyes a little.

Doroz laughed. "Scoff if you must, but we have to protect things and people here. Our little game isn't as much in the public eye as *you've* been recently. First that dust-up at Arlington, then your testimony at the Senate hearing. I watched the whole thing on C-Span. I think the entire squad did. You got some cheers when you took Senator Moore apart."

"Thanks. Look where it got me."

"Oh, it's not *that* bad, and you have the advantage of replacing a real jerk. I haven't been in place long, but I've been here long enough to know that your predecessor, John Woodley, was a chinless, gutless wonder. We had to essentially keep him locked up in his office all day for fear he'd leak classified stuff to Main Justice if he heard somebody talking in the hallway. Instead of trying to cover us, he'd always look for 'legal' reasons why we *couldn't* do something, and would threaten to rat us out to the AG or one of her underlings if we went around him."

"What made him leave?"

"Life for him here wasn't pleasant. There *may* have been additives in his coffee from time to time that kept him in another office." Doroz pointed to the men's room across the hall.

Trask chuckled. "So if I get the squirts suddenly—"

"Nah. *You* don't have to worry." Doroz paused to take a sip of his own coffee from a cup on the desk. "Want some? I have a pot over here."

"I think you talked me out of it for now."

"Suit yourself. How's my old team doing with the police murders?"

"Still a good group, and Grog's a good sub for you, but they're up against a brick wall. We have an ID on at least one of the killers: a hulk named Barrett from Kansas City. Our problem has been finding him. Lynn ran him through every set of indices she could think of, and got zilch."

Doroz was suddenly serious.

"She *won't* find anything, either."

He stepped out into the hallway and called out a name, then stepped back into the office and closed the door.

"Everyone here is security-cleared to hell and gone, but I'm still careful to do everything on a need-to-know basis. Jeff, what I'm about to tell you fudges on that a bit, but because I know you'll do the right thing with it, you're in. You just can't go any farther with this than to tell Lynn she's spinning her wheels. She did some great work for me when I ran that squad, and I won't sit back and know that she's wearing out her computer for nothing. All that means is that none of the details you're about to hear leave this squad. Clear?"

"Perfectly." Trask smiled. "This is going to be an interesting role reversal for us. She was always the OSI undercover whiz, flying off somewhere I couldn't know about to do something she couldn't tell me about. Now—"

He was interrupted by a knock on the office door. A tall man with a mustache entered the room without waiting for permission. Trask figured he was at least four inches taller than six feet, and he had the easy, confident manner of a pro athlete.

"Jeff, this is Howard Buckley," Doroz said. "He's from the CIA, and part of our squad here."

"Call me Buck," the tall man said. "Never Howard. That's a family historical accident."

Trask turned back to Doroz with a questioning look on his face.

"He's a great nephew of Bill Buckley of National Review fame, who was once a CIA man himself for a short time, working for another CIA man by the name of E. Howard Hunt. They were close friends, so the story goes, so Buck's dad thought he'd close the loop when he filled out the birth certificate."

"Like I said, call me Buck," the tall man said.

"Anyway," Doroz continued, "Buck comes to our little party here from CIA SAD/SOG. Know what that means?"

"Special Operations Group?" Trask asked. "We had those in the Air Force, too. So Buck's a real spook."

"The spookiest," Doroz confirmed. "The SAD stands for Special Activities Division. So he's special twice. Black ops."

"I thought all that work was done *out of* country," Trask said.

Buckley looked at Doroz and raised an eyebrow.

"I told you he was the best we could get," Doroz said. "Tell him. He understands that it stays here. He has a top secret clearance, and I'll vouch for him until they put me in a body bag. He's no John Woodley, Buck."

"He'd better not be," the tall man said. "Woodley was a waste of motile sperm."

Buckley turned toward Trask and held out his hand. "Welcome. It's good to have a prosecutor assigned who's actually *on* the team instead of fighting us. Helluva thing you guys did out there at Arlington."

"Thanks. I would say I'm happy to be here, but I'm not sure yet."

Buckley shrugged.

"Understood. Anyway, a few nights ago, I paid a visit to a friend of yours in the hospital—that little punk Rusean Short. I slipped him a mickey, something the Russians developed called SP-117. It's their new-and-improved truth serum, a thiopental sodium blend with some special sauce thrown in. Short didn't know a whole lot, but he coughed up enough info to let us add two and two, and when we looked at some satellite data, we were able to locate the camp where Short, and your target Barrett—whose name is now 'Hassan,' according to Short—had been training."

"It was way the hell out in West Virginia, in the mountains in a national forest," Doroz explained. "I went out there two nights ago with Buck's special ops team."

"We called it 'Operation Pest control.' We cleaned the nest out," Buckley said. "All pests exterminated, but your man Barrett wasn't there."

"We did find some uniform materials, some old M1 drill rifles, and lots of Islamic reading material," Doroz added. "What we didn't find was a single shred of anything that would link the camp to anyone in the outside world. No computers, tablets, cell phones, not even a piece of paper with a phone number scrawled on it. No names, addresses, nothing. These guys were asleep when we hit them, Jeff. They didn't have time to throw papers or maps in a fire. They were just disciplined enough to be totally off-grid."

"That explains a lot," Trask said. "But I can only tell Lynn and her guys not to spin their wheels on a data search."

"That sums it up," Doroz agreed.

"Back to Rusean Short," Trask said, looking at Buckley. "We heard he was improving, then all of a sudden he's dead."

"I didn't dose him," Buckley said. "I wouldn't have thought twice about it, thug that he was, but it wasn't me. Somebody else got something by the guards."

"Will it show on the autopsy?" Trask asked.

"We won't tell Kathy Davis anything, either," Doroz said. "But the answer is no. There are several things the pros use that are essentially untraceable. Speaking of Kathy, that was horrible news, hearing about Willie Sivella."

"Good reason for not giving up on Barrett, even if he's off-grid," Trask said.

Doroz nodded. "We may have options here that weren't available to you before."

"Good," Trask said. "I thought I was being sentenced to six months of filing motions for FISA orders."

He referred to the paperwork required by the Foreign Intelligence Surveillance Act before electronic surveillance could be initiated against foreign agents or "lone-wolf" terrorists.

Doroz laughed. "You'll be doing enough of that, too, but it'll be a good cover for you. In the meantime, someone wants to meet you off-campus."

"What now?" Trask asked.

"We'll let you get settled, we'll get some lunch, and then you have a date with a scorpion."

———

Doroz drove the sedan, with Buckley stretching his long legs in the shotgun seat while Trask rode in the back.

"Where are we heading, if you don't mind me asking?" he asked.

"Here's the drill," Buckley said. "We rent a hotel room, somewhere in town, text the location in code to our source, then we get to the meet site first and wait for him to knock on the door. That way nobody sees us together in public, and since we always change the location, no nosy hotel clerk starts solving puzzles in her head or flapping her lips about it. Today it's a hotel in Crystal City."

"How long has this guy been cooperating with you?" Trask asked.

"He's a source, Jeff, not a cooperating target or defendant," Doroz corrected. "The actual new Bureau speak is 'CHS' for confidential *human* source. I guess the clowns in our headquarters think we talk to plants and animals or machines on occasion, but in this case, it's not just terminology. We have a different mindset with a source. Most of the time, there's no potential prosecution for leverage, so we just thank them for their help without leaning on them. As long as they're useful, anyway. Sometimes they even get paid."

"Are we—the JTTF—paying Saleem?"

"No," Buckley said. "The White House is doing enough of that for all of his religious conference work, probably high six-figures."

"What does he gain by helping us?" Trask asked.

"You get to form your opinion on that," Doroz said as he turned into the hotel garage. "Buck and I each have our own. I won't taint yours by giving you ours up-front. I'd like your honest evaluation on that point after you've met with him a couple of times."

"Fair enough."

"He's an Afghan by birth, Jeff." Doroz explained. "But from one of the northern tribes. Unlike many of his countrymen, he remembers and appreciates the assistance we gave his people in helping them kick out the Russians. You know, the whole *Charlie Wilson's War* story."

"Good flick," Trask noted.

"I thought so, too. Saleem's a conundrum, though. Smart enough to play it one way for the politicos on the hill, then he'll tell us something that seems 180 degrees in the other direction. I've interviewed hundreds of folks—bad and good—over the years, and I go home with my head swimming after talking to this guy. There are nights I stay up trying to decide what I've decided. Still, some of his info has been very helpful."

Doroz stopped at the hotel desk to get the key to the room while Trask and Buckley waited for him in the lobby gift shop. When Buckley saw Doroz moving toward the elevators, he paid for a pack of gum and Trask followed him as he followed Doroz. Once inside the room, they waited about ten minutes before hearing the knock. Buckley checked the peephole, then opened the door.

Trask recognized the face from the appearances he'd seen on the TV newstalk shows. Saleem wore glasses, a full beard, a well-tailored business suit, and a Rolex. He was about five-nine, and Trask guessed 175 pounds or so. Saleem smiled broadly when he saw Trask, and extended his hand immediately.

"This is a privilege for me, sir," the imam said. "A true privilege."

Trask noted no accent in the voice at all. He saw Saleem's eyes reading his mind.

"College at the University of Colorado," Saleem said, "Not far from your Air Force Academy, and an American high school before that. I am Afghan by birth, American by education, and a moderate Muslim by faith."

Trask nodded and felt himself smiling back at the man.

"I've enjoyed watching you spar with that lunatic on some of the talk shows."

What do I call this guy? Imam? He's not mine, and I'm no Muslim. Would that be an insult? Amal? Too familiar? I'll try 'Mr. Saleem.' Seems safer.

The imam again anticipated the question.

"Please call me Amal, Mr. Trask. May I call you Jeff?"

"Certainly."

"Excellent. Our mutual friends here told me that I could meet you this afternoon, Jeff. I jumped at the chance to meet one of the heroes of Arlington."

"Thanks, but I didn't feel like a hero then, and still don't," Trask replied. "We were faced with a serious problem and took the only course of action open to us. I would much rather have seen those events take a less serious turn. One good friend would still be with us."

"Yes. Major Williams. I know how you feel, Jeff. I had many good friends die in our battles to expel the Russian invaders of my country."

Saleem hung his head for a moment, and Trask could feel a genuine sense of loss emanating from the man.

"I have some questions for you, Amal," Trask said.

Saleem looked up and then glanced, smiling, toward Doroz.

"He is very direct, Barry. I like that." Saleem returned his gaze to Trask. "What are your questions, Jeff?"

"I heard you mention the term 'prison Islam' on one of your TV appearances. Tell me more about that, please."

"Of course. It is a major problem for those of us who are called 'reformists.' In truth, we believe that there is nothing in our faith that *needs* to be reformed, other than the misunderstanding—by those *outside* the faith—of what Islam is all about. At any rate, 'prison Islam' is an aberration of the true faith, much as ISIS is an aberration. In fact, I believe that agents of ISIS are using their false interpretations of the faith to draw the disaffected within your prisons into their ranks."

"Is your sparring partner on TV—Asalati—an agent of ISIS?" Trask asked.

Saleem shrugged. "He could well be. I don't know. He talks like one of those mongrels."

"I interrupted you," Trask said.

I'll learn more about you while you're talking and while I'm listening than the other way around.

"We were discussing 'prison Islam,'" Saleem said. "About eighty percent of those in your prisons who convert to a religion—whether to *any* religion after being an atheist, or going from one religion to a *new* one—are converting to some form of Islam. It is such a distinctive fact of life that your federal prison stores—I believe they are called 'commissaries'—are selling Muslim *Kufis*—our woven skull caps—as a result of the high demand.

178

"Moderates like myself—I prefer that term to 'reformist' for the reason I mentioned—are trying to present the true Islam as an option to your prisoners. I have volunteered to be a Muslim chaplain in your federal prison system, I have been vetted to perform that role, and I am trying to teach the true faith in prison religious services. But you have to understand the mechanics of how the extremists like Asalati are gaining access to the prisoners who wish to hear *them.*"

"I'm listening, and I'm interested."

"An inmate in your system has the right to request a 'pastoral visit' by the practitioner of his choice. He can file what is called—in prison terminology—a 'cop-out,' asking that he be permitted to have a religious consultation with—for example—Imam Asalati. There is little or no screening of these other imams for the pastoral visits. The inmate makes the request, and he is granted time in a room with Asalati. Who knows what they discuss, or what plans they make for the time after the prisoner is released? I am convinced that ISIS looks for those who are violent or who are inclined to extremism by nature, like some of those in your Black Lives Matter movement."

"I didn't hear you say *that* on television," Trask noted.

But I bet you heard me say enough on C-Span to believe I'd appreciate it.

"I don't believe the president would have appreciated it if I had said that," Saleem said, smiling. "I believe that I play a constructive role on his council, and I would like to keep that position. One must be mindful of one's superior's agenda."

And the check that comes with it, Trask thought. *You have a mortgage just as I do, just like those career guys on the capital crimes committee.*

"Do these converts to 'prison Islam' always change their names?" Trask asked.

"Almost invariably. Some do so officially, some do not. Most assume an Arabic or Muslim name as a testament of their new faith. If I were investigating someone in those circles, as you are, I would assume this to be the case."

"Back to this Asalati character," Trask said. "What can you tell me about him?"

"A native of Afghanistan, like myself, but from one of the tribes in the south. His father was an air force pilot, trained here in the states, and Aashif spent a lot of time here as a boy. His father's love of flying rubbed off on him, and he is also a pilot. It gives him quite an advantage over the others like myself."

"The others?" Trask asked.

"The other Muslim chaplains. More accurately, those requested by the prisoners."

Saleem paused for a moment, thinking.

"I will share with you a theory," he said. "Many times, I will conduct a service in one of your jails. It could be a federal prison, perhaps a state facility. It is not uncommon for one of the inmates to express an interest in the more violent or 'prison' Islam. I can see them getting frustrated with my message as I speak. When they find that I am *not* condoning violence or jihad, when I am trying to teach Islam's message of peace, they often challenge me. Sometimes they walk out; sometimes I have to ask them to leave, and sometimes I have to have them removed by the guards.

"I have found that on more than one occasion, Asalati—or one of the other imams of his extreme circle—will visit the facility within days of my visit. The other inmates who accepted my message will invariably tell me upon my return that the inmate who left my service—or who had to be escorted out—asked to meet with Asalati or one of his friends after my first visit. I mentioned Asalati's advantage. I have to travel by commercial aircraft, car, or train. I know of occasions when Asalati has flown his private plane to a nearby airfield to meet with such inmates. He is able to respond quickly when someone expresses an interest in converting to *his* brand of Islam."

"That would mean that someone in the prison is marking them for recruitment by Asalati and his group," Trask observed.

"You are most perceptive, Jeff." Saleem bowed his head slightly as he spoke.

"So it is your impression that Asalati runs this circle of imams?" Trask asked.

"Oh, no, quite the opposite," Saleem said, shaking his head. "I have heard from several in our community—those who have been recruited on occasion but who have declined his invitation—that he will speak of someone he calls his *saaqhib*. That is a word in our language meaning 'master.' Some in your old movies just pronounce it 'sahib.'"

"Tyrone Power. *King of the Khyber Rifles*," Trask offered.

Saleem laughed heartily. "Yes. Precisely."

"And you have no idea who Asalati's master might be?" Doroz asked. "This is the first time I've heard you mention him."

Saleem shrugged.

"It is the first time the topic has arisen. No, he is what your other old movies and novels would call a 'shadowy figure,' although I think the more precise use of your language would be a 'figure in the shadows.' I have only heard the term, *saaqhib*. I have never heard his name mentioned. It is not unusual for a cleric in our faith to have a spiritual mentor—one who trained him in the faith—and many would use that term for their teacher. I have never had a pleasant enough conversation with Asalati to dig that deeply into his history."

"But you'll keep your ears open for an opportunity?" Buckley suggested.

"Of course," Saleem said. "Whatever I can do to assist you. There are many in our mosques who *do* speak to me in confidence, and I am often able to fit some loose ends together to form some theories."

"Any theories about terrorist training camps in this area?" Trask asked. He felt both Doroz and Buckley tense up a bit as the question was asked.

Don't worry guys, nothing more singular than that. I know this is a one-way street. He gives us the info, and we give him zilch. I'm just seeing what kind of response we'll get, and how deep it might go.

"I have heard of such a place somewhere out 66 highway," Saleem responded. "Nothing more particular than that, I'm afraid."

"Do you recall who mentioned that to you?" Doroz asked. "Any way to follow up on it?"

"I do not recall at this moment. I will try to remember and contact you. If it was someone I can contact again without raising suspicion, I will do so."

"Thank you, Amal," Buckley stood, marking the end of the session.

"Yes," Trask said. "I enjoyed meeting and speaking with you. I do have one final question, if you don't mind."

"Of course. Anything."

"Why did you suggest to the president that he keep me around?"

Saleem grinned. "The president always tries to be mindful of what your press calls the 'optics' of his situation—at least ever since that round of golf following the ISIS beheading of that reporter. I reminded him that many regarded you as a hero after the events at the cemetery, and that many of his political enemies liked you even more after your Senate testimony. I suggested that he could maintain some control over your situation by keeping you in his Justice Department, under the supervision of his appointees. I also reminded him of the old saying by Sun Tzu in *The Art of War*: 'Keep your friends close, and your enemies closer.' He agreed that by keeping you in his employ, he could at least control your access to the press."

Trask laughed. "My banker and my wife thank you, at least. I'll have to see what I think down the line."

"I'm glad I could help," Saleem said. "Who knows? Maybe you can do a favor for me sometime."

The men shook hands. Saleem left alone. Trask and Doroz followed Buckley down to the parking garage a few minutes later. Trask climbed into the back seat again.

"What did you think?" Doroz asked as he started the car.

"Very disarming," Trask said. "I think you should change his code name. He's a chameleon of the first order. I'll have to reserve judgment on 'the scorpion' and most of what he said for now. We'll see what materializes to either support or contradict him."

"You said, 'most,'" Buckley noted.

"Yes I did," Trask said. "He needs to brush up on his Sun Tzu. *The Art of War* is mandatory reading for us military academy types. That quote about keeping your enemies close is *not* from Sun Tzu."

"Who said it, then?" Buckley asked. "I've heard it before, and it makes some sense."

"Michael Corleone in *The Godfather, Part II*," Trask answered.

Buckley looked across the car at Doroz.

"You're right. He's sneaky-scary."

Doroz nodded and smiled.

"Told ya."

Chapter Twenty-Two

"So you're telling me I'm wasting time, doing what I'm best at doing, while I'm trying to find this guy?"

Lynn stared across the dinner table at Trask with a scowl on her face.

"Sorry, but that's about all I can tell you," he said smiling. "Everything else about my day and my new life is very highly classified." His smile grew wider. "Isn't this fun?"

"Not a damn bit."

"I do have a suggestion, though," he said. "Assume that since his release from the Kansas pen, Barrett's been off the grid, but assume that he was on it before he left."

"What will that get us? He was in the Kansas state prison for ten years!"

"One specific suggestion, then. Have Val cut a subpoena to the Lansing prison for Barrett's visitor list for the last two years while he was on the inside. See if any of those visitors had ties to this area. Maybe that will point to where he's hanging his clothes at night now."

"That makes sense," she shrugged. "We sure don't have anything else to go on at the moment."

"Oh, and do a basic profile on our moderate talking head, Amal Saleem. And as far as the visitors for Barrett, I get to see those names when you get them."

"I'll have to ask my squad supervisor about that," she said. "Since you're no longer officially assigned to our investigation, he might find that it's outside your 'need-to-know.'" She looked up at him and smiled. "Isn't this fun?"

DeAnthony Barrett—or Hassan Abdullah as his associates now called him—was in a foul mood. He understood that he could not go out in public for a time. He had seen the bulletins on the television news. An image of his face—at least a younger version of it, but still unmistakable—had been broadcast multiple times across multiple channels, with a very large reward offered for information leading to his arrest.

There's some wisdom in the imam's caution, but how long do I have to rot in this basement? I've been let out of one prison cell only to be locked up in another one. I'm getting sick and tired of it. I need another job to do, and quick. The TV helped for a while—I hadn't seen one since Lansing—but it's still just another cage with a TV.

He turned off the television and climbed the stairs to the door on the main floor of the building. He pounded hard on the door, three times. A much smaller man with a beard unlocked and opened the door.

"What is it, Hassan? How can I help you?"

"I'm just goin' stir-crazy, *Saaqhib*. I need to get out of here and go somewhere, anywhere. I just can't look at those basement walls no more. At Lansing I could at least go into the yard and work out, see the sun, move around some."

"I understand. You have been a faithful soldier, Hassan. Please be patient. You understand why you must remain hidden for now?"

"Yeah, yeah. I really do. I seen the TV. I just don't know how much longer I can stay down there."

The smaller man nodded. "We'll take the van out after dark; go somewhere in the country, perhaps. We'll take some food. Would that help?"

"Yes, *Saaqhib*. I'd like that a lot. Thank you."

The big man turned and headed back down the stairs. He heard the door being locked behind him.

Many more days like this, and I won't be getting back in the damn van.

———

Trask downed his morning cup of coffee, and sat at his new desk in a cubicle in the JTTF SCIF, reading. He turned to see Barry Doroz standing behind him.

"The Qur'an?" Doroz asked.

"'If you know the enemy and know yourself, you need not fear the result of a hundred battles,'" Trask said. "Sun Tzu *did* say that."

"Any danger we'll see you wearing a *kufi* any time soon?"

"Only if this bald spot on the back of my head gets any bigger. What's up?"

"Brainstorming. Sometimes I just want to shut the door and think. This morning I've been thinking about your battle at Arlington."

"I wish I could stop thinking about it. I keep seeing my head shot sail past Rusean Short, then he pulls his rifle up, and a round explodes out of the muzzle and goes into Chet Williams's gut. It's all in slow motion, right out of a Sam Peckinpah flick, really graphic."

"You did what you could. Stop beating yourself up."

"I suppose. What are you thinking about the cemetery?"

"I'm not sure. Just a feeling that it wasn't the master stroke in the plan of our evil *saaqhib*."

"Why do you say that?"

"Think about it, Jeff. If that was the end-all of everything they were working toward, why still have that camp in the mountains? Why not have all the other bad-ass little terrorists on the scene, dressed as other marines, or even as cops? They could have had one helluva crossfire going once all the mourners sat down."

"I see your point."

"They had to be planning some other ops. If what Saleem told us the other day is accurate, their master planner is still on the loose, and we need to think about what direction he may be taking this."

"You're convinced that Asalati and his *saaqhib* were behind the camp and the attack at Arlington?"

"That's what the gut is telling me. I always trust my gut, and since retirement, there's a lot more there to trust."

"If that's the *question*," Trask responded, "I always start with the worst-case scenario for an answer. What's the most credible nightmare if we get outsmarted?"

"I've asked Buck the same question," Doroz said. "Conventional wisdom says it's a dirty bomb somewhere here in the District. You know, spread nuclear waste all over the place with some conventional explosives and wait a few thousand years for the stuff to wear out. It would be a lot easier for them to fly that kind of plot under the radar than setting off a real nuclear blast. Those nuke devices don't come or travel cheap, and every government operator in the Western world is always on high alert for them."

"Even with a dirty bomb, we'd have to move the government out of town," Trask mused. "I suggest Omaha. Wonder how many lobbyists would follow the center of power out there to a cold Nebraska winter in the center of the country?"

"They'd find a way to follow the money, I suppose." Doroz laughed. "I just pictured lobbyists in mukluks or duck boots."

"Any way to follow the money to your dirty bomb?" Trask asked.

"Not really. Not that much cash required. Getting their hands on the explosives would be a piece of cake. The problem for them is getting the nuke waste to spread with the blast."

"A big problem, I hope."

Doroz snorted. "I'll bring you a file to read. It'll at least change your nightmare."

Moments later, he dropped seven inches of written material on Trask's desk.

"Sweet dreams," Doroz said. "Just remember not to take it home with you."

Trask opened the folder and absorbed the fact sheets as he flipped through them, speed-reading at the rate of about five pages per minute.

A dirty bomb, or radiological dispersal device—RDD for short—is nothing like a nuclear weapon, which could destroy tens of square miles and spread radiation to hundreds of square miles. The RDD, by contrast, is composed of conventional explosives, with a much more limited blast used to disperse radioactive material in an effort to cause fear and panic and contaminate the affected area.

Okay, so wouldn't the size of the affected area be determined by the size of the explosion and the amount of radioactive matter dispersed? Of course it would. So if I'm a terrorist, where would I look to acquire radioactive materials? Here it is. They're routinely used at hospitals—amounts are probably not that big relative to other possible sources—research facilities—that would depend on the sort of facility—industrial activities—same caveat—and some construction sites, where they might be used for inspecting welding seams. None of those seem very promising.

Yeah, yeah, yeah. All our propaganda from the Nuclear Regulatory Commission says that all the stuff is "very tightly controlled" to keep it from falling into the wrong hands. Of course, the next page admits that they've lost some. The important thing here is that the combined total of all the stuff they've lost over the last decade wouldn't be enough for one RDD. THAT's good news, at least.

Wait a minute. What about the nuclear power plants? Where's the stuff on those?

Trask flipped through the folder's contents until he found the section he was looking for.

Here we go. A single, average-sized nuclear power plant produces . . . WHAT?! Twenty metric tons of nuclear waste in a single year? And we have nearly eighty-thousand metric tons of it spread around the country? Where? Stored in what? Who is guarding this stuff? I thought we were going to bury all that junk out in Nevada.

Trask flipped through more pages of the material. *What was the name of that place?*

Yucca Mountain storage facility. Nevada. Yep, that's what I remembered. What happened to it? Let's see; we spent twelve-billion dollars on the place, but Harry Reid—he was majority leader then—and the administration defunded it in 2012. That's where we were going to bury all this junk, but now we can't. The Government Accounting Office—hardly a conservative group—admitted in its report that the closure of Yucca Mountain was for purely political reasons, not for safety or technical problems. Wonderful.

So where is all this stuff now?

Trask turned back to his computer terminal and entered a search phrase. The machine responded, and a photograph appeared on the screen.

Unbelievable. Only a government could come up with a 'solution' this bizarre. They're keeping the radioactive slag on-site at the power plants. All eighty-thousand metric tons of the stuff, spread out in sites from coast to coast. What do they call these silo-looking things? Dry storage casks. Big concrete cylinders weighing hundreds of tons themselves. Sitting right out in the middle of might-as-well-be nowhere with some fences around them. Bear was right. New nightmares tonight.

He stepped out of his cubicle into the hallway.

"Bear?"

———

"Is this better, Hassan?" the bearded man asked him.

"Much better, *Saaqhib*, thank you."

Hassan, also known as DeAnthony Barrett, propped his massive feet on a stump as he leaned back in the lawn chair that was struggling to support his weight. He looked out over the small mountain lake. The moon was reflected in the water, and he could hear the bullfrogs croaking at the water's edge. The night air in the mountains was cool.

"We are actually not far from the old camp," the older man said. "This was an alternate site that I explored when we were choosing the location for the training facility. It's a nice spot, but a little too open. We were afraid the camp might be seen from the air, and that the lake might have proved to be too much of a temptation for the trainees. They could have been spotted swimming or fishing from the air. The site we finally chose had the creek for a water source, and offered much better coverage."

"I understand."

"I'm sorry it was such a long drive for you in the back of the van, but we had to make sure we got far enough away so that you would not be seen. I had to drive carefully for the same reason. I did not want to be stopped for speeding."

"I know, *Saaqhib*. I appreciate it."

"We will need to head back soon. It's a long drive back as well."

"Just a few more minutes, please."

"As you wish. We will leave in half an hour. Please do not go to sleep. That chair looks as if it will collapse, and if you were to be injured, I could never lift you."

"I'll stay awake." Hassan leaned forward a bit so that his weight was supported by all four of the chair's legs.

The older man stroked his beard and felt the bulge of the pistol concealed at his belt, his only hope of controlling his huge pupil if he became unruly. *I am glad that you are in an agreeable mood, my friend. You are too valuable to us. I would regret having to dispose of you at this early stage.*

———

Trask turned fitfully in the bed, subconsciously trying to limit the range of his thrashings so as not to wake Lynn. Having been plagued with a recurring nightmare as a child, he had been able to train himself to recognize the bad dream while still immersed in it, and to wake himself on cue if he recognized the dream and felt it becoming too disturbing.

He had not had the nightmare in decades, but it was back. He was about twelve, and back in his backyard in south Mississippi, finishing his mowing chores near dusk on one of those muggy summer evenings. He knew the script of the dream all too well, and knew that when he killed the growl of the mower by turning it off, another growl would come from another direction—the direction of the trees that lined the property to the north. He would be surprised at first by what he thought was the continued running of the mower engine, and would realize too late that the noise was not from the mower. He would turn again—for what might have been the fortieth time—to see his little cocker spaniel Taffy running to intercept something behind him, only to be tossed aside by the larger animal like a rag doll. The wolf would then leap—fangs bared and snarling—for his throat.

Oh no; I've seen this movie before, and I don't like it one bit.

He sat up in bed, waking at the point where the little dog went running toward something behind him.

I don't want to see her get killed, or that damned wolf jumping at me again.

He got up and headed up the stairs of the split foyer to the kitchen. He didn't drink water at times like these, preferring instead the slight sting of something carbonated. He grabbed a diet soda from the fridge and sat down at the dining room table in the next room, waiting for the sweat that still coated him to cool.

A furry head brushed his bare leg, and he looked down to see Nikki, the oldest of their rescue dogs, looking up at him.

"I'm okay, girl," he said quietly. "Just a bad dream."

He looked at the old dog while he stroked her head.

You're the same color as Taffy. You have the same temperament, the same eyes, even the same bark when you feel a threat from somewhere. Sometimes I think you're a reincarnation of my first dog—my first birthday present—my little guardian angel who's come back to watch over me.

He thought about the little cocker again. She was always watching him, following him around, ready to stand between him and any threat. It was a role she had played since the time when they both were babies.

She hadn't been killed by a wolf. The only real wolf in Hattiesburg at the time had been confined to a pen in the zoo. He had found her under her favorite bush one day after coming home from school. She hadn't been in the driveway to meet him. She had died at the age of fifteen. He buried her under that bush the same afternoon, deep enough so that no wolf could ever dig her up.

He spent a few more minutes petting Nikki's head. He was cooler now, the sweat having dried. He went back down the stairs to the bedroom, with Nikki following in his footsteps.

Good. Lynn's still asleep.

Nikki settled back in on her pillow against the wall. Tasha, the little mini-schnauzer, was asleep on the foot of the bed.

Boo's on the couch in the den. She sleeps inside in the summer while the air conditioner's running, outside in the winter. He smiled. *Probably does that to guard against wolves.*

He crawled in between the sheets, careful not to disturb either Lynn or the little dog snoring at her feet. He glanced at the clock.

Wonderful. Three-fifteen. I might get four hours of sleep tonight.

Another dream took him back to his twentieth year, while he was at the Air Force Academy. He saw himself standing at attention, waiting for the Retreat Ceremony—the lowering of the flag and the playing of the national anthem—just prior to the Cadet Wing marching to Mitchell Hall for the evening meal. Piles of snow surrounded the terrazzo, the plows having pushed it aside to allow the squadrons to form and begin the ceremony.

When the last strains of "The Star-Spangled Banner" echoed away, he thought he heard another sound. The cadets around him began to look from side to side, breaking ranks, running from the formation. He recognized the sound. It was that growl again, only much louder. He saw them on the edges and in the center of the terrazzo, standing atop the piles of snow, their fangs bared and snarling. It was the largest pack of wolves he had ever seen.

———

Chapter Twenty-Three

"How about surveillance of Asalati's house?" Trask asked.

"Been there, done that," Buckley said. "Drive-bys, stakeouts, pole camera. All we see is the imam himself coming and going. No girlfriends, associates, deliveries, nada."

"That in itself tells us something, doesn't it?" Trask suggested. "I mean, think about the care that they took at the training camp to leave us nothing. Is it a coincidence that one of their leaders is following what looks like the same careful protocol?"

"That's what my gut's been telling me all along," Doroz said. "You just explained it better."

"He doesn't have to do a damned thing at his house, anyway," Buckley explained. "Your department had given all these clowns their very own safe spaces, even before the little college kids started asking for them."

"Explain, please." Trask leaned forward in his chair.

"The mosques," Buckley said. "We used to be able to send undercovers or cooperators into the mosques, and identify those who were going hardline radical. Back in 2011, the ACLU joined with CAIR—the Council on American Islamic Relations—and sued us for allegedly violating the civil rights of mosque-goers in Los Angeles because we sent an undercover in to try and flush out the nut-jobs.

"Now we have our *own* stupid DOJ committee, kind of like that capital crimes committee you told us about. The Sensitive Operations Review Committee. SORC. I always thought they should have named it the Dare-not Operations Review Kommissars: DORK. The acronym would have been more accurate. We have to spell out everything ever known about a target mosque in order to justify any surveillance whatsoever. Most of us don't trust the DORKs at DOJ enough to hand them that information for fear they'd tip off our targets."

"Before that committee was set up, the FBI had a lot of successful under-cover and sting ops against some homegrown jihadis," Doroz said. "Now, our hands are tied. We had *after-the-fact* reports that the Tsarnaev brothers had been tossed out of their mosque in Boston for being radicalized. If we had known that *before* the marathon bombings, we could have saved some lives."

The First Amendment conundrum, Trask thought. *How far does the Constitution go to protect a religion that advocates the overthrow of the Constitution, and the supremacy of Sharia law?*

"Anyhow, that's the stone wall we run into," Buckley continued. "Let's assume that Asalati is hiding Barrett and God knows who else in his mosque, and maybe even this mystery man, the *saaqhib.* We can't begin to get inside the joint. I'm still convinced that if we asked the DORKs, by the time they ever said yes—probably the twelfth of never—our targets would be moved to another mosque. This whole administration seems more concerned about protecting Islam than they are the rights of anyone else."

"So that's a restriction on *federal* law enforcement," Trask thought out loud.

Doroz smiled. "I told you, Buck. He's about solutions, not road blocks."

"Just a thought," Trask said.

And one I don't want to drag these guys into. They'd pay the price for the end run if they got mixed up in it. I'll ask for volunteers on the side.

"How about aerial or satellite shots we might already be getting without targeting the place?"

"We'd have to get 'em on the sly, and our hands would get spanked pretty hard if the DORKs found out about it," Buckley said. "Any little thing specifi-cally targeting a mosque is off-limits."

"How about asking your friend Saleem?" Trask asked Doroz.

Doroz shook his head. "No. Think that through with me. If Saleem was wel-come in Asalati's mosque—and he's probably not—we've talked about Asalati enough with him to where he'd probably have already checked that square for us. He *hasn't* checked it, and if he's telling us the truth, Asalati and company would probably toss him out on his ear, or worse. More importantly, do you trust Saleem enough at this point to even make that request? If we trust him, and we're wrong, it's just like Buck here going to the DORKs. They pack up and move the perps and any assets to another mosque and we still get nowhere."

"Got it." Trask nodded. He took a sip of a Diet Coke. "That stuff on the nuclear waste scared the hell out of me."

"It *should* have," Doroz agreed. "Plug in 'terrorism' and 'nuclear waste' into a Google search, and it spits out lots of concerns that the anti-nuke power lobby has had about any and all of the plants. I remember one saying it was like we've spread our own dirty bombs all over the continent, and are now just waiting on the detonations. I'm a fan of nuclear power, when it's managed correctly, but I wouldn't trust the crew in charge at the moment to babysit my cat."

"You have a cat?" Buckley asked him.

"No. Hate 'em," Doroz said. "That further illustrates my level of trust for these clowns."

"Shutting down Yucca Mountain sure seemed like a bad idea," Trask noted.

"Even if they hadn't, they were planning on shipping all the waste out there on trains," Buckley said. "That's who-knows-how-many miles of track that could have been sabotaged to hijack a few tons of those half-spent glow bars. They used to rob trains on horseback a century or two ago, so it couldn't be that hard an op to plan. Now, they don't even have to do that. They can just use Google Earth to locate every dry cask facility in the country, and plan their assaults accordingly."

"How's the security at those facilities?" Trask asked.

"I'm not really sure," Doroz said. "It's supposed to be a secret. I hope those casks are more secure than they look. They're *supposed* to have several layers of security around them. That *probably* means fences, other barriers, ground sensors, rapid response teams, maybe some other measures. It's hard to say. I've never heard of any of the response teams—assuming they're actually out there—doing prep drills, and I keep my ears pretty close to the ground.

"The casks are thick and heavy as hell, with three-feet-thick concrete walls. The other problem the bad guys would have—besides security—is transportation. They'd have to almost steal the casks themselves in order to have a container safe enough for transport, and the things weigh 115 tons apiece. I know the *jihadis* are willing to die for their cause, but a slow painful death from radiation sickness might be a hard sell, even for Asalati and the other recruiters."

"Let's hope our targets have something less drastic in mind," Trask said. "I hate having good cops bite the dust, but that's a lot easier to deal with than this, and I can sleep a little easier if I *don't* think about it."

———

"You're in luck," Lynn said, placing the plate of beef stew in front of him.

"No need to tell me that," Trask said. "I could smell it when I walked in the house."

"I'm not talking about the stew."

She put a copy of a document on the left side of his plate.

"The Grog okayed you to see it. It's Barrett's visitor list from the Kansas State Prison at Lansing."

"Excellent! Thank you." He kissed her on the forehead, nose, and mouth. "It's typed," he said.

"Is that a problem?"

"It would have been better if we had a sign-in log or something. We could have had signature or handwriting samples to compare to exemplars. It's still a lot better than nothing."

He scanned the dates and names listed by the prison as having visited the prisoner then known as DeAnthony Barrett.

"Bingo. Aashif Asalati. On more than one occasion, too."

He went back to reviewing the pages.

"What are you looking for now?" she asked. "It seems like Asalati's name would be your proverbial smoking gun."

"It's enough of one, even if there's nothing else," he said. He paused and stared at her, a serious look on his face. "The other thing is classified, babe. Can't talk about it."

"I completely understand. Don't sweat it. I just hope it helps, and that there's something you can give back to our squad as a result. Poor Val's going nuts trying to think of something to do since we've had no way of finding Barrett."

"You're not going to like all of this, either," he said, "but I need you to have Dix, Tim, and Val meet me for lunch tomorrow. Make it the FOP. Just those three. No Bureau or federal types, so that means you're out for now. It's for your safety and the others involved, alright?"

"Just as long as you and Val have chaperones."

He laughed. "I'm glad you're okay with it. Trust me on this."

She kissed him. "Always have."

He went back to the list of visitors. He scanned until he found the earliest entry for a visit by Asalati. He then took a finger and slowly traced the entries before that visit until he found the name.

Just who the hell is Abisali Ghilzai?

————

Barrett knocked on the door at the top of the stairway. Hard. When there was no answer for ten seconds, he knocked again. This time, he heard the lock turn and the door opened.

"What is it, Hassan?"

"I have to get out of this basement, *Saaqhib*. We have to do something to get me out of there more often. I can't stay down there this long. I just can't."

The bearded man nodded.

"I have not seen the announcements seeking your arrest on television for about a week now. The interest of the media is at least dying down. They have other stories to cover with the elections coming up. It is after dark. There is no one in the courtyard, and it has high walls. I do not think it would be too risky for you to spend two or three hours outside every night after sunset. Would that help? It would have to be when all of the others have left."

"That would help a lot, *Saaqhib*. Thank you."

The older man stood aside to let him pass. Barrett walked to the door that led from the main section of the mosque to the courtyard. He sat on a bench and breathed in the outside air like it was a tonic. The air was warm and muggy, the atmosphere of a Washington summer, not like the cooler mountain breezes of his last outing.

A couple of hours every night. That will work for a while, but just a while.

———

Trask was waiting at the table when they came through the door to the FOP dining room. He stood to shake hands. There were four of them instead of three.

"Give us just a minute, guys," he said to Carter, Wisniewski, and Val, as he motioned Nick McCarver away from the table.

He walked a short distance away before speaking.

"Why are you here, Nick? I asked Lynn to send only the other three. What I'm about to say and ask these folks to do is risky enough with them acting just in a local capacity. It gets real dicey for a federal officer."

"I'll take the risk, Jeff. I owe it to Jackie. I saw the Barrett visitor list when it came in, and now you're having a sit-down, so I know this is related."

"You're right; it is." Trask thought for a moment. "The Park Police are under the National Park Service, correct?"

"Yeah. Why?"

"So you don't usually get all the DOJ bulletins, for example, telling the FBI what they can or can't do about this and that?"

"Separate agency."

"I'll take that as a 'yes,' meaning you don't get them."

"Separate agency."

Trask smiled. "Okay. You're in. Risk accepted."

McCarver nodded. "Thanks."

They returned to the table and joined the others.

"Here's the scoop," Trask said. "You've all seen the visitor list for Barrett while he was in Lansing. You've seen that Aashif Asalati, the radical talking head from TV, visited him there. Asalati is the only link we know of between Barrett in Kansas and this area. We have reason to suspect that Asalati, being the *jihad* apologist that he plays on TV, may be an actual recruiter for Islamic extremists in the U.S.

"Now here's the rub. There's nothing to prevent us from surveilling Asalati at his residence from now until doomsday. The problem with that is we would see nothing. The reason we would see nothing is that the department that Val and I work for has forbidden *federal* agents who work for DOJ from targeting or putting any surveillance whatsoever on mosques, for fear of offending our Muslim brethren. So we've in essence issued an open invitation to the extremists to do everything they shouldn't be doing in the mosques. Everybody with me so far?"

"I'm ahead of you," Carter said.

Wisniewski nodded. "I get it."

"Like I said, I'm in." McCarver shrugged. "All in."

"Val," Trask said, "There's a risk for you in this that I can't deny—"

"None that I'm not willing to assume," she said. "This guy needs doing."

Trask smiled. *Your judge-of-character score just went up, Jeff old man.* "Good. Very good."

He reached into the inside pocket of his sport coat and unfolded a printout of a satellite view of a building.

"This is the mosque that our man Asalati calls his place of worship. Odds are that Asalati—being well aware of our department's suicidal blind spots—is using his mosque as a safe house for his henchman Barrett."

Trask looked across the table at McCarver.

"Since our department has forbidden any surveillance of this place of worship by federal agents who might be working *for our department,* I was wondering whether any local *or other* law enforcement officers might volunteer to keep a lookout on this place for a few days to see—you know—what they could see."

"I was thinking of going back to my regular job for a few days," McCarver said, "meaning that I would not be available for the FBI task force assignment for a while."

Trask smiled. "Nick has volunteered to take the day shift. That might free up some evenings for anyone who is NOT working assigned hours on the books as a deputized member of an FBI task force."

"There's a hotel adjacent to the mosque here," Carter said, pointing to the eastern side of the structure. "The upper floors would give us a good view of

A Winter of Wolves

the place. If we got a room toward the street, we could see the front of the mosque and the courtyard from the window. Tim and I can alternate night shifts *after* performing our hours and duties as federal officers."

"What's my job?" Val asked.

Trask shook his head.

"For now, it's just keeping a low profile. Keep on keeping on. You've got one hell of a good career ahead of you. We won't put that on the line unless we have to. If I get burned because of this, so be it. I've made my choice. I'm disqualified anyway because of the Arlington thing. If we do see Barrett, we've got to think of a way to flush him out of the mosque. They won't let us hit the place with a warrant, and we couldn't tell them how we got the probable cause for one, anyway. I'm out of ideas for now. Work on that. If we get him out, he's your case to try."

She nodded. "Hurry it up if you can. I'm supposed to keep Mr. Eastman in the loop. I think he's close to pulling me back to one of the court details if nothing happens soon. He knows I've been twiddling my thumbs."

"Our man Barrett hasn't been out of the can that long," Trask said. "Unless I miss my guess, he'll show somewhere around this place."

Trask looked at Val. "Ross can't know about this at all, at least for now."

She nodded. "Understood."

Trask looked at the satellite image again before rolling it up and handing it to Carter.

He looked at his watch.

"It's twelve-thirty and we haven't even ordered. Anybody hungry?"

———

Trask walked into the acting squad supervisor's office. Doroz and Buckley were waiting on him.

"We have volunteers," he said. "Non-FBI volunteers. Now we wait."

———

Chapter Twenty-Four

"Absolutely nothing," McCarver said as he greeted Carter at the door. "I've got a camera with a good zoom lens set up at the window. It looks down on the courtyard in case anybody does go out there. I'll leave it in place for you guys. It's set up behind the gap in the curtains, far enough back that nobody should be able to see us."

"How about the front of the place?" Carter asked. "No oversized hulks coming or going?"

"Not that I've seen."

"Maybe we'll get lucky tonight, then," Carter said. "Go home and enjoy your evening."

"You sure you're okay working these double shifts?"

"Been doing them for years now, Nick. That's probably why I'm single again. At any rate, I've got no one to go home to. You do. Do it."

"On my way, then. Good luck."

McCarver opened the door to find Timothy Wisniewski standing in the doorway, his hand poised to knock.

"Looks like you have company, Dix," McCarver said over his shoulder. "I thought you guys were going to alternate on this shift."

"So did I," Carter responded. "Let him in. He just can't stand to be without my mature guidance for more than twelve hours at a time."

"Good luck," McCarver said again as he left.

Carter shook his head as he looked at his partner.

"Young man, if I had Randi Rhodes waiting for me at home, I sure as hell wouldn't be here. What's wrong with you?"

"I'm devoted to my duties, and to my mature partner," Wisniewski quipped. "I just figured I'd get the lay of the land for a bit before I took my turn tomorrow night."

"We're getting it *together*, then," Carter said. "Nick set up the camera for us. I haven't even had a chance to peek through it yet. How's the zoom?"

Wisniewski stepped to the window and peered down into the courtyard of the mosque, adjusting the lens on the camera to magnify details of the scene below.

"Pretty damn good," he said. "I can make out some kind of bug on the big plant down there in the yard."

"Good. We shouldn't have any problem then if our man Barrett is in the house and decides to take a stroll. Since you're *here*, you get the first hour. I'm going to take a mature nap."

———

"Did you find anything on this Abisali Ghilzai character?" Trask asked her.

"Just that his name means 'warrior,' and he's probably from one of the southern tribes in Afghanistan," Lynn answered. "I got that from googling his name. Other than that, and a single car registration about four years back, he's another phantom. I'm getting tired of trying to mine data on ghosts in this case."

She took another bite of her salad.

"This place has the best food," she said. "Good idea. We haven't been here in ages."

"I agree," he said. "Best food in Georgetown. You found a car registration on Ghilzai?"

"Yeah, a van. Local. That's it."

"Any address associated with it?"

"Sure. A vacant lot. Totally bogus. I would have told you if I found anything worth finding. He must have paid off the DMV clerk to get the plates. Everything else on the form was either worthless or blank."

She looked up and gave him a stare that he knew all too well.

"What have you got Dix and Tim doing?" she asked. "They've been acting weird today, like they couldn't wait to get out of the squad room."

Trask sighed.

"I try and protect you by keeping you *out* of the loop when I have to, babe. I *really* can't tell you yet. You'll be able to put it all together when I do."

"Or maybe before."

She smiled as she raised her wine glass in a mock toast.

"Or maybe before," he agreed. "You already figured out that they were doing something off the books, and yeah, it's for me."

"Is your neck on the line again?"

"Probably," he admitted. "But just professionally this time. Not physically."

"My salary won't cover our bills if you get yourself fired," she said.

"I know. We may have to go back to being poor, ignorant, and happy again."

"Works for me." She shrugged. "As long as we're together. Ignorance of all this stuff might actually *be* bliss."

He nodded. "You have no idea."

———

"It's dark, now," Wisniewski said, jostling Carter as he lay on the bed. "Wake up, Dix. I gave you an extra hour. It's your turn."

"Anything?" Carter asked him.

"Hell, no. Just about fourteen, different, normally-sized humanoids wearing various forms of bedding walking through the courtyard from time to time."

"How do you know they were different?" Carter asked. "Could you make out faces?"

Wisniewski snorted. "No, master detective, sir, but unless they had reason to believe that I was up here watching, I didn't figure that they had reason to change those sheets they've been wearing just for my benefit. It hasn't exactly been the desert version of a GQ fashion runway down there, and my conclusion was based upon the garb I observed."

"Sorry, point taken." Carter rubbed the sleep out of his eyes and walked over to the camera. "Good clear images. If our man shows, we'll at least have proof when he looks up."

"I am, as you suggested, heading home to Detective Rhodes now," Wisniewski said. "Can I make a burger or ribs run for you before I head west?"

"Thanks. Good idea, Tim. We don't need to be ordering pizzas up here. Might not get the most discreet delivery guy in the world. That camera stand over there would be hard to explain."

He reached into his wallet and pulled out a ten.

"A burger and fries will get me by tonight, thanks. The Mickey D's down the street is good." He handed the bill to Wisniewski. "Diet coke. That'll make up for the calorie count on the fries."

"Back in fifteen."

Carter stepped back to the window. The courtyard was a Moorish design, a tiled area about fifty feet square surrounded by arches that supported a walkway along the borders above the open area.

Kind of pretty. Wonder what the inside of the place looks like?

A man wearing what Carter thought must be traditional desert clothing walked from one side of the courtyard to the other.

Just like Tim said: a normally-sized humanoid. Certainly not DeAnthony Barrett.

He left the window and grabbed the remote control for the television.

The Nationals are playing tonight. Might as well see how they're doing. I'll keep the sound just loud enough to hear in the hallway. Make it seem like a normal businessman has the room rented.

The knock on the door was Wisniewski. He handed Carter the sack and soda cup, and walked to the window while Carter took the food to a desk beside the bed.

"Master Detective Carter, sir," he said. "Perhaps you should take a look, if you could tear yourself away from the baseball and burger, that is."

Carter jumped up and headed for the window. Wisniewski stepped aside to give him room to look through the camera's viewfinder.

"Got him. I'll be damned. First night, too. Did you get the shot?"

"I did. He came out and looked straight up at the night sky, like he was tokin' on a tank in one of those oxygen bars. We'll email it over to the squad—"

"The *hell* we will. Remember, we're off the federal books. Send it to our regular desks at our metro office. Call Jeff, and send a copy of the pic to Nick McCarver. Good catch."

"Thank you, master detective."

"Knock that crap off. I would have seen him after I got done with the burger."

"If he was still outside."

"Good point, junior. *Now* you get to put him on the clock. See how long he stays out there. We need to have an idea of his schedule. It might help us figure out how the hell we're going to flush him out of that place."

"I was about to go home to Randi, as you previously ordered."

"That was before you called me 'master detective' three times in one night. Since you were *diligent* enough to spot him and take the pic, you get to write the report, too. No good deed goes unpunished."

————

"He's in the mosque, as we suspected," Trask said.

"Great idea you had, and good work by Dix and Tim," Doroz said.

"So we know where he is," Buckley said. "We still can't arrest the SOB. Not in the mosque, anyway; it's off-limits. We need to figure out a way to flush him out of there."

"Agreed," Trask said. "Dix had a good idea. He and Tim are going to stay on the night watch for a while to see if there's a schedule to Barrett's playground recesses. In the meantime, we get to come up with a master plan."

"Any ideas yet?" Doroz asked.

Trask shook his head. "Not a thing. How about you?"

"Nope."

"Me either," said Buckley. "But he's got to come out of there some time."

"Does he, Buck?" Doroz asked. "Would *you* come out of a safe-space if a wanted poster with your face on it was streaming on every TV screen in town?"

"No," Buckley said. "But he's not me. He's a thug who likes to kill, and who just got out of the pen. That's a caged brute down there. He'll need to prowl again. We just don't know when."

"Maybe we'll figure that out," Trask said. "In the meantime, we get to keep thinking. Maybe we can *lure* him out with something."

"Any idea what?" Doroz asked.

"Not a thing," Trask said. "How 'bout you?"

———

"Anything happening?" Carter asked as McCarver opened the door to the hotel room.

"I *did* get plates on a van as it pulled into the garage down there," McCarver replied. "It's registered to our other mystery man, Ghilzai."

"Good. That's something Lynn can put in our file on *him*, if she doesn't already have it. She's already got info on all kinds of vehicles, including Asalati's plane. Jeff told her he had a private pilot's license."

"I'll have to get a private *fighter* pilot's license, then," McCarver said. "Give me a little time, then tell me when he takes off. Anyway, I wrote the plate info down on the note pad on the table, in case you need it."

"Thanks. Have a good night."

"Yeah. You, too. Keep an eye on our target for me."

"Will do."

Carter watched the early evening news on one of the cable channels, checking his watch from time to time.

He usually doesn't come out until after eight, waits until it's completely dark out.

He walked over to the camera, scanning the scene below.

There's an SUV coming out of the garage. Wonder if it's the one Nick ran?

He checked the plate numbers on the note pad.

Same one. I bet the saaqhib *felt the need to have a prayer session with our man Barrett. Maybe they're planning to kill another cop.*

He checked the courtyard again.

No sign of him yet.

———

"We can only do this once in a while, Hassan."

"I know, *Saaqhib*. Thank you."

The big man looked out over the lake as he finished the bucket of chicken.

"Thanks for the Popeyes. I always liked it. Missed it at Lansing. I don't think I can ever eat meatloaf again. Seems like that's all they ever fed us, meatloaf and mashed potatoes."

"Are the visits to the courtyard helping?"

"They do, but I'm still goin' nuts. Basement walls, courtyard walls: they're all still *walls*. They may not have bars or razor wire on top of 'em, but they're still walls. This helps more."

"We'll try to get out once a week or so, then. I like it out here as well. It is peaceful, and gives me a chance to think."

"Do you have any more work for me to do?"

"Soon, Hassan. Soon. We have plans for something very big."

"Why are we waiting so long?"

"We are waiting on the very breath of God, Hassan, a change in the weather. When the right pattern materializes, Allah himself will aid us by spreading destruction all over this land of infidels."

———

Trask dialed the number.

"Hello, Jeff. What's up?"

"Sorry to bother you this late, Bear. Any chance you could set up another meeting with Saleem tomorrow?"

"I don't see why not. He's usually available when we ask him to be. I'll call him, and Buck can get us another hotel room. Something burning a hole in that fevered brain of yours?"

"Not really. Just another square I think we need to check. I'll see you at the SCIF in the morning."

"Okay. Tell Lynn I said hello."

"Will do. Goodnight."

———

Trask walked back into the den. Lynn was surrounded by the pups, watching television.

"What's on?" he asked her.

"Just the weather. I'm glad it's something besides cops getting killed. First, those five in Dallas, then the ones in Baton Rouge. We'll be flying the thin blue line flag out a lot more than I ever wanted to."

Trask nodded. He took a few steps toward the front of the house to check on the light. The solar spot was working well, highlighting the police memorial version of Old Glory. Instead of a blue field and red stripes, the flag showed a black field and alternating black and white stripes, with a thin blue line replacing one white stripe and running between the others.

He returned to the den. Lynn had switched to The Weather Channel, and a map of the entire country was displayed on the screen. The jet stream had taken an unseasonal plunge southward, with a low pressure system above the dip and a high pressure ridge hovering below and to the east.

A pretty meteorologist wearing a dress with a plunging neckline was predicting severe winds for the east coast for the days to come.

"The combination of the jet stream flow, accented by this low to the west, and the high pressure to the east, means that we will have strong winds flowing from the south-central and southeastern United States up through the Carolinas into Virginia, and from the nation's capital all the way to New York City," she said.

"Are you staring at her dress, or at the map?" Lynn asked him.

"The map," he said, staring intently.

She looked at him, frowning.

"You really are, aren't you?"

He snapped back to the moment.

"I'm sorry. What were you asking, babe?"

———

Asalati watched as the pretty woman described the patterns on the screen. He was not alone.

"Allah is with us, Aashif. Look at this. The low pressure system turns counter-clockwise, pushing the winds from southwest to northeast. The jet stream has dipped all the way down to Texas. The high pressure to the east is rotating clockwise. It is as if gears on either side of the jet stream were squeezing it in the middle and accelerating the airflow northward and eastward through a huge wind tunnel. It is the perfect pattern, the one for which we have prayed. In three days, the center of the funnel will be over our target. The winds will carry the results of our attack straight over Washington, then to Philadelphia and on to New York."

"I see it, *Saaqhib*. I will be ready. My aircraft will be fueled, and the other cargo will be aboard. It is a short flight, and the enemy will have no time to react. I believe your plan is perfect."

"Your cargo will be ready and waiting, Aashif. I will have Hassan at the field tomorrow night to help with the loading."

"How is his mind, *Saaqhib*? Is he still claustrophobic?"

"I'm afraid so. The trip in the van tomorrow should help, and I have promised him another trip to the mountains on Saturday. The traffic is too heavy to make the drive on a weekday. How much cargo can your airplane handle?"

"My maximum payload is about 2,500 pounds. With my own weight and the extra fuel, a good figure is 2,000 pounds—about a ton, or just over 900 kilos, depending on the system of weight that our suppliers are using."

"Good. Hassan will be very useful with the loading, then. You fly on Sunday, the same day of the week as the attack on their Pearl Harbor. Very fitting."

———

Chapter Twenty-Five

"I've been doing a lot of reading lately, Amal."

Trask leaned forward. He was sitting on the bed in the hotel room, facing the chair occupied by Saleem. Doroz and Buckley sat at the table across the room in the mini-suite.

"In trying to understand these zealots, I keep coming across verses in the Qur'an which seem to empower them—to justify what they're doing in the name of Islam. These verses would be ideal recruiting tools for someone like Asalati to use in our prison system. If you match these verses up with a predisposition to commit violence, or even murder, you get home-grown *jihadis* without having to water those plants very often."

"I probably know them already, Jeff, but just to be sure, which verses have you discovered?" Saleem asked.

Trask brought out a pocket notepad.

"Verse 2:191 commands a Muslim to slay the unbelievers wherever he finds them. That reads a lot like verse 9:5, which says a Muslim should—when the opportunity arises—kill the infidels wherever he finds them. The only difference is an apparent qualifier that seems to suggest that you don't have to kill infidels unless there is an opportunity to do so. Then there's a lot of talk about beheadings. There are over a hundred similar verses.

"Verse 3:85 says that any religion other than Islam is not acceptable; verse 8:12 instructs Muslims to terrorize and behead those who believe in scriptures other than the Qur'an; and verse 47:4 tells believers not to hanker for peace with the infidels, but to behead them when you catch them. How do you preach a religion of peace with those commandments coming from your holiest text?"

Saleem nodded and smiled.

"You quote the Qur'an correctly, but only partially, Jeff. That is understandable, as your contact to the faith is new. The verses you cite are just as appealing to those in my world who are predisposed to violence as they are to some in your prisons. Every society on the planet has criminal elements. I would argue, however, that for every verse such as those you have cited, there are others that moderate them. For example, the holy book in verse 25:63 tells us to respond to enmity with peace. Verse 2:178, coming shortly before one of the verses you cited—2:191—tells us to choose forgiveness rather than revenge even after blood has been spilled; and verse 60:7 says that we should embrace former enemies as friends.

"It is undeniable that the extremists would say that some of the verses commanding peace would only apply to other believers in Islam with whom a Muslim has had a dispute. These sects would also say that the very term 'moderate Islam' is an oxymoron, since the commands of Allah are clear in the verses you cited, and need no explanation or moderation. They do not consider themselves to be extremists; they believe they are simply following the plain instructions and will of God."

"I'm just trying to understand why some in Islam say that ISIS and others like them have hijacked a religion of peace when these verses do not seem to be immediately qualified, either literally or in context," Trask said. "I'm trying to understand what we're up against. You quoted Sun Tzu at our last meeting. He also wrote that 'If you know the enemy and know yourself . . .'"

"'You need not fear the result of a hundred battles,'" Saleem finished the quotation, smiling. "I understand and applaud your motivation."

Saleem took off his glasses and polished the lenses with the sleeve of the robe he was wearing.

"Let me try it this way," he said. "If we have to rely on labels like 'moderates' and 'reformists' to explain our faith to those outside it, we may never find an explanation that is sufficient. Some who believe in the Islam of peace actually call *themselves* 'radicals,' because they advocate *radical degrees of love.* They advocate reconciliation instead of revenge, service to their fellow man instead of selfishness, compassion over the barbarism we see in ISIS and their kind, and wisdom instead of warfare."

"What you have just outlined *should* give us common ground," Trask said.

"It is more visible when one studies more than just the Qur'an," Saleem added. "You must read the *hadiths* as well. They are similar to some of your New

Testament gospels, in that they recount observations of Mohammed and his actions by his followers while he walked the earth. They tell, for example, of the mercy he showed to his former enemies at Hudaybiyyah and Mecca, when he chose peace over further warfare."

"Thank you for that explanation," Trask said. "Changing the subject a bit, were you able to recall who told you about this *saaqhib* who pulls the strings on Asalati?"

Saleem shook his head.

"I'm sorry. I have tried to remember, but could not."

"How about the names of the other extremist imams—if I can call them that—who are helping him recruit in our prisons?"

"I must again apologize, but I do not travel in those circles. I *do hear* about them from other Muslims, and from other prisoners I meet in your jails, but I have no names."

"Do you recognize the name 'Abisali Ghilzai?'"

Saleem paused for a moment. "I have heard the name *somewhere*. I cannot recall where I heard it, and it was not recently." He smiled and shrugged. "I am sorry that I cannot be more helpful."

Trask returned the smile. "You *have* been helpful, Amal. Thank you for your time. Please call us if something else comes to mind."

———

"Dry well?" Doroz asked from the driver's seat as they drove back to the SCIF.

"Could be," Trask answered. "What do you think, Buck?"

"It's either dry, or the bucket hit quite a snag on its way back to the top."

"If you had to pick?" Trask asked him.

"I guess I'd pick dry. Why else even talk about Asalati if you're on the other team?"

A very good question, Trask thought. *But if the question is good, where's the answer?*

———

"It was an excellent idea to use another truck, Aashif. I do not think that mine has been compromised, but it is always wise to vary our routine. The frame of this vehicle is also stronger, and we can make a single trip instead of two."

"Thank you, *Saaqhib.*"

Asalati turned his head to the rear of the ton-and-a-half. A window in the rear of the cab was open, and he could see the huge figure in the forward section of the bed of the truck, sitting on a tarp and hanging on to some cargo straps for stability.

"Are you comfortable, Hassan?"

"Yes, Imam."

"The payload is mixed and ready for pickup. It is a short drive away from your airfield. The material is somewhat unstable, but it should be safe for the brief transport and then for your flight on Sunday. I instructed the suppliers to pack the mixture in small drums. Each one should weigh 100 pounds or less, and should be easy for Hassan to lift."

"Will that be a problem for you, Hassan? Twenty canisters weighing 100 pounds each?"

"Piece of cake, Imam. As long as they ain't greasy, I won't drop 'em. I used to lift a lot more than that in the yard at Lansing. All day long."

"Excellent," Asalati said. "Where did you get the formula for the explosives, *Saaqhib?*"

"On-line."

"From one of our specialists?"

"No," the older man chuckled. "From one of theirs: Timothy McVeigh. It is the same mixture of ammonium nitrate and fuel oil that he used in Oklahoma City. Our canisters should be more stable because of the material we are using for the containers and the lighter weight in each one. He had more than three tons in the truck he used. You will have one ton on your aircraft."

"You are sure it will be enough to penetrate the storage containers at the power plant?"

"If Allah guides your hands on the controls as he did for our pilots at the World Trade Center, it will be more than sufficient. There are twenty-seven casks on the ground, and they contain tons of waste. The weather pattern on Sunday will mean that the winds will carry that waste from Washington across Philadelphia and all the way to New York and beyond. The panic will be something to behold, and it will be anything but temporary. The half-life of that waste is about 24,000 years."

"It will be a magnificent victory for us," Asalati said, nodding. "It is my honor to deliver the blow, and I will be watching their panic with the prophet himself."

"Have you re-checked your flight plans, Aashif?"

"Yes, *Saaqhib*. The distance from the airfield at Manassas to North Anna is about 70 miles. I will be fighting some headwinds, which will slow me down a little, but the flight time will be very brief. The enemy should have no chance to respond."

"We will proceed as planned on Sunday, then," the older man said. "If, however, you get the signal from me that something has gone wrong, you should execute the plan immediately. The winds may not be quite as favorable as they will be on Sunday, but they are already good."

"I understand, *Saaqhib*."

"Very good."

The truck traveled west on Interstate 66 before turning south on US Highway 28.

"Turn here, Aashif."

Asalati steered the truck westward along a paved road until he came to a barn beside a farmhouse. As the truck stopped, three tattooed men with shaved heads came out of the farmhouse. Each carried an automatic weapon.

"The money?" one of them asked Asalati. The man's accent marked him as a Latino. His tattoos marked him as a member of the MS-13.

Asalati turned and retrieved a briefcase from behind his seat. He handed the case to the largest bald man.

"We'll be back after the count," the bald man said.

It took fourteen minutes.

"The stuff's in back of the barn," the bald man said. "Mixed and ready to go."

Asalati nodded and started the truck.

The man in the passenger seat turned toward the back of the truck.

"Time for you to go to work, Hassan. Be careful with our cargo."

Carter looked through the peephole of the door to the hotel room, expecting to see the face of Tim Wisniewski. He saw the face of Val Fuentes instead.

"What are *you* doing here, young lady?" he said, opening the door.

He stuck his head out into the hallway to make sure she was alone.

"I made Tim tell me where you were hiding. I need to talk, and I need to be a part of this," she said. "I can't sit in that office all day and do nothing to contribute. I know everyone's trying to protect me, Dix, but I'm a big girl. I want to help, and I can take care of myself."

"Have a seat." He motioned toward the bed. "Sorry, but we only have one chair."

He looked through the camera's viewfinder down toward the courtyard of the mosque. It was empty. He took a pen from his shirt pocket and jotted the time and an entry on his surveillance log. He looked up at her.

"What's on your mind?"

"Those poor officers in Dallas and Baton Rouge," she said. Tears welled up in her eyes. "I watched them on TV, Dix, running *toward* the shooter trying to protect the very demonstrators whose message was *attacking them*. And then the ones in Louisiana. Black and white . . ."

"And blue," he reminded her. "All blue, Val."

"I've been so wrong about all this."

"No, not about *all* of it. There are bad apples in every barrel. You just can't make the same mistake about all police officers that others made about all us poor, stupid black folks once upon a time. It's the fallacy of generalization, as prejudiced in one direction as it is in the other. The difference is . . ."

"The difference is what I saw in Dallas. The group who's getting all the hate slung at them is out there protecting the haters, Dix, guys like you and Tim and Jeff and everybody on that task force. I just had to tell you that I get it now. I really get it and I had to apologize to someone."

"No apologies required," he said. "It's called growing up, or *growing out* of the box that somebody put you in while you *were* growing up. Sometimes it's a parent; sometimes it's a professor; a lot of times it's a politician. Everybody makes choices. You either climb out of the box or crawl back in it. Welcome to the real world.

"For what it's worth, I've been watching the coverage of all of that, too. Most of the BLM demonstrators in Dallas weren't thugs. I still think they are being misled by the organization's message, but they were rational folks who seemed to appreciate that the officers on the scene were actually trying to protect their right to march and protest."

"I need to call that prosecutor in Baltimore," Val said.

"The state's attorney?"

"Yeah, the one trying to prosecute all the cops."

"Why do you need to call *her*?" he asked.

"To tell her she's put herself in a really big box. Seriously."

Carter laughed. "A box or a hole. I hear there's a petition to disbar her now."

The ringtone on his cell phone interrupted them.

"Hello, Jeff," Carter said.

He paused to let Trask talk.

"No, I haven't seen him tonight. Not yet, anyway."

Another pause.

"Got it, tomorrow morning. Let's do it at the task force, and bring *everybody* up to date. I think they deserve to know, don't you?"

Another pause.

"Yeah, Val should be there, too. The more players involved, the more ideas we might get. We'll come up with something."

A final pause.

"Good. See you then."

He ended the call and returned the phone to his belt.

"Let me catch you up on our little observation post here, so that you'll be a knowing and meaningful participant in our meeting tomorrow."

She smiled and wiped the remaining tears from her face.

"Thank you, Dixon."

———

Chapter Twenty-Six

"Yeah, he's holed up inside the mosque," Trask said. "I figured I'd get that out in front, just in case there was someone here who wasn't in on the world's worst-kept secret."

The snickers came from all around the table.

Trask looked around the conference room. Seal, Carter, Wisniewski, Lynn and Val from the violent crimes squad, Doroz and Buckley down from the SCIF, and McCarver from Park Police. All present and accounted for.

"The question on the floor for discussion is this. How do we get him out of there without starting a political firestorm and ending all of our illustrious careers? In Val's case, before hers really gets started."

A few more chuckles.

Good. The less tension, the more ideas.

"Let me start with the volunteer, *non-federal* surveillance team members who've been working around the clock to document the whereabouts of DeAnthony Barrett," Trask said.

"Behind my back and without approval," Seal growled. A smile followed the growl. "I'm proud as hell to know you."

"Synopsis, please, Dix," Trask said.

"Sure."

Carter pushed a button on the console and a screen dropped from the ceiling. A second button push resulted in the display of a surveillance photo of Barrett relaxing on a bench in the courtyard of the mosque. A third button push yielded the close-up of his face magnified from the first photo. The final button push displayed the surveillance close-up beside the mug shot from Barrett's arrest in Kansas.

"Other than age and some prison weight, I don't think there's any doubt we're looking at the same guy," Carter said. "Oh, and my partner gets all the credit for the pics."

Wisniewski stood and took a mock bow.

"He's been there every night after dark?" Seal asked.

"Almost," Carter responded. "He missed last Saturday night, and he was a couple of hours late last night. Must have been under the weather or something. Every other night for the past nine he's made a regular appearance about an hour after sundown."

"And this is Asalati's mosque?" Seal asked. "That radical asshole from TV?"

"He doesn't own it, boss," Lynn said, "but it *is* where he conducts services as an imam."

"And we can't just go in and grab this Barrett guy?" Seal shook his head. "You pirates find the thug who murdered at least three cops, maybe more, and we can't arrest him?"

"We'd be violating a presidential directive to enter the mosque, Rich," Doroz said. "I'm retired, but you're not and a lot of others here aren't either."

"Might be worth the early departure," Seal said. "Let me think about that for a minute."

"I'll go in with you," Buckley quipped.

Trask raised an eyebrow, thinking.

"I saw that," Carter said to Trask. "Something always happens when that happens."

"What happened?" Val asked.

"Dix, do you have your surveillance logs with you?" Trask asked, ignoring Val's question.

"Of course," Carter said, shoving a clipboard across the table. He turned to Val. "Shhh. Jeff's thinking again."

"You said he usually hits the courtyard about an hour after sunset," Trask said. "It looks like that's been running about eight p.m. or so every night, every night except last Saturday. What *did* happen last Saturday night—also at about eight p.m.—was the departure of a Chevy van from the garage. Thanks to Nick, we got the plates on the van when it arrived earlier that day, and thanks to the ever-vigilant eyes of Dixon Carter . . ."

"When the Nationals aren't on TV," Wisniewski said.

"Ignore him, Jeff," Carter said.

"Thanks to Detective Carter," Trask continued, "We know that the same van left the mosque's garage about eight, and after running the plates, Nick found that the van is registered to none other than mystery man number two, Abisali Ghilzai. I mention this for no other reason than tonight is Saturday night. What if the courtyard is becoming too small a place for our very large suspect, and his sponsor is taking him out for a night on the town? Traffic's lighter on Saturday, especially to the west."

I better stop there. Don't want to say too much about the camp.

"The town, or the country, or to kill more cops." McCarver mused. "Can we grab the van if it leaves the place tonight?"

"I wouldn't, Nick," Doroz said. "If Barrett *isn't* on board, it puts the whole target group on alert, and they move him to who-knows-where."

"The 'whole target group?'" McCarver asked.

Doroz glanced at Buckley, who looked at Trask, who looked back at Doroz.

"Since the dots on my neck are already perforated, let me try this," Trask said. "Nick, Rich, Lynn, Dix, and Tim, this is for you. Without totally throwing classified stuff all over the wall, let me just say that—based on facts that those of us sentenced to the SCIF have observed, and on theories not yet proven—we think we're into a cell of jihadists, that Barrett was recruited by them before he left Kansas, that he's here working with and for them now, and that they have something far worse up their sleeves than killing a couple more of us."

Trask looked at Buckley. "Safe?"

"Yeah, safe. For now."

"Good." Trask collected his thoughts before continuing. "Besides those considerations, we have Bear's very real concern—that Barrett might *not* be in the van, and that we would sound the alarm for the whole cell by taking it off—*and*, if I can play lawyer for a minute—we don't have probable cause yet to arrest either Asalati or even Abisali Ghilzai, whoever that is. If Barrett's not in the van with *whoever* the driver may be, we *still* won't have probable cause for an arrest of that driver."

Trask's left eyebrow went up again.

"I saw that *again*," Carter said. "Spill it."

Trask shrugged. "I just have a theory about Abisali Ghilzai. I think he has another name: Amal Saleem."

Doroz did a double take. "How do you connect *those* dots, Jeff?"

"It's still just a theory," Trask said. "And one I can only discuss with you and Buck for now, for obvious reasons."

"Obviously," Seal said sarcastically.

"Classified stuff, Rich." Trask said.

"Yeah. I got that."

"Let's follow the damned van," Doroz said.

"To where?" Buckley asked him.

"To wherever the thing goes, Buck," Doroz said. "What have we got to lose at this point? We've got enough bodies and cars, and enough people who know how to do it. We've even got a couple of ladies on the team to make it look like we have couples out for a Saturday night drive, or a trip to an in-law's house. If we're lucky, we spot our hulk with whoever the driver might be, and grab 'em both. I have a hunch that he's heading west, too. Like I said—what do we have to lose?"

"Nothing that I can see. Somebody will have to stay back in the hotel room to let us know if Barrett's not in the car," Lynn said.

"You're right," Carter said. "Tim just volunteered. He needs the practice."

"What!?" Wisniewski protested. "Why do I have to hang back? I'm the one who saw him down there in the first place!"

"Making you the most qualified to recognize him again," Carter said. "Besides, you're a non-federal, off-the-clock volunteer, remember? Some of these fine *federal* folks aren't *allowed* to look at the mosque. Got it?"

"Shit." Wisniewski slumped back in his chair, arms folded.

"Don't forget to keep the log and write the report," Carter added, sliding the clipboard over to him.

The laughs from the rest of the group finally made even Wisniewski crack up.

"Car assignments," Trask said. "If I can make some suggestions?"

"Shoot," Seal said. "I think I'm just along for the ride on this anyhow. You might as well tell me who I'm riding *with*."

"Thanks," Trask laughed. "I need to be in the c-car with Bear and Buck."

"The c-car?" Lynn asked.

"Classified, babe," Trask said. "Even Hillary knows what that means. She just won't admit it."

Some moans joined the giggles.

"We really might have to make some decisions based on the confidential info we can't share yet," he continued. "Plus, if I'm right, we'll want to hang back a little from the target car."

"Twenty bucks says you're wrong," Doroz said.

"Get your money ready," Trask responded. "Val can ride with Dix. They'll look like a couple. They're both black."

Carter roared.

Val just gave him a look and a shake of her head.

"Nick drives alone. He looks like a loner anyway. Lynn, you're with your boss, okay?"

"*We* look like a couple?" she asked.

"Any *other* questions?" Trask asked.

"If this works and we see Barrett . . .?" Doroz asked.

"It's his option as to how he wants to come in," McCarver said. "Much as I'd like him to pick door number three, it's his pick."

"By the book," Trask agreed. "If my hunch is correct, we'll have a presidential advisor to deal with, and if he's *not* a target, he'll be a witness."

"Cars assemble at seven-thirty," Doroz said. "Let's do it right. Nobody gets too close until we make our move. *Not* like the movies. No following right behind him for miles."

"Amen to that," Seal said.

"We'll take our cue to roll from our eye-in-the-sky, or at least a high floor of the hotel," Doroz continued.

Wisniewski just saluted.

———

Two blocks away from the mosque and the hotel, Trask sat in the back seat again. Doroz was driving, with Buckley in the front passenger seat as usual. The car was different this time.

"We should hang back on the surveillance relay until well after dark," Trask said, "just in case I'm right, Bear. We don't want Saleem or Ghilzai or whoever he is making our faces."

"I'm agreeing out of an abundance of caution only," Doroz said. "You should have that twenty ready for me. Why do you think Saleem isn't being straight with us, anyway?"

"A number of factors. One, for a so-called 'man of peace,' he has studied Sun Tzu and *The Art of War* enough to quote it, sometimes even accurately. Two, it should have been easy for him to remember *either* who told him about the *saaqhib*, or to provide us the names of some of the other radical imams surrounding Asalati. He couldn't, *or wouldn't*, because it would have given us something to check that would have spun back on him.

"Three, I had Lynn do a basic background profile on Saleem. As you know, being her former squad supervisor, she's damned good at those. Even though he claimed to have attended an American university and high school, we couldn't find any records to back that up. Saleem doesn't seem to have existed prior to twenty-seven months ago. Granted, things have been pretty chaotic in Afghanistan over the past several years between the Russian occupation, the Taliban, and our own combat ops there. I doubt very much if there's a bureau of vital statistics in Kabul that could come up with a birth certificate for *anyone* at this point.

"In addition, the names are just too coincidental. 'Abisali Ghilzai' loosely translates to 'a warrior' from one of the southern tribes in Afghanistan. Those are the ones near the Khyber Pass, the tribes that are still giving us fits. Some of the northern tribes were our closest allies after 9/11. If you're going to pretend to be a moderate Muslim, you couldn't find a better name than 'Amal Saleem,' which—again loosely translated—means 'hopeful for peace.' You don't want to carry a name that means, 'I like to fight and I hate Americans.'

"At any rate, a month or so before Amal Saleem springs into life out of thin air, Abisali Ghilzai visited DeAnthony Barrett at the state pen in Lansing, Kansas. Two weeks before that, he registered the van that I hope we'll be following tonight here in D.C., using a vacant lot as an address."

"You still don't have anything tying Saleem to Barrett, or the Kansas visit," Doroz said. "I'm not buying it."

"Just a slip of the tongue is all," Trask remarked. "During our first visit with him, he mentioned that he'd heard something about the camp 'out 66 Highway.' He didn't say 'I-66,' or even 'Highway 66.' He said '66 Highway.' Thanks to my roving JAG days, I think I visited almost every area of the country in my five years as a circuit prosecutor. I tried a couple of courts-martial at Whiteman Air Force Base, about an hour south and east of Kansas City.

"Every time I turned on the local news in my quarters at Whiteman, I heard Kansas City reporters talking about 'Seven Highway' or '40 Highway.' It's the *only* part of the country where I heard people flipping road and highway names like that. My guess is that our man Ghilzai-Saleem actually spent some time around Kansas City before migrating here."

"What about all of his knowledge of the moderate Muslim theories?" Buckley asked. "He seemed pretty convincing slinging that doctrine. I might want a piece of this bet, hoss."

"You're on, then," Trask said. "I have forty in my wallet, and it's just itching to turn into eighty."

"What about the moderate theories?" Doroz echoed Buckley's question.

"Even before he recommended that I do so, I'd been reviewing the *hadiths*," Trask said. "One of the prominent ones includes the doctrine of what the Muslims call *taqiyya*. Most Muslim clerics and scholars teach that the faithful should be truthful when dealing *with other Muslims*, but they make and even *urge* an exception when a believer is dealing with an infidel. If the lie advances the cause of Islam by earning the trust of gullible infidels—like the two in the front of this car—then the deception is not just tolerated, it's *encouraged*.

"Think about the opportunities that all this deception gives him. He sits at the hand of the president, maybe even soaking up loose remarks about our military intentions. He goes to the prisons—maybe even spouting moderation theories—and if some Black Lives Matter or other irate inmate wants to walk out, the good imam himself identifies them to Asalati for recruitment.

"I have some Qur'an citations that support my argument, too, not just the *hadiths*. Verse 16:106 says that there are circumstances that can even compel a Muslim to lie. Verse 3:54 mentions that Allah is the best of schemers, and the word actually used in the Arabic text is *makara*, which literally translates as 'deceit.' The *hadiths* I mentioned just expound upon the doctrine of these verses."

"I thought you were a history major," Doroz said.

"I actually had a double major," Trask responded. "History and humanities. Humanities was a catch-all for every other course the Academy offered which was not related to math, engineering, or flying. I had to take 'em all to stay on the dean's list so I could leave on the weekends, the only way to balance out the Cs I was getting in science and engineering. It included several courses in philosophy and comparative studies of various religions. Wanna hear about karma and Hindu reincarnation?"

"Probably not," Buckley said. "We could use some good karma tonight, though."

The radio in Buckley's lap chirped. Buckley hit a button, the radio came to life, and Wisniewski's voice came through the speaker.

"Open channel now, folks," Buckley cautioned, signaling the end of any classified conversation in the car. "What's up, Tim?"

"The van's rolling, people," Wisniewski said. "Good luck. Dix, if our target's confirmed, you damned well better let me know asap so I can get on the road to catch up."

"I'll think about it," Carter said from the car closest to the mosque. "There's a pretty prosecutor sitting next to me and I might get distracted. Jeff?"

Buckley held the radio up over the seat so that Trask could speak.

"Yeah, Dix?"

"Can I get in on the bet on Saleem?"

"Sure. I'm taking all comers. Anybody else? Lynn?"

"Oh, no. Been there and done that. Burned too often," she said.

"You're that sure he's right?" Seal asked as he pulled the car into traffic.

"Go ahead; join the pool, boss."

"No. I'll take your word for it. You're married to him."

"Car number one, what are we doing?" Doroz asked.

"We're apparently taking the scenic route out of town," Carter said. "Turning south on Louisiana, probably west on Constitution if Barry's hunch was right. Yep. Target van westbound on Constitution. We're about three cars behind him."

"Rich?" Doroz asked.

"About half a block behind Dix," Seal responded.

"Nick?"

"Five behind the Grog."

"Good. We've got eyes on *you*, about four cars back. Let's all stay in touch. We'll leap-frog when the lead car calls the shot. Keep us posted, Dix."

"Will do, Bear. Passing Main Justice now. Want to stop in, Jeff?"

"Hell, no."

"Didn't think so."

Trask looked to his right as the car he was riding in passed the Justice Department building.

If this goes badly tonight, the only reason I'd ever be in there again would be for a very high-level ass-chewing.

"Passing the Washington Monument," Carter said from the lead car. "Still about half a block behind the van."

The monolith came up to the south.

Closed until sometime this fall while they fix the elevator. Not many tourists are in shape to climb five-hundred feet without it.

Trask looked to the south as his car passed the Reflecting Pool. The Lincoln Memorial stood guard over the west end.

Here's where all the mess started, at least as far as we knew at the time. Now I think it started somewhere a lot farther west—in Kansas.

"We're across old Teddy's bridge, and he's staying on I-66 west," Carter said.

Trask nodded as his car crossed the Theodore Roosevelt Bridge over the Potomac.

Ghilzai, Saleem—whoever's driving—is calling it '66 Highway' in his head.

"Radio's off," Buckley said from the front seat. "We may be headed to the mountains again, Bear."

"That far? How do you figure that?" Doroz asked.

"No reason. Just a hunch," Buckley said, pulling a handgun from a holster on his belt. "You carryin' again, Jeff?"

"My little pocket Sig. The cops in Virginia still haven't released the one I had to use at Arlington."

"Good. Better than nothing if it's needed. How does it shoot?"

"I'm decent with it inside 25 feet."

Buckley laughed. "An honest man. Radio's back on."

"We're leaving Falls Church, still heading west," Carter said. "Traffic's light for this road."

"Everybody tighten the line," Doroz instructed. "We may have to play leap-frog in a little bit."

"Roger," McCarver said.

"Got it," Seal responded.

"He's pulling off for gas," Carter said. "We'll follow him in to the pumps. I'll fill up and Val can use the restroom—"

"But I don't need—"

"Like I said," Carter continued, "Val can use the restroom, because that's what females do when guys stop to fill up. We may be able to get eyes on the driver."

"Do you need to use the restroom?" Seal asked Lynn.

"No!"

"Everybody else take the next exit past the gas station and wait on a side road. We can't all pull in there at the same time," Doroz said. "We'll roll again when Dix gives us the cue."

"I'll flip on the side road and pull in behind the van when he comes by," McCarver said. "He hasn't seen me in his rear-view yet."

"That works." Doroz was nodding with approval in the front seat. "Got your twenty ready for me, Jeff?"

"I have my wallet open, but it's programmed to receive," Trask answered.

Programmed to receive. "Hotel California," if I'm not mistaken.

"I have the driver in sight at the pump," Carter said. "Mr. Trask just won sixty bucks."

"I'll be a son-of-a-bitch!" Buckley exclaimed.

Doroz just shook his head.

"Should've known," he said, handing a twenty backward. His action was duplicated shortly thereafter by his passenger.

"A pleasure, gentlemen," Trask said, inserting the bills into his wallet.

They passed the exit where the van and Carter had turned off. Trask looked to his right and saw in the distance that the van was still parked under the lights of the pump island.

Doroz pulled the car off at the next exit. They headed north about 100 yards before Doroz waved at McCarver as they passed Nick's car, already turned and ready to get back on the interstate.

"We'll flip and get behind him in a minute," Doroz said. "There's Lynn and the Grog."

The car driven by Seal passed them on the way to line up behind McCarver.

"Decent technique, even for cops and Bureau guys," Buckley noted.

"Glad you approve," Doroz said. "Jeff, do we need to notify anybody in your chain that we're following a presidential advisor and confidant?"

"Probably, but we're not going to. If Barrett's in the back of that car, I want hard evidence—hopefully with photos—of Saleem harboring that known fugitive before we give anybody a chance to try and put another political lid on anything."

"I like this guy, Bear," Buckley said. "A lawyer with common sense. Who'd have thunk it?"

"I'm with you, Jeff," Doroz said. "Just wanted to make sure we were on the same page."

"He's rolling again," Carter said over the radio.

"I'll pull in behind him when I see him pass," McCarver said.

"I'm rolling," he said a couple of minutes later.

"Space it out again, folks," Doroz cautioned as they began moving. "We're driving in the country now."

"I'm a quarter-mile back of him," McCarver said. "He's got it set on three over the limit, being very careful. I'll have to vary speed and probably pass him, or he'll get suspicious."

"Do what you need to do," Doroz said. "Rich and Lynn can pull up the line."

"I'm passing, then," McCarver said.

"We have him," Seal acknowledged. "We'll come up real slow on him for a while—should be okay for a bit."

Fifteen minutes later, Seal was back on the radio.

"He's turning north on I-81."

Doroz shot a look at Buckley, who simply nodded.

"All cars abort for now," Doroz said. "Find a place to sit and wait. Sorry, boys and girls, but they're heading to secretville, and we can't tell you anything yet."

"Shit," McCarver said.

"Ditto," Carter said.

"Jeff, be careful, damn it," Lynn said. "I love you."

"Dix," Doroz asked, "before we go off-radio for a while, can you check with Tim . . ."

"Already did. No sign of Barrett at the mosque."

"Thanks. Everybody sit tight for a while. This could take some time. We'll be back in contact when we can."

———

Chapter Twenty-Seven

Abisali Ghilzai, also known as Amal Saleem, pulled the van into the clearing beside the lake. He walked to the edge of the water and waited for Hassan to bring the chairs. His would still be a light, aluminum and plastic contraption. He'd sprung for a wooden Adirondack model to provide better support for Hassan.

They settled into their seats, Ghilzai going over the weather maps he'd brought, checking the wind patterns again and again. Barrett just leaned back, closed his eyes, and breathed as deeply as a man could breathe.

Doroz pulled the car slowly along the back road into the George Washington National Forest.

"Better go dark," Buckley warned him.

"Good idea."

Doroz switched off the car's headlights.

"We'll have to go in on foot," Buckley said. He turned around toward Trask. "Got your hiking boots on?"

"Afraid not. Comfortable street shoes."

"Want to stay with the car?" Doroz asked him.

"Not a chance. Besides, we only have one radio."

"That's a point," Buckley said. "Can you keep up?"

"Watch me."

"We will." Buckley got out of the car and headed for the trunk. "Let me put my toy together."

He popped the lid and pulled out a case that opened to reveal an ominous-looking assault weapon. He attached a suppressor to the end, inserted a magazine, and grabbed a spare one, shoving it down into a front pocket of his cargo pants.

"No disrespect to your pocket pistol," he told Trask, "but I'd rather have this if we run into your man Barrett in the dark."

Trask looked at the weapon.

"MP5?" he asked.

"We have a winner." Buckley's smile was visible in the moonlight. "Let's go find 'em."

Trask peered through the dim light at the rough, unpaved road leading into the woods.

"How far do we have to go?"

"Couple of clicks," Buckley said.

Buckley led the way, half-walking, half-loping up the trail. Doroz followed, taking four strides to Buckley's two. Trask found himself gasping for air as he brought up the rear, trying to make his rapid breathing as quiet as he could. After fifteen minutes that seemed more like forty, Trask saw Buckley's hand rise in a stop signal.

"I don't think they went to the camp," he whispered to Trask and Doroz. "The van tracks peel off this way."

He pointed to the right down an even narrower, unpaved road. Trask peered into the darkness at his feet, trying to make out the clue. Failing, he just shrugged.

Glad you're in front, big guy. Didn't know I'd need my glasses tonight.

"Real slow and quiet now. Watch your step; roll your feet." Buckley warned. Trask thought he saw Buckley flip the safety on the submachine gun.

———

Ghilzai looked at the weather map for the hundredth time.

We have planned well. Tomorrow will be a day for the history books, for history books centuries from now. I shall miss Asalati. He has been a good companion and pupil. He will be honored by all the faithful.

"Saaqhib?"

"Yes, Hassan? What is it?"

"I'm staying here. I'm not going back to the mosque tonight. I can't stay there anymore."

"Are you sure, Hassan? We have other missions planned for you."

"I can stay at the camp. I lived there before. You can always come and get me."

Ghilzai nodded. He was about to reach for the pistol in his waistband when he heard something. He reached instead for his cell phone, and typed a brief text message before pressing the 'send' icon.

———

Buckley turned when he heard Doroz trip behind him. He put his finger over his mouth, cautioning both Doroz and Trask not to move or speak.

They remained frozen for several minutes, hoping that the continued silence would quieten whatever concerns the sound of Doroz's fall might have generated in their targets.

Buckley broke the freeze. He pointed down the trail, silently asking Doroz if he could go on.

Doroz grimaced, pointing toward his ankle and shaking his head from side to side.

"Think I sprained it," he whispered.

Buckley looked at Trask, again pointing and asking the question with his eyes. Trask nodded and stepped around Doroz, patting him on the shoulder as he passed.

They moved forward even more slowly now. Trask thought about ditching his shoes, answering his own mental question in the negative.

I never went bare-footed, even as a kid. If I stepped on a pebble, I'd yell like a little girl. I'll just be careful.

Buckley had the stop sign up again. Then he waved Trask forward with one hand, following that signal with another—both hands palms down—to come up slowly and stay down.

Trask crouched forward and pulled even with Buckley, coming up on the taller man's left side. The van was parked a few feet in front of them and to their left. To the right and twenty yards in front of the van, two men sat in folding chairs facing a small lake, their backs to Buckley and Trask. One of the men in the chairs was small; the other was huge. The break in the pines above the lake let the moonlight illuminate the scene.

Finally. That's like a spotlight compared to the gloom we've been tromping through for the last hour.

They froze again, Buckley training his weapon on the targets. He motioned Trask toward the van.

He wants me to take cover behind the truck.

Trask started to rise from his crouch, gripping the little Sig Sauer with his trigger finger along the slide of the pistol and watching the targets in front of him as he began to move. What he saw next froze him again, this time in complete surprise.

The smaller man in the chairs was suddenly holding a pistol, pointing it not at the hunters behind him, but at the much larger man in the chair beside him. Trask saw the bright flame from the muzzle flash as the pistol fired at DeAnthony Barrett's head. Instead of falling, however, Barrett moved like a huge cat, knocking the gun out of Ghilzai's hand, and grabbing the smaller man's head with two monstrous hands.

Trask heard a scream, followed by a sickening, crunching sound. Barrett threw the body of his *saaqhib* into the shallow water at the edge of the lake, then turned toward them, reaching for the wound on his ear.

He saw them just as Buckley opened fire. Trask thought he saw at least one round strike Barrett's leg before the giant figure was out of sight, limp-running to their right around the edge of the lake.

Buckley pointed again toward the van.

"Use it as cover. I'll follow him, maybe drive him around to you. He'll want the truck to get out of here. If I don't get him, you do. Wait until he's inside your effective range, but don't let him get close. I think I nicked him, so he shouldn't be moving too fast, but don't take any chances. Empty your mag."

"Got it," Trask said.

If I don't have a heart attack first.

Buckley moved off like a cat around the right side of the lake.

Trask positioned himself behind the van, gazing at the left side of the lake through the darkness. He rested the little pistol on the hood of the vehicle, figuring that it would stabilize his aim, and hoping at the same time that he'd never need it. Some clouds moved in front of the moon, reducing visibility to mere feet.

I have to be as still as possible, as quiet as possible, like I was in church during a prayer, or at the movies. The movies? I forgot to silence my cell phone.

First the bat phone.

He reached for his shirt pocket. It wasn't there.

I must have dropped the damned thing. Probably never find it. That's a few hundred I'll owe for a worthless, useless piece of junk. Wonderful.

He kept his gaze across the hood of the van while reaching for his belt, the Sig in his right hand, his own phone in his left. He took the Samsung, held it close to minimize any light from the device, pulled the top menu bar down, and killed the speaker.

A noise behind him made him turn quickly. Spinning to his right, he saw Doroz limping slowly down the trail toward him, his handgun in one hand, his left hand up in a caution sign. It was what he saw behind Doroz that sent a chill down his back.

DeAnthony Barrett was barely concealed by the trees on the far side of the road, making his way slowly but steadily toward the limping Doroz.

He's too close. Bear won't have a chance.

Trask froze for a second, but saw something shiny, about ten feet up the trail behind both Doroz and Barrett.

The bat phone!

He pushed a symbol on his Galaxy, and the cell phone's obnoxious, generic ringtone sprang to life. Barrett spun around just as he stepped into the trail behind Doroz, trying to see who or what was behind him.

"Bear! Down!" Trask yelled as he tried to draw a bead on Barrett with the little Sig.

Doroz dropped to the ground.

Trask never got the chance to fire. A steady stream of forty-caliber rounds screamed over Doroz's head, slamming repeatedly into the huge figure of DeAnthony Barrett.

"Nice work for a lawyer," Buckley said as he came around the other side of the van. "He must have circled around behind me. See if you can find the keys to this thing on your friend in the water. Bear's not in any shape to walk very far. We'll throw the bodies in the back. You drive the car; I'll get the truck."

———

Aashif Asalati finished his time in the bathtub of his quarters in the mosque. He had shaved every bit of his body—at least every area he could reach—and felt clean enough to meet his maker. He dried himself, put on white robes, and knelt—facing the east—to offer his prayers.

I am ready. Tomorrow will be my day. No, that is a selfish thought. It will be a day for all of the faithful, for Allah.

He passed the little table where he ate his meals, and where he charged the cell phone. A light on it blinked, indicating that he had received a message.

The saaqhib has called to wish me luck tomorrow.

He picked up the phone and noticed that the message was a text, not a voicemail. When he read the message, he dropped the phone and ran to find his car keys. He bolted for the door, leaving the phone on the table. He would never need it again.

———

Chapter Twenty-Eight

"Meet us at that truck stop in Winchester," Doroz said into his radio as he tried to find a position more comfortable for his sprained ankle.

"We're all already there," McCarver said. "We were about to come looking for you guys. It's past midnight."

"Are you okay, Jeff?" Lynn's voice was the next to respond.

"I'm fine, babe," Trask said from the driver's seat of the car. He looked out at the West Virginia hills as the car approached the Virginia state line. John Denver's "Country Roads" was playing through his mind.

"Everybody else good?" Carter asked.

"All the good guys are still good," Doroz said. "Buck's driving the bad guys' van, and their condition is not good at all. They're both dead, and in the back of the van."

"Anybody nicked on our side?" Seal asked. "I have a first-aid kit in the car."

"I just rolled my ankle, Grog. I'm good, really," Doroz said. "Rest of our team is totally unscathed. Just a little dusty."

"You didn't want to call somebody to process the crime scene?" Seal asked him.

"We're still swimming in very classified waters, Rich. Besides that, they would never have found us before daylight, and there may be more dominos to fall. Dix, can you call Tim and see if he's seen Asalati tonight?"

"I'll do that."

"Good. We'll meet everyone in the parking lot in about fifteen."

The car and the van crossed the line into Virginia.

Trask steered the car as he followed the van off the interstate and into the parking lot. The rest of the surveillance team had parked on one side of the lot, away from the pumps and the all-night restaurant.

Buckley bounded out of the van as Trask pulled the car beside it.

"There was a briefcase under the driver's seat, Jeff. It kept sliding out and hitting my heel every time I braked. You and Bear might want to help me see if there's anything worth seeing, now that we've got enough light to see with."

"Those weather maps around the chairs at the lake worried me enough," Trask said.

"Classified, remember?" Doroz limped around the side of the car to the van.

"Oh yeah." Trask held up his hands as the rest of the team approached. "Give us five, guys."

"Nothing to see here, people," McCarver quipped from the group. "Our self-contained termination and clean-up crew is comparing notes."

"Really, Nick. Five minutes," Doroz said.

Buckley popped the case open and pointed a flashlight at the contents. Trask took the lead in examining the papers inside.

"Jeff?" Val called from the group behind them. "Do we need any kind of warrant for that? Just asking."

"Warrants are for people who have reasonable expectations of privacy," he answered. "The guys in the back of this truck are dead. They don't have an expectation of breakfast."

"Sorry," she said.

"No problem. Thanks for the input."

Trask examined the contents of the case.

The first few pages on top were more weather maps, with red markers showing that the low pressure system in the center of the country was flowing eastward, above the dip in the jet stream. The counter-clockwise rotation of the low's airflow was circled, and the wind direction marked with an arrow pointing to the northeast. The high to the east of the jet stream was similarly marked, the vector of the wind currents from that system pointing parallel to the direction of the winds from the low. Another red arrow was marked between the fronts, running southwest to northeast, along the eastern edge of the jet stream, pointing directly toward the District of Columbia.

"What's with all the interest in the weather?" Buckley whispered.

"Don't know yet," Trask said, leafing through the other related pages on the top of the stack. "These look like maps for tomorrow. They're almost identical to the ones we saw at the lake, but marked up. Did you grab those maps by the chairs, Buck?"

"Yeah, right after we loaded Saleem's soakin'-wet corpse into the van. You need 'em?"

"I don't think so."

Trask turned over another page. The diagram he saw appeared to have been downloaded from the Internet. It explained in detail the composition of the bomb used by Timothy McVeigh to destroy the federal building in Oklahoma City.

Trask winced. "This isn't good."

He turned and called over his shoulder to the group still standing twenty feet away.

"Dix, did you reach Tim?"

"Yeah. He's headed this way in case we needed him. He said Asalati left the mosque in his own car about an hour ago."

Trask returned to the briefcase. The page under the McVeigh recipe was a series of calculations. Trask recognized the chemical symbol $N2H4O3$.

"Shit!" he said.

"What's up?" Doroz asked.

"These are calculations for ammonium nitrate mixtures. Somebody's been building a bomb."

Trask turned the page over. The light hit a satellite photo of a row of silo-like structures arranged in rows of two, surrounded by a tall fence. A short distance away, two large, globe-like structures rose along the banks of a river.

"Oh, no. Oh, no!"

He grabbed the first page again from the stack, and traced the arrow pointing toward Washington back down to its base. He whirled around and called for Lynn.

"Babe? Do you remember where Asalati parked his plane?"

She started to step forward. Doroz had his hand up holding her back, but Trask pulled it down.

"We don't have time for that now, Bear. I think Asalati's planning to hit a nuclear waste storage facility tonight. If he cracks these casks open and the weather pattern does what he wants it to do, Washington will be glowing in the dark for the next millennium."

Doroz waved her forward.

"I remember," she said. "Manassas Regional. He has a Beechcraft 60, twin-engine, the model they call 'the Duke.' His aircraft number has a '247' in it. I remembered that 'cause it was like a business being open twenty-four-seven. I don't remember the rest of the numbers or letters. The number's painted on the side of the plane, not on the tail."

"Somebody google that plane model on their phone, please," Trask requested. "What's its payload?"

"Payload?" Seal asked, pulling his cell phone out of its case.

"You know," Trask said. "How much weight can it hold when it takes off with a full tank of gas?"

"Working on that," Seal said.

"Thanks. Dix, start Tim toward the airfield, lights and siren if he's got 'em. He's closer than we are by a long shot. Ask him to contact the Manassas police and see if they can cut off Asalati before he gets that plane airborne."

"I'm on it," Carter said.

"Wikipedia says that Beechcraft can lift about 2,500 pounds," Seal reported.

Trask shook his head. "So he's probably got at least a ton of explosives on board, plus his fuel in the plane."

McCarver stepped up beside Trask.

"I'm missing some things here, Jeff. We've been out of your classified loop. Where's he going?"

Trask put the weather map with the markings next to the satellite view of the power plant.

"This is the nuclear power plant at North Anna, in Louisa County, Virginia. This fenced pen down here has twenty-seven of these dry storage casks. Each one is designed to hold thirty-two spent fuel assemblies. There are 264 rods in each fuel assembly, and each of those rods of spent fuel is twelve feet long and holds hundreds of pellets of nuclear fuel. We're talking tons of stored nuclear waste with a half-life of well over two thousand years. There's a fence around the joint and probably additional security of some sort, but there's nothing *covering* it. Nothing at all over the top, meaning it's vulnerable to an air attack, and Asalati has a plane. If he has a ton of explosives loaded on that plane and crashes it into those casks, whatever leaks out will be picked up and carried by these winds—"

Trask grabbed the map with red markings and pointed to the base of the center arrow.

"That's North Anna, there, at the bottom of the arrow. The current winds are indicated by the markings, and will take whatever goes up in the blast straight over Washington, then to Philly, then to the rest of the population centers up the coast, including New York."

"I've got a light bar in my car," McCarver said. "I can lead the convoy. Where do we need to be?"

"At an airport in Manassas," Trask said. "Three hours ago."

———

Aashif Asalati was second-guessing himself. Instead of taking I-66 west out of Washington, he had opted for the back roads through Burke and Fairfax Station, reasoning that the police might be looking for him on the main roads. The *saaqhib's* message had just instructed him to go immediately, with no other details, and he did not know what state of alert the enemy might be in. He was not familiar with the route he had chosen, and had already been forced to backtrack twice, as he repeatedly found himself headed north or south, instead of west toward the airport in Manassas.

He checked his watch. It read 1:46 a.m.

The tower will not be operating, but that is not my concern. All I have to do is reach my aircraft.

He passed a sign reading "Compton Road."

Finally. I know that route. It will take me to Highway 28. I can take the highway south through town and to the airport.

———

McCarver was second in the row of cars as they raced south and east back toward Manassas and the capital. They were doing just under a hundred miles per hour, and had picked up another escort, a Virginia State Trooper who had initially wanted to write them all a series of tickets, but who had taken the lead after seeing several different kinds of badges and having a heated thirty-second conversation with McCarver and Buckley.

"Tim has a lookout for Asalati's car on the air," Carter said over the radio. "Red Ford Fusion, DC plates: OPM-202."

Doroz was looking at his phone, which was in the process of another Internet search.

"If this is accurate, Manassas Regional's tower ops closed at 2230, hours ago. If he gets to his plane, he'll have to take off dark. Probably no runway lights operating."

"Hell, it's not like he would have filed a flight plan," Trask said.

"You're right," Doroz said. He entered another search phrase. "North Anna is close to a little town called Mineral. It's only seventy miles south of Manassas. If he gets the plane up, we won't have much time, even if he gets slowed down a bit fighting the headwinds. What the hell do we do if he gets off the ground?"

"Hold the radio up for me," Trask said.

Doroz put it close to Trask's head as Trask steered the car.

"Buck? Do you or your national JTTF headquarters have a direct line to the DOD folks?"

"Yeah, of course."

"Better get 'em patched through, quickly please. Highest level possible. Hell, get the Secretary of Defense on the line. We may not have time to climb any chain of command. Pull every emergency string you've got."

———

Asalati took the exit south and eastward onto the Prince William Parkway, running in front of the Manassas Regional Airport. He looked in his rear-view mirror and saw that a police cruiser, with lights flashing, was nearing the cloverleaf behind him on Highway 28.

I must assume that they are looking for me.

He turned off his headlights and took a left turn, *away* from the airport. He parked the Ford, got out, and took a pair of bolt cutters from the trunk. He pulled a leather flight jacket over his Afghani *qmis* and jogged toward the border of the airport, heading for the concealment offered by groves of trees behind a furniture store.

———

"Lynn, where is Asalati's aircraft parked at the airport?" Trask asked over the radio.

"I just got the registration info. I didn't get any hangar information, Jeff. It would have required talking to the people at the airport, and—"

"—And we didn't want them alerting him. Got it. The place will be all shut down now; no way to call and ask."

Doroz held the radio back close to his own face.

"Tim, are you in range?"

"Roger," Wisniewski said.

"Are you still in contact with Manassas PD?"

"Can be in no time. I'm following one of their units now, rolling in front of the airport."

"You're there now? You don't see any planes taking off, do you?"

"No, the place looks deserted."

"See if the PD has an emergency contact number for an airport manager or something. We need to know where Asalati hangars his plane."

"Will do."

"How far away are we?" Trask asked.

"If we don't slow down, and don't all die in a pile up because something pulls out in front of that trooper, we should be there in about twenty minutes," Doroz said.

"Tell our lead car to speed up, then," Trask said. "Buck, how are we doing with that DOD contact?"

———

Asalati reached the gate to the rear of the building bearing the sign, "Dulles Aviation." He used the bolt cutters to snap the chain padlocking the gate, opened it, and stepped through. He ran toward the Beechcraft that was already parked outside the hangar, on the apron of the tarmac.

It was a good idea to leave it outside overnight. We tied it down securely and left the windows cracked a bit in case the fumes from the fuel oil started to seep out of the containers. I will not have to deal with the hangar doors now. Just cut the tie-down cables and take off.

––––––

"Airport manager says that Asalati's Beechcraft is usually hangered in one of the Dulles Aviation hangars on the far side," Wisniewski reported. "Manassas PD and I are rolling toward that building now."

Buckley's voice came over the radio. "Jeff, I can have SecDef on line in about two minutes."

"We're turning off toward the airport," Doroz said.

"We should know whether we'll need his help very shortly, Buck," Trask said. "Hold for now."

He took the airport exit hard behind McCarver's car, the tires squealing as he made the turn.

"Oh, shit!" Wisniewski's voice screamed.

"Details, Tim!" Carter's shout over the radio was just as loud, just as on edge.

"He has the plane out already, props running! He's on the end of the runway, about to take off!"

"Tim, can you ram him, cut him off?" Trask's tone was quieter, flat. He was all too aware of what he was asking.

"Just a ton of bombs on board? Yeah. Why not? Wish me luck, folks."

Wisniewski gunned his car from behind the Manassas Police unit and passed it, speeding across the infield of the dark airport toward the main runway.

––––––

Asalati sat in the pilot's seat and pushed the throttle forward. The engines of the Beechcraft roared louder. He released the brakes and the plane lurched forward.

There's a lot of wind. I'll have to watch out for the shear. I'll be fighting the headwinds once I'm up.

He was pushing the plane forward at its top speed when he saw the car screech onto the runway at the far end. It turned hard, almost rolling over, then the driver gained control and Asalati saw the headlights coming toward him.

He tried to force the throttle even farther forward, and grabbed the controls, ready to pull backward and lift the plane into the air.

———

"Just a big game of chicken now!" Wisniewski yelled as he floored the accelerator, heading straight for the oncoming plane.

Two propellers! I'll point it between them. Oh, I forgot. There's a bomb on board that thing, too. Hell, no time to jump. Sorry, Randi.

He held the steering wheel steady as he raced toward the oncoming plane. At the last second before impact, he involuntarily ducked and closed his eyes. He heard the roar of the aircraft's engines as the plane lifted off and passed inches above his windshield.

He hit the brakes and skidded to a stop.

"Sorry, folks, he's up. I missed him."

"We saw," Doroz answered. "We're rolling in now, buddy. Helluva try."

"Dammit!" Wisniewski yelled. "Dammit!"

"We're working on our last contingency, Tim," Trask said. "It's not over yet."

———

Asalati turned the Beechcraft southward and into the wind, which was picking up rapidly.

It would be good if Allah could hold his breath for just a few moments. He can exhale again when I reach the target.

The plane bucked as he tried to find an altitude where the buffeting was not so severe.

I do not want the cargo to detonate before I get there!

He found quieter air at about 5,400 feet.

I should be there soon. Counting the time to line up the target, I have about twenty-five minutes left.

He began to sing an Islamic call to prayer.

————

The convoy pulled to a stop on the tarmac. They were out of their vehicles, watching helplessly as the blinking lights of the Beechcraft disappeared southward into the dark, early morning sky.

"The secretary's on the horn, Jeff," Buckley said. "Take our last shot."

Trask took the radio.

"Sir, this is Jeff Trask. I'm a federal prosecutor in the DC office working with Mr. Buckley and the JTTF. . ."

"Aren't you the guy from that Arlington shootout, Mr. Trask?"

"Yes, sir. I'm the guy from the Arlington shootout. Mr. Secretary, we don't have a second to waste, so I'm going to get to it.

"There is a Beechcraft 60 in the air now. He just took off from Manassas Regional Airport. You can confirm that with any of the air traffic control towers in the region—Dulles, Reagan, Langley, Richmond—somebody should have him on scope. The pilot is Aashif Asalati . . ."

"Isn't he—?"

"Yeah, the nut job from TV. That's right. Sir, our investigation tonight has confirmed that this guy and a terrorist cell he helped manage are responsible for the recent police murders in the area. We also have proof that he has a ton of explosives on board that aircraft, and that he intends to fly it into the storage casks stored at the nuclear power plant at North Anna, Virginia."

"The *what*!?"

"Sir, North Anna is a major nuclear power facility. They have twenty-seven silos full of nuclear waste sitting out in the open. They are vulnerable to an aerial attack like this. If they go up in a blast, the wind currents are going to carry that gunk straight to the capitol building and beyond."

"You said 'proof' . . ."

"Maps and documents. Maps charting the weather patterns from North Anna. Documents showing how to make a fertilizer bomb, the same kind McVeigh used at Oklahoma City. He has a ton of the stuff on board, and there are hundreds of tons of nuclear waste at North Anna."

Trask thought for a second.

"The papers were found in a van with the guy who killed the officer at the Lincoln Memorial. We saw him kill Amal Saleem tonight, the president's advisor."

There was a very brief pause.

"Suggestions, Trask?"

"Call the air base at Langley, sir. Quickly, please. They're the closest to his target. If they have fighters on alert they might be able to respond."

"Thank you, Mr. Trask. I'll issue the order."

Buckley looked at Trask with a scowl on his face.

"We're making Saleem a *hero*?"

"Would you rather him be a martyr for the radicals?" Trask asked. "If the secretary has to call the president first, do we get an order faster if a trusted advisor has been murdered, or if we have to answer for him being an un-vetted mad scientist who may have had a hand in whacking police officers? If we get through this night, Abisali Ghilzai will be remembered by another name as a tragic, heroic voice of moderation. Hell, we may have to attend *his* funeral. I just thought we'd get faster approval this way."

"What do we do now?" Doroz asked.

"Wait and pray," Trask said.

"The hell with that. I'm going to go get our dogs," Lynn said. She held out her hand, and Trask tossed her the keys to Buckley's car. "Head straight back here, and please be careful."

Buckley stared at him. "What the hell?"

"Those dogs are her kids. You try and stop her," Trask said.

———

Major Michael Wims of the 1st Fighter Wing, Joint Base Langley-Eustis, roared off the runway and climbed rapidly. His F-22 Raptor turned hard to the west. He had to make up as much of the hundred miles between the coastline and North Anna as possible in order to make the air-to-air launch as successful as it could be.

"You have authority to engage," the voice said over his radio. "Engage as soon as you can make the shot."

"Roger."

Every detail about the AIM 120D missiles hanging on his aircraft went through Wims's mind.

Once I launch, the missile will run at Mach 4. Max range about 112 miles, so with a perfect shot, I could even fire now. Just have to make sure the target's acquired and locked on.

He checked the radar screen.

There he is. Target acquired. Close to the damn power plant already. They said these AMRAAMs were "fire and forget" weapons. Hope they're right about this one. It hits or we'll have a lot to try and forget.

"Missile away," he announced. "I'll follow to assess."

———

Asalati fought to maintain control of the aircraft as he descended toward his target. The surface winds were even stronger than the ones he had battled at higher altitude, and he realized that he had flown slightly to the east of his intended course. The turn back into the west would be too sharp to make.

No matter. Instead of attacking from the north, as I had planned, I can turn past and come back in from the other direction. I will have to account for the wind shear from the south, and include that in my approach calculations.

He saw the complex passing by off to his right.

They left just enough lights on for me to line up the target. They are so huge I could have probably seen them in the moonlight.

He steered the Beechcraft south and to the east, and then began a slow turn back toward the two rows of huge casks. He put the plane into a shallow dive, fighting to maintain a level horizon indicator as the winds tried to push him north of his target. A sudden reduction in the velocity of the gusts allowed him to make a last-second course correction as he approached the southern fence line.

Allah is with me. I will go in just over the top of the barrier. My impact point will be immediately between the two rows.

"Allahu—!"

The missile struck from the rear just as the plane crossed the top of the fence, detonating the explosives on board and sending a huge fireball into the night sky. The southernmost four storage casks rocked outward from the initial force of the blast, their reinforced concrete walls collapsing under the pressure. They then rebounded inward to the center of the enclosure, completely collapsing into each other.

The winds began to blow with increased velocity, carrying the gigantic cloud from the explosion northeastward, directly toward Washington, D.C.

———

Epilogue

Two hours later, Trask's bat phone rang. He spoke for a moment, then returned the device to his shirt pocket.

"I just talked to the Secretary of Defense again," Trask said. "The pilot from Langley said he was too late."

Trask felt his knees starting to buckle. He sat back, resting on the bumper of the van with the bodies still in the back.

"He said the fireball was massive, and then he saw collapsed casks blown all over the compound."

The rest of the team stood in silence, still on the tarmac at the Manassas Airport, unable to move, not knowing what action to take next.

Trask's regular phone—the one on his belt—rang next.

"Yeah, babe. Just head on back to the airport. Keep heading as far west as you can before the dirty air gets there. We'll figure something out when you get here. Be careful."

Buckley's radio beeped. He changed frequencies and walked a short distance away from the group. McCarver was looking at Buckley with his hands extended and palms upward, a gesture eloquently asking a question that could not be repeated in polite circles. Buckley saw him and started walking back to the group.

"Sorry," he said. Habit."

Suddenly, he stopped in his tracks.

"Are you sure? Don't say it unless you are, damn you, Hank! Are you really sure?"

He let out a whoop and started whirling around, doing a strange but very happy dance.

"The casks on that end were empty! The asshole hit the south end of the row where nothing was stored yet! The security team at North Anna said they have a crack in one cask that might have to be sealed up, but no major leaks! There's nothing in that air blowing toward DC *except a bunch of freakin' air!*"

Trask slumped forward and put his head in his hands.

I have always believed in one God. One God for all of us. He was with us tonight, and I don't care what name He uses.

They all met at the center of the line of cars and huddled together for several minutes, hugging, laughing, and catching their breaths.

Buckley's car pulled up with Lynn driving and three dogs in the back seat.

"Buck," Trask almost giggled. "I think my ride's here. At least your car's here."

"Hell, keep it 'til Monday," Buckley said, waving off the suggestion. "I still have bodies to bury, maybe literally. I'll take the van."

Trask waved to Seal. "I'm riding with Lynn. We're going home."

Seal waved back. "Tell her to take Monday off."

"I'll ride with Buck," Doroz shouted, limping toward the van.

"I'm outta here, too," Wisniewski said. "I think I need a change of underwear."

Carter and Val rolled slowly by in the other car, and waved as they drove toward the airport exit.

"So how do you like the mundane routine of federal law enforcement?" Carter asked her.

"I've got such an adrenaline rush going right now, I know I'm not going to be able to sleep for two days. When I finally collapse, I'll sleep for a week."

"I'll drop you at your place," Carter said. "I have some stuff I need to pick up at the hotel."

"I'll go back there with you," she said, reaching for his hand. "I've been wanting to take a chance with you and to ask you to take one with me. It just seems like this might be the right time. We *do* have a room already."

"Dixon, you guys left your radio on," Trask said.

Lynn laughed and turned on the car's FM radio. Johnny Nash was singing something about the rain being gone.

Author's Notes

I hope that you have enjoyed reading *A Winter of Wolves*, the fourth novel in the Jeff Trask crime drama series. I'd like to offer a few remarks by way of explanation concerning some of the issues raised in what I hope you found to be a compelling, contemporary historical novel. Many of these issues are important to me, and I hope you'll spend a few more minutes with me as I explain why.

In 2015, I retired from the United States Department of Justice after more than 25 years of service as an Assistant United States Attorney. Counting five additional years as an Air Force JAG circuit prosecutor, I am proud to be able to claim three decades of service helping to enforce the laws of this country.

I had planned to serve longer, but instead retired a year short of my full retirement date, as that date was defined by Social Security computations. The reasons for my premature departure had nothing to do with the extraordinary people with whom it was my great pleasure to work, at least in the "worker bee" ranks. I loved almost all of the other prosecutors, administrative and support staff, and especially the heroic men and women of law enforcement at the local, state, and federal levels.

The reason I left the job I loved had everything to do with the corruption of the Department of Justice by the Obama/Holder/Lynch administration into something almost unrecognizable. Instead of honoring their oaths to uphold the laws of the United States, these individuals and their minions chose to *ignore* the laws with which they had political or philosophical differences, whether those laws concerned immigration, national security, or drug or weapons crimes. It seemed as though every policy decision inflicted upon the nation by the administration was driven—not by a motivation to keep the country safe and secure—but by this clique's stated desire to reform the nation into something that they preferred for political—and often racial—reasons.

I am not naïve enough to believe that the criminal justice system is never influenced by politics. Unfortunately, it always has been, at least to some degree. I served in the Air Force during Nixon's Watergate cover-up and the infamous Saturday Night Massacre. I was in the United States Attorney's Office in Washington D.C. when members of Ed Meese's anti-pornography task force asked for my assistance in doing legal research to determine whether subscribers to *Playboy Magazine* could be prosecuted for possession of pornography. They never got it. I watched in disbelief when Janet Reno's regime presided over the unmitigated disasters at Ruby Ridge and Waco, and when she snatched a young boy from loving relatives and sent him back to Castro's Cuba. I shook my head in sorrow when Alberto Gonzalez attempted to throw good career men and women under the proverbial bus rather than take responsibility for his own purge of dozens of United States Attorneys. I then saw these collapses of judgment amplified exponentially by Holder's idiotic Operation Fast and Furious, in which DOJ and ATF sold hundreds of weapons to criminals and drug cartels, resulting in murders on both sides of our southern border.

In short, neither of our major political parties has had clean hands in the recent management of justice. Much of the tortured history of this series of collapses is, in my opinion, due to the placement of the Department of Justice within the president's cabinet. It should have been obvious at the beginning, and it is painfully obvious now, that the nation's chief law enforcement officer (as the attorney general is often called) cannot be expected to perform his or her duties in the ethical and independent manner required *as long as* they are operating as a political appointee and an arm of the president. The position of the attorney general, and the department that he or she supervises, must be independent of the president and the cabinet if they are expected to operate with only justice in mind.

The fictional reference in the novel to the case of Rusean Short is, unfortunately, a re-telling of a very real disaster caused by the Obama/Holder/Lynch regime. The early release of hundreds of hardened criminals from prison by this president has already resulted in an uptick in violent crime, and in the murder of innocents. There will be more to come. The very real case of Wendell Callahan, for example, parallels the description of the Rusean Short matter in the book.

Callahan was released early from federal prison and went home to butcher his former girlfriend and her two young daughters, slitting their throats. He was charged with their murders, and is now facing the death penalty in Ohio, only because the State of Ohio—and not the federal government that turned him loose—had jurisdiction over these brutal homicides.

The imposition of longer, mandatory sentences in the 1980s was a response to a climbing violent crime rate, one that affected our minority neighborhoods the most adversely. It was (and remains, see south Chicago today) the poor, black neighborhoods that suffered the most when street gangs and drugs took over their streets and buildings. Congress' responses to the alarming murder and assault rates worked. Violent crime rates dropped for decades as the worst criminals remained behind bars, where they could only harm each other.

Unfortunately, those who blame every social ill on racial prejudice (rather than bad life choices) have convinced many that the same laws that were enacted primarily for the protection of minority neighborhoods were *unfair* to them. Now, members of both political parties pander to the families *of the convicted* by clamoring about "draconian" or "unfair" sentences, and the president and attorney general return the thugs to the streets, falsely claiming that only "non-violent" defendants, or inmates convicted only of drug "possession offenses" are being returned to their homes.

Liberals brag about the sentence reductions as an achievement of fairness, and conservatives claim that they are saving millions in the budget because of the reduced costs of incarceration. None of them bother to ask the families of the new victims what *their* costs have been, or whether they feel fairly treated by the release of the predators back to their communities.

I sat in a Capital Crimes Committee meeting in Washington, D.C. (very similar to the one described in the book), and witnessed a newly-minted political hire from Mr. Holder's office essentially veto a death penalty vote concerning murderous meth heads who had invaded the home of illegal immigrants. These thugs tortured a seventeen-year-old, executed him in front of his mother, killed her boyfriend, and then shot a ten-year-old boy, who jumped in front of the same mother trying to save *her* from being killed. His mother died anyway, but the heroic little boy fortunately survived. Politics, not justice, won that day.

Politics—and not justice—also won when FBI Director Comey wrote sub-section (f) (the section criminalizing gross negligence) OUT of the applicable statute in the Clinton email investigation. While he may have exercised prosecutorial 'discretion' in some of his prior posts as an Assistant United States Attorney or Deputy Attorney General, he was *not a prosecutor* at the time of the email scandal. He was—at that time—the nation's chief investigator, sworn to uphold the laws of the country *as written by Congress*, and he was *neither* sworn *nor entitled* to re-write those statutes to his own satisfaction. His explanation that he had worked all his life to "decriminalize negligence" and thereby would not recommend prosecution was nothing short of ridiculous, and was a cop-out. There has always been prosecution of criminal negligence at every level of our legal system, and with good reason. Negligent homicide by reckless driving is one example that should come readily to mind. Starting a fire in a fireworks stand would be another. Intent is not required for convictions in either case for obvious reasons. If our system ultimately collapses, those charged with providing the checks and balances contemplated by the Constitution—but who could not find the courage to apply them—will have to answer to history.

The lack of independence and integrity in the attorney general's office could not have been more drastically displayed than it was by Attorney General Lynch's conference with former president Clinton in the now notorious tarmac meeting. A first-year law student would know better than to engage in such a meeting after the first two hours of ethics class. This political tryst was inexcusable on any level.

Following all these amazingly horrid exercises in poor judgment by political operatives posing as prosecutors, I strongly believe that the time has come for the creation of an independent justice arm for the nation, one that could be trusted to investigate even the office of the president, if necessary, without fear of political retribution. It would also obviate the need for the appointment of supposedly independent special prosecutors. We have tried to achieve this result in the creation of the post of Director of the FBI, whose term limit lasts beyond that of the president who appointed him. Unfortunately, we chose to leave the director under the thumb of the attorney general, who still reports to the president. In the end, achieving an adequate re-structuring will require honest and non-partisan work by both sides of the political aisle. Time will tell if they are capable of such efforts.

The issue of Muslim assimilation is a current major concern, not only for the United States, but for the entire non-Muslim world. We must realize at some point that a concept such as *Sharia* law, which seeks by its own definition to overthrow and supplant the Constitution in favor of a theocracy—a theocracy that would ban every other religion and even execute those who attempted to practice them—is NOT entitled to Constitutional protection. We ignore this threat to the peril of civilized society. Worrying about political correctness in the face of the brutality seeking to impose this tyranny upon the world is nothing short of stupid.

Are there "moderate" Muslims wishing to live with the rest of the world in peace? Of course. The numbers speak for themselves. The billions across the world who believe in Islam are not *all* devotees of ISIS or the Taliban. The problem is that of these billions, even the small percentage of Muslims who *are* radical jihadists is horribly significant. To remain Americans, and to keep any real concept of America as it exists today, we must develop methods for recognizing the difference between the radical and the peaceful, enforcing a Constitutional assimilation of the latter, and *destroying* the evil of the former. We need the assistance of peace-loving Muslims to achieve this goal, and to prove that they, and not the *jihadis*, are the true faithful of Islam.

The final major issues with which the novel deals are the ever-climbing tonnage of our nuclear waste, and where we can safely store it. Closing Yucca Mountain was yet another purely political decision by Obama, Harry Reid, and company. I initially had reservations about exposing the threat of an aerial attack on a storage facility as clearly as it is described in the book, not wishing to provide a guide for such an attack. Those reservations disappeared when I discovered—not only the danger presented by local, dry-cask storage, but also the very method by which terrorists could spread it—in an Internet search that took less than five minutes. The threat is undeniably real, and the invitation to this destruction should be removed before it is exploited. If the book achieves nothing more than an increase of security at sites such as North Anna, I would be delighted.

Thanks again for reading *A Winter of Wolves.* Stay safe, and may God bless you and our nation.

Marc Rainer

Acknowledgements

My thanks to my informal editorial board for their eagle eyes and excellent suggestions in the completion of this book. These include Lea, Jennifer, Alta, Tania, Mary Jo, and Jamie. Each of you brings a different perspective to your review, and all of you are very much appreciated.

Thanks also to the good folks at CreateSpace for the formatting and cover work.

A final thanks, as always, to the brave men and women who continue to protect and serve.

Made in the USA
Middletown, DE
30 September 2016